THE PERFECT SCREAM

Lynn had pulled around the corner and parked, then got anxious and started to drive around the block. The rain had stopped, but the road was still slick. Almost no one was on the uneven sidewalks. As she came up the street on the east side of the pub, Lynn saw someone on foot come out of the narrow alleyway between the buildings. It took her a moment to realize it was Zach.

The street was empty beyond her and there were no cars parked next to the sidewalk. She slowed the Suburban and saw Zach glance over his right shoulder before he took a step into the road. She punched the gas and felt the big vehicle lurch forward.

Almost like it had happened with Alan Cole, Zach froze midstride and looked up at the fast moving SUV.

Lynn couldn't keep the smile from spreading across her face.

She just wanted to hear the scream. . . .

Books by James Andrus

THE PERFECT WOMAN

THE PERFECT PREY

THE PERFECT DEATH

THE PERFECT SCREAM

Published by Kensington Publishing Corporation

The
PERFECT
SCREAM

JAMES
ANDRUS

PINNACLE BOOKS
Kensington Publishing Corp.
www.kensingtonbooks.com

PINNACLE BOOKS are published by

Kensington Publishing Corp.
119 West 40th Street
New York, NY 10018

All Kensington titles, imprints, and distributed lines are available at special quantity discounts for bulk purchases for sales promotions, premiums, fund-raising, educational, or institutional use. Special book excerpts or customized printings can also be created to fit specific needs. For details, write or phone the office of the Kensington special sales manager: Kensington Publishing Corp., 119 West 40th Street, New York, NY 10018, attn: Special Sales Department; phone 1-800-221-2647.

ISBN-13: 978-0-7860-2770-5
ISBN-10: 0-7860-2770-3

First printing: February 2013

10 9 8 7 6 5 4 3 2 1

Printed in the United States of America

ONE

Detective John Stallings shifted in the seat of the county-issued Impala so his Glock didn't bite into his hip when he turned to look at his partner, Patty Levine. It had taken him a while to get used to the blond hair and pretty face, but now he viewed her like any other cop—only meaner and with a better punch. The Police Memorial Building, or PMB, rose in front of them.

Patty was studying a document in the battered gray-metal pad case where she stored notes and calendars that went back years. She held up a photo and said, "Zach Halston, twenty-one, senior at the University of North Florida. May be out at the beach with some fraternity nerds. Mom hasn't heard from him in ten days and she's worried."

"Great, so now we babysit frat boys?"

"What else do we got going on? This is a nice, lower-stress change of pace."

Stallings gave one of the noncommittal grunts that had gotten him through nineteen years of marriage.

Well, eighteen with a year sabbatical. What he didn't say out loud, what he'd never mention to another cop, was that he *did* have better things to do. He had conducted a relentless, secretive search for his daughter, Jeanie, who had disappeared three years earlier when she was sixteen. If his bosses at the Jacksonville Sheriff's Office knew he was working his own daughter's case he'd have a lot to explain. As it was, the command staff and his immediate supervisors had gone above and beyond the call to help Stallings. The case was open and a detective still did some checking, but Stallings had a schedule of talking to other missing-persons detectives across the country and searching the Internet for any clues on sites about missing kids and runaways. That's why he resented this jerk-off assignment.

After a minute of brooding, Stallings said, "Any idea where the frat boys are?"

"The father says they're at one of the mom-and-pop hotels over in Atlantic Beach. It might be slow checking on partying college kids in the morning. Maybe we should grab an early lunch if we don't find the right hotel in the first few tries."

Stallings nodded and sighed.

"You look tired. What's wrong?"

"Usual."

"What's your favorite phrase? Is today the day?"

"C'mon, I know you went through the academy ten years after me, but they had to still be preaching it."

She shrugged her muscular shoulders.

"Is today the day that changes your life?" Stallings shook his head. "Just a way to keep you alert and not fall into complacency." He had said the phrase at the start of every assignment since his early road patrol days. Lately, he'd taken an active role in changing his life and it was showing results. His wife, Maria, had been much more open to talking and his father, whom he had not seen in twenty years, was now part of the family again. Sort of.

Patty looked out the window and said, "You think we should consider another assignment for a while?"

"Why?"

"It doesn't bother you that the other units call us the 'spring break patrol' or 'runaway round-up'?"

He snorted. "And looking for burglars in Hyde Park is better?"

"You know nothing we do here can undo the past."

Stallings looked down and sighed. "But it can make me feel better about the present."

Patty didn't answer, but he sensed her frustration. This was his choice. She'd had to take any detective bureau assignment she could to get off road patrol. She didn't have the same perspective as him. At least she had gotten some homicide experience with a few cases that required all the detectives in crimes/persons to work together. No one would've guessed that Jacksonville, Florida, was the crossroads of the South for deviants and killers.

Stallings said, "Let's see what happens today and worry about tomorrow later."

Lynn mumbled the common "yeahs" and "un-huhs" as she absently listened to her mom go on and on about the problems she was having with the built-in vacuum system at their house in Hyde Park. Then she heard her mother say, "Are you still there, sweetheart?"

"Yeah, Mom, I hear you." She may have heard the words, but all of her attention was focused out the windshield of the blue Chevy Suburban she'd borrowed from work. The Thomas Brothers Grocery and Supply chain treated her well. They paid her top dollar to keep their books, gave her time off when she needed it, and did little things like loan her a giant killing machine without asking any questions whatsoever. Again she heard her mom say, "Can you hear me, sweetie?"

Lynn smiled. She could tell how old she was when she'd met someone based on if they called her by her first name, her middle name, or a nickname. Her parents and siblings as well as anyone she knew as a very young girl, before she started school, never called her Lynn. Everyone else did. Her mom called all the kids "sweetheart" or "sweetie."

Before she realized it, the conversation was over and her mother said, "All right, sweetheart, you be careful." Lynn knew her mother was paranoid about her children's safety, even a twenty-four-year-old child like herself. The slight tremor in her mother's voice ate away at Lynn a little bit at a time.

She closed her cell phone and looked down the nearly empty street leading out to International Speedway Boulevard, one of the main roads of Daytona Beach. And she thought downtown Jacksonville was shitty. This hellhole seemed to be nothing but rednecks and bikers. Every block along US 1 was jammed with strip bars and tattoo parlors. She couldn't believe she'd liked this place when she was a kid. Even the board-walk down by the beach was a second-rate parody of a real boardwalk like Atlantic City's.

But she had to remember why she was here and what she was trying to accomplish.

This was a mission, not a pleasure trip.

The morning was a wash, but looking for the miss-ing frat boy got easier after lunch when a lot of the fall break crowd started to stir after a night of club hop-ping. That's what caught Patty's eye as they drove past the Pelican Harbor Inn—a line of buff, tanned young men leaning against the cheap metal rail of the two-story motel along the eroding beach east of Jack-sonville.

Patty smiled. "Fraternity nerd alert."

Stallings whipped the Impala into a spot at the next hotel a few feet away from the hedge that separated the rundown buildings. "Don't kids go home for Thanks-giving break anymore?"

"Not when there are a few extra days off school. Now they party."

"Hey, you can't park there," called a dark-skinned, Middle Eastern man when he saw the two detectives turn toward the Pelican Harbor Inn.

Stallings held up his badge from his belt without a word and the man waved him on. He could hear the music blaring from an open door as he and Patty took the outside stairs up to the second floor. The windows pulsed to the heavy bass as the detectives approached the boys in the outdoor hallway.

The closest boy, wearing a T-shirt that said REHAB IS FOR QUITTERS, turned his head slowly toward them, his eyes moving to the guns and badges on their belts; then he hopped off the railing to greet them.

"Is there a problem, officer?" asked the young man in a voice loud enough to be heard over the music as he waved his hand behind his back to get the others off the railing.

Stallings shouted, "Cut the music," and waited as one of the boys scampered into the first room. A few seconds later there was silence. His ears still rang, but now he could hear the waves break over the narrow beach. He smiled and said, "That's better."

"Was that it?" asked the group's spokesman.

Patty often used the imposing Stallings to get someone's attention, then handled the details. The young men were obviously nervous around her stern-looking partner.

Patty stepped forward and said, "What's your name?"

The boy paused.

Stallings stared at him.

"Bobby Hollis." He couldn't say it fast enough.

Patty calmed him with a smile. "Well, Bobby"—she held up a photograph she slipped out of her metal case—"he here with you?"

The young man took the photo and said, "Zach Halston?"

"That's right."

"No, I thought he was home visiting his parents. Haven't seen him in a while."

"We stopped at your apartment complex. No one was around." The apartments acted as the fraternity houses for all the small, local universities.

"Everyone either went home for a few days or came out here."

"Why vacation so close to J-Ville?"

Bobby gave Patty a sly smile. "We grab these rooms cheap, then make up stories about being graduate students from Stanford or Harvard. The local chicks eat that shit up."

Patty just nodded. She knew all the scams guys put on to meet women. This was just a tad more shallow than most. She said, "Got any idea where he might be or anyone who's close to him?"

"Why? Is he in trouble?"

Now Stallings stepped forward. "Does it matter? We need to find him. Is there anything about that you don't understand?"

"No, sir."

"We're gonna look around. Which rooms do you have?"

The young man pointed to the open door and the room next to it.

Patty said, "Just two for all of you?"

He smiled at her and stepped closer. "We're struggling college students. This was all we could afford."

The detectives each took a room. There were sleeping bags piled on the floor and the bed, separated so the box spring and mattress could each hold bodies. After peeking in the empty bathroom, Stallings headed back out to the crowd on the railing. Before he reached the door, he heard a crash. As he stepped outside, a shirtless, muscle-bound young man flopped out into the hallway. Patty stepped out behind him.

"Problem?" asked Stallings, already knowing what had happened.

Patty smiled. "I just had to show him that you don't make cracks to the police."

"What'd he say?"

She looked down at the dazed young man and nudged him with her petite foot. "Go ahead, tell him."

The young man shook out the ringing in his ears and mumbled. "I didn't know who she was. I asked her if it was true that lots of fun came in small packages."

Stallings shook his head and said, "Dumbass." He turned back to Bobby Hollis, knowing that Patty's little demonstration would've loosened some tongues. "Tell me who could help us find Zach."

Bobby's eyes shifted up from his friend on the cement walkway. He didn't hesitate. "Connor Tate. He was left at the house to keep an eye on things, plus he's trying to save some cash, so he didn't come over here with us. He shares an apartment with Zach some of the time."

"What do you mean 'some of the time'?"

"Zach has an apartment away from the apartment complex that houses the fraternity. It's closer to Arlington." The boy sketched out a map to the apartment at Stallings's urging.

"He has a place at the fraternity complex too, right?"

The boy nodded. "That's the one with Connor."

Patty asked, "Why two places?"

The kid shrugged. "You'd have to ask Zach."

Now Stallings said, "Give me Connor's number."

Patty understood Stallings's personality after a couple years of working with him. He had lost the ability to ask for information a long time ago. It was faster to just tell people to give him information.

Bobby blurted out a cell phone number.

"Where was Connor when we went by the frat house?"

The boy shrugged. "You know how it is. We got time off, we party. He's a hard sleeper."

Stallings threw a glare over the scared young men. Patty had to smile. He had gotten his point across without saying a word. If they had to talk to these boys again they'd be too scared to hold anything back. It was like bringing a big, mean dog with you on interviews. She wanted to reach over and pat him on the head.

Lynn waited, her eyes glued to the front of the bank, considering her actions. She knew there were consequences to everything someone did in life. That's what drove her. It wasn't like this would be the first time. She hated to admit the satisfaction she'd gotten from the fire she'd set in Atlanta. The Internet really did have the answers to everything.

Movement caught her eye and she sat up straight in the seat of the big SUV. Someone was at the front door to the bank. It was him. Lynn didn't know why she was so certain it was him. He paused at the door, looking back inside. His face was not visible, but she knew exactly who was stepping out of the crappy little bank a block off International Speedway. She'd already scoped out his BMW parked across the street in the parking lot that served the strip mall as well as the businesses grouped near the bank.

She felt a wave of excitement at the prospect of what she was about to do. This was going to be sweet.

TWO

Alan Cole paused for a moment as he was about to burst through the front door of the bank and into the bright, beautiful sunshine of Central Florida. It was two o'clock and he wasn't going to close any more loans or open any more investment accounts today. It was time to hit the beach and put in some time on his board. But he had to stop and turn to make eye contact with the hot little Puerto Rican chick working behind the far end of the counter today. She had a wild-ass look in her eye that matched the outrageous fake boobs she liked to show off. He'd love to roll into the next big fraternity party and show the young punks what an alumnus like him could find if he trolled the right waters.

He waited at the front door just long enough for her to give him a flash of those dark eyes with just a tad too much makeup around them. Somehow in just that casual glance she said to him, "Come for me whenever you're ready." At least that's how he chose to interpret the look. He probably wasn't wrong. She had seen him race up in his tight 320i and noticed the tailored suits and the way his arms popped in them, because of all the time he put in at the gym.

He took a final, quick glance around the lobby and noted only one decent-looking MILF waiting in line for the next teller. He wouldn't mind moving to a branch farther east and picking up more customers with bodies made for the beach. But at least out here he had a chance to show off his ability at writing loans and hooking investment clients.

The humidity wasn't as bad as it usually was when he cleared the door and stepped out onto the cracked sidewalk. He barely looked as he stepped into the street. Why should he? Even though they were near the Daytona Speedway no one ever drove above twenty on this twisting side street.

Then he saw it. A big blue Chevy Suburban. It seemed like it was right on top of him and moving fast down the middle of the street. He thought about sprinting forward but then turned on the ball of his Bruno Magli shoes instead.

That was his mistake.

The massive SUV didn't swing wide to miss him as he thought it would. It rolled directly toward him like a shark about to hit a helpless swimmer in the open sea.

He caught a flash of the driver's smiling face. Could it be? No shit. He knew her. But in that second of recognition he could not recall exactly where he knew her from. He had a clear idea it was not a positive connotation as the steel bumper of the Suburban struck him just above his right knee and the grille swept him up like the teeth of a shark. For a moment he had the sensation of flying as he tumbled through the air toward the uncut grass swale in front of the bank. He lost sight of the truck as the ground filled his field of vision and rushed up to meet his face.

Then everything went black.

Lynn was disappointed all she heard was a short yelp of terror instead of a more satisfying scream. She had been spoiled by her first victim. That had been a healthy scream. She glanced in the rearview mirror to see his crumpled heap lying across the strip of grass and sidewalk in front of the bank.

One more asshole dealt with.

A smile crept across her face as she casually pulled out onto International Speedway Boulevard and turned toward I-95. In about an hour she'd pull back into the main parking lot of Thomas Brothers, toss the keys to the fleet manager, and go back to work like she had only been out running a few errands.

No muss, no fuss, no regrets.

Now she could focus on who was next.

THREE

John Stallings was still annoyed at his assignment finding the wayward fraternity nerd. As far as he was concerned Zach Halston was a spoiled rich kid whose friends couldn't keep their yaps shut. They had given up his secret apartment off campus with hardly any argument at all. Now that Patty had sweet-talked the key out of the manager, Stallings thought the boy was just trying to keep a low profile and stay off his parents' radar for some reason. Patty and he had jointly decided to come here before going by the fraternity house again. Their first visit to the Tau Upsilon house had been a bust except they had discovered most of the brothers were over at the hotel on the beach. One of the brothers who stayed at the house, a young man named Connor Tate, was supposed to be close to the missing Zach Halston. They had a few questions for Connor.

Stallings glanced around at the tables and kitchen counter and immediately picked up signs of relatively serious marijuana use and sales. Small plastic Baggies were stacked in one corner next to a scale and ashtrays were filled with half-smoked roaches.

Patty said, "This keeps getting better and better. This halfwit must be stoned every hour he's awake and it looks like he sells fifty bags a day. That must be how he affords this place off campus and he doesn't have to answer any of Mom or Dad's questions. Too lazy to work, too stoned to be bored. This boy is a real credit to society."

Stallings let out a snort of laughter, but that was it. This was not a good use of his time. A shiftless pot-head who hasn't checked in with his parents. Fucking great.

Patty said, "Jackpot," as she pulled a Toshiba laptop from under a pile of *Playboy* magazines.

Stallings recognized the key to many missing young people's whereabouts lay in their personal computers. The odd email or Facebook entry had led them to more runaways than all the phone tips to a hotline combined. Technically, at twenty-one, Zach Halston wasn't a run-away. He was classified as a missing person, and if his parents hadn't been educated and influential, Stallings doubted anyone at the Jacksonville Sheriff's Office would have told him to look for the kid. In fact, Stall-ings was thinking about turning the laptop over to nar-cotics when Patty had gotten everything she needed, since he figured it held the names of the kids' cus-tomers. But that undermined the whole concept of a warrantless search to find a missing person.

Patty started to rustle through the kitchen drawers as Stallings glanced up at a long hallway filled with cheaply framed photographs on the wall. He flicked on the overhead light and slowly started strolling down the hallway. Most of the photos were of Zach with his drunken frat brothers at wild parties and in bars. They were more than a few bongs and other drug paraphernalia prominently displayed. Stallings started understanding the concept of a second, secret apartment more clearly.

There were a number of photographs with young women posing in different states of drunkenness. He briefly thought about trying to talk to some of the girls but figured it would take more time to identify them than it would to actually locate the missing frat brother.

Near the end of the hallway, Stallings was about to turn and join Patty when one photo of Zach Halston with his arm around a young woman caught his eye. He stepped to one side so the light would fall on it. He reached into his breast pocket and quickly yanked out his cheap, cheater reading glasses he'd been forced to use over the past year. He stared at the photo and every detail, slowly reaching up with a trembling hand and pulling the four-by-six photograph off the wall. He fumbled with the frame, roughly pulling the back off it so he could look at the photograph without any distortion from cheap glass.

He stared until he realized he was certain of what he was looking at.

The girl in the photo was his missing daughter, Jeanie.

FOUR

Jacksonville Sheriff's Office homicide detective Tony Mazzetti was in a miserable mood. A mood that had lasted for months. That was one of the reasons he was looking at the case file of an open homicide with such contempt. A simple shooting in Arlington. Some poor schmuck manager of an auto parts store. No robbery, no known enemies, no motive. Just a nice middle-class kid shot for no apparent reason. And Mazzetti had been unable to solve it. He felt like shit.

But it wasn't just a blot on his immaculate homicide clearance rate. Three articles of his had been rejected by various history magazines in the past three weeks. That had never happened before either. He'd pulled a hamstring at the gym and now wobbled around like an arthritic old man. Mazzetti thought he could trace back the string of bad luck and sustained bad mood to breaking up with Patty Levine.

No matter how he spun it in his head or talked about it with his mom or sister, Patty was the only one who'd done any breaking up. He'd just sat there like a mute dolt and let the best thing that ever happened to him walk right out of his life. While she had been polite and professional in the office, he had no indication she was remotely interested in hooking back up with him romantically. Now the problem had to do with him needing a girlfriend. He had gone years without a steady girlfriend and thought he was getting by just fine. But Patty had shown him the wonders of a committed relationship and now he found himself chatting with women more and interested in starting a new relationship. It was exhausting.

His immediate concern was finding who had pumped three .38 rounds into Kirk Topps, manager of the Independent Auto Parts store in Arlington. This was a real puzzler. The young man was a graduate of the University of North Florida, came from a nice, middle-class family. Both of his parents were teachers. He'd had the same steady girlfriend for three years and no history of drugs, alcohol, or gambling. Those were usually the big three culprits in an unexplained shooting.

Mazzetti's partner, Sparky Taylor, had used that enormous brain of his to find unbelievable video of the street coming and going to the auto parts store. Sparky was a technical genius who knew how to talk to other tech geeks. He'd found security cameras at different businesses that covered the street from a number of angles. Then Sparky spoiled some of his efforts by finding JSO policy regarding the use of unrelated videotape. It made him fill out way too many forms and permissions.

Sparky had been driving Mazzetti batty with his constant citation of policy and investigative ideas. Mazzetti didn't care what the former tech agent made him do as long as it helped solve a goddamn homicide.

His cell phone rang and he snatched it up absently, barking into the receiver, "Mazzetti."

A flirty female voice said, "Hey there. You think you could find a reason to run over to my office sometime today?"

Mazzetti immediately recognized the voice belonging to Assistant Medical Examiner Lisa Kurtz. The cute, redheaded graduate of Syracuse Medical School had been playing a game of *catch me if you can* with Mazzetti for weeks. Now Mazzetti was ready to catch her.

"I'll be over in a little while."

Sergeant Yvonne Zuni felt like she was up to speed on the squad after only a few months in the position. The biggest factor in her getting a handle on everything was the slowdown in homicides during the last part of summer. She wasn't going to argue with how she'd found herself in the very favorable position of being the sergeant in charge of the crimes/persons unit; she was just going to enjoy it.

The sergeant had never seen herself as a career woman. Growing up in a warm and loving family from Trinidad, she'd thought about following in her father's footsteps as a veterinarian. But mainly she'd dreamed about having kids. Her sisters both had families. Her cousins all had children. And for a brief period she'd thought she had it all. She was married and had a baby boy at home. But a rare blood disease had taken her son before his first birthday, and then everything else went to hell.

But she hadn't given up on life. She'd recently started to date again, even if her taste in men had turned out to be poorer than her ability to command police officers. She enjoyed her job and the people she worked with, and most of all, Yvonne Zuni had not given up hope. There was no reason she couldn't have it all again.

In a way she felt like she was the mother on the squad. She worried about the detectives in her command as well as the cases they worked on. Maybe it was a way to make up for the fact that she'd only gotten to act like a real mom for a short time.

Sergeant Zuni looked through her glass-enclosed office at the far end of the squad bay and saw the intimidating form of Lieutenant Rita Hester strolling toward her. The lieutenant made a daily appearance but had little to do with the operational control of cases since Yvonne had become the permanent sergeant. The lieutenant now focused on some of her other duties, which seemed to include climbing the command ladder. Sergeant Zuni had seen the lieutenant take more credit for cases and be harsher on detectives as a way of getting recognized by the sheriff and command staff. It didn't bother the sergeant as long as the lieutenant continued to get the detective bureau the resources it needed to solve cases.

Lieutenant Hester stopped at the office door and said, "What's new, Yvonne?"

"Nothing really. Tony is still working the robbery of the auto parts manager, Luis Martinez is looking into a reported gang robbery, Stall and Patty are looking for the missing fraternity boy. You know, the usual."

The lieutenant shook her head and said, "Wouldn't mind breaking something big and catching some news coverage."

"Sorry we haven't had a decent murder to solve."

"Funny. You know what I mean. Patrol gets all the attention because people see them out there in uniform. We have to fight for anything we need." The lieutenant looked across the squad bay and said, "That's the nature of police work. Feast or famine. It's hard to tell the bosses things are slow but you need more resources. Know what I mean?"

Sergeant Zuni nodded her head. She could imagine how tricky politics were at the upper ends of the Jacksonville Sheriff's Office. Rita Hester was a legend in the agency for her toughness and intelligence. She was a role model for women like Sergeant Zuni even when she talked politics and not police work.

The lieutenant turned her head and gave a rare, warm smile as John Stallings entered the squad bay and waved to her. Sergeant Zuni knew that two had been partners on the road many years earlier. Stallings could say and do things that would get most cops fired and the lieutenant would just find them amusing. Right now the veteran detective looked worried as he slipped something into an envelope and left it on his desk before he approached the lieutenant

The lieutenant said, "What's wrong, Stall?"

"Nothing, just tired," mumbled Stallings.

"The family doing okay?"

Stallings nodded.

"How are things with Maria?"

Stallings just shrugged and said, "Same."

Sergeant Zuni and the rest of the squad rarely asked Stallings about his shaky relationship with his estranged wife. She realized now it was a two-way street between Stallings and the lieutenant. He may be able to say things to her, but she could say things to him no one else could.

Sergeant Zuni still thought Stallings was acting strangely.

Lynn had worked out all the permutations and probabilities of being caught by the police. That's what she did. She was a numbers girl. And she wanted to see numbers and information on paper. Her days at Florida State had taught her the value of research and understanding a subject from all angles. Her bachelor's degree was in general business but her minor was in statistics. She thought the possibility of her being stopped before she completed her grim task was statistically unlikely. That was if she stayed on the same cautious, prepared, and determined path. She had once heard that soldiers with those three traits are the most effective fighting units. In a way she felt like she was in a war. There was a clear enemy and a clear goal, and she had already killed for her cause.

But she didn't want to lose herself in this mission. Lynn knew for a fact that she was different. Different from other people. Different from other bookkeepers. And different from other killers. Because, if she had to be honest with herself, that was what she was: a killer.

The first time she had done it she'd been shaky. It

was too elaborate and unpredictable. But it worked. It worked like nothing she'd ever expected. The flames. The screams. The satisfaction.

The second time seemed harder. More personal. She recalled every detail. Holding her father's blue metal Smith & Wesson Model 36 revolver in both hands. Her dad had so many guns she knew he'd never notice one was missing from his safe for a few days. She'd been shocked he could tell the gun had been fired just by the smell of it. He knew it been fired and not cleaned. Luckily, with all that had happened, he just wrote it off as a lapse in memory. He never thought his baby girl had used it to pump three bullets into Kirk behind the auto parts store he managed.

The act of killing someone, of taking his life, no matter who it was or how much he deserved it, had changed her. The shooting had been tough. Lynn had trembled almost as badly as Kirk did when he started to plead for his life. Lynn had made it a point to look him in the eyes and let him know what she was doing. She wanted him to realize the consequences for his actions just as she understood the consequences for hers.

In the final moment he recognized her and just as he said, "Aren't you . . ." she pulled the trigger. The initial shock of the gunshot and the blood had stunned her into silence; then she stepped up and pumped two more rounds into his chest to make certain he was dead.

She had seen it on the news two days in a row but never heard another word about the incident. There were no witnesses, no clues and, as far as the city was concerned, no justice.

She had spent almost a month assessing what she

had done and how. She was careful to use different ways to kill her victims because she wanted to minimize the possibility of being caught because, unlike many killers, she still wanted to have a normal life.

Once all this business was done.

John Stallings drove directly to the tiny, lonely house he had rented while he and Maria worked out issues with their marriage. The stress of losing Jeanie, work, and life had been too much for Maria, who had hidden a serious drug problem from the world for years. Now that she had her head screwed on straight she'd decided he was the root of many of her and the family's problems. His obsessive nature and dedication to the Jacksonville Sheriff's Office had left him distant and emotionally unapproachable. That was the phrase some shrink had fed into Maria's head and she blurted it out whenever things got tough.

All that seemed unimportant right now as he stared at the photo he'd taken from Zach Halston's apartment. He had examined every detail again and knew it was his daughter after she'd disappeared. The photo, coupled with his father's vague, Alzheimer's-confused recollection that Jeanie had visited him after she disappeared, was proof she was still alive.

But what to do with it now? That was the question that roared in his brain and threatened to tear his heart apart. He couldn't risk mentioning this to anyone at JSO for fear of being removed from the case. It was too personal and he could not be objective. All the same reasons they'd used to keep them from looking for

Jeanie when she disappeared. Sure, he had slipped back onto the case. But it took time and emotional capital to keep all of his activities secret from his coworkers. He didn't care if it clouded his judgment. He just wanted to find his daughter—and to do that he had to find Zach Halston to learn more about this photo.

Patty Levine felt her lungs burn as she picked up the speed of her nightly run. With a slower pace around the office she'd started to exercise much more regularly. Although she felt better aerobically and had lost weight, the pounding of running tended to aggravate her back pain and caused her to use more painkillers than she should. It all seemed to be a cycle. She'd work herself off the Ambien, then get so exhausted from no sleep she'd hit it twice as hard for a few days. She would cut out painkillers altogether, then double her dosage of Xanax. She just couldn't get out from under the cloud of prescription drugs. She'd hoped the lull in cases, part of the common roller coaster of police work, would allow her some perspective. She thought it might be a chance to work on her drug use. She'd been wrong. It felt like she needed the pills just to make it through the day.

Her biggest regret was breaking up with Tony Mazzetti because of her drug use and her concern that she'd always be second to homicide investigations with him. Anyone she met in the sheriff's office would be tough to date. Police work did not lend itself to smooth relationship building.

She glanced at her watch and realized she'd already

gone forty-five minutes and needed a few minutes to cool down and stretch. She stopped at her favorite park bench, which overlooked a small pond and had shade from the late afternoon sun. This was where a lot of runners ended up because of the workout area with bars for pull-ups and grass for abdominal exercises.

As Patty leaned forward with her foot on the back of the bench, she made a wide sweep of her arm like she was a ballerina stretching before a recital. It was a goofy ritual she'd done since her early days in gymnastics. It made her feel more graceful and feminine while fulfilling an important fitness requirement. She noticed the guy in the grass to her right finishing up a set of crunches. She'd seen him in the park before and smiled as he stood up and started to stretch his back. He was about her age and awfully cute. She'd seen his long strides and knew he was serious about his afternoon runs.

Patty took a moment to gather her courage and finally said, "How far today?"

He smiled and said, "Four miles. You?"

"I go by time. I did forty-five minutes." She took her foot off the park bench and stepped toward the man. She held out her hand and said, "I'm Patty."

FIVE

Stallings had agonized about what to do with the photograph of Jeanie. He wanted to rush over and show Maria, but the longer he considered it, the worse idea it appeared. He had no idea what the photograph meant or how it might affect Maria and her fragile recovery. As much as it hurt, he'd have to keep the photo from her for now.

The one person he could show it to, the one person whose memory it might help, was his father. Stallings had been surprised how quickly he had gotten past twenty years of estrangement from the man who had bullied and terrified him in an alcoholic haze for most of his childhood. These days, James Stallings was a fixture in the Jacksonville homeless scene. Since going on the wagon he'd done all the things any twelve-step program could ask. And that included starting up and moderating a number of support groups for alcoholics and addicts.

But in the past six months Stallings had reestablished contact with his father and found the old man was worth the effort. He had immediately dazzled Stallings's children, who were thrilled to meet their long-lost grandpa. Without even trying, he'd helped Stallings with his own issues of anger and sorrow over his missing daughter. The biggest surprise by far was an off-the-cuff comment his father had made at lunch one Sunday afternoon in front of the entire family. This was about the time they realized he had a serious memory issue, which was diagnosed as Alzheimer's disease. Over pizza, his father commented that Jeanie had visited him twice. Under questioning, the old man came up with enough details to make it sound plausible, and the next week Maria had found Jeanie's old diary in which she'd written that she knew her grandfather lived in downtown Jacksonville based on comments she'd overheard between her mom and dad.

But James's faulty memory kept him from providing any useful information. The old man had babbled something about her name being Jeanie and then later said she liked to be called *Kelly*. She'd told him not to tell anyone she had visited or she'd never come back. When the old man remembered brief snippets of the meeting, he knew the pain he had caused his son. It racked him so badly that Stallings hated to bring it up. But today, armed with a more recent photo of Jeanie, he hoped to pry more details from his father's defective brain.

Stallings chatted briefly with the priest who ran the community center where James Stallings volunteered. The short, pudgy priest never seemed to do anything but watch the various tables of adults talking about their problems on one side of the giant room and the boys playing basketball on the other. But he liked Stallings's father and seemed to keep a pretty good eye on the old man.

Stallings said, "Notice any changes in my dad?"

"I'm sorry to say I do. If you listen to him he doesn't call a lot of people by name. He uses names like *Sport* or *Bud*." The priest took a second to clear his throat and wipe his eyes. "He doesn't even call me Doug anymore, just Father."

"Thanks for letting him keep working with his groups. It means a lot to him."

"It means a lot to everyone in the groups too. I think they'd continue to meet only if to keep your father's mind occupied. He really did a lot for them the last few years."

Stallings couldn't answer because of a catch in his throat. Instead he saw the group start to disperse from around the table and walked toward his father, the photograph of Jeanie in his right hand. He felt his whole body tense as he got closer and tried to work out the small talk with his father before hitting him with hard questions.

He stopped a few feet away from the table and waited until his father looked up and saw him. When James Stallings looked up and smiled, he had a strange expression on his face.

Stallings was about to ask his father what was wrong when the old man said, "Hello there, young fella. What can I do for you?"

He just stared at his father for a moment trying to

think what to say and figure out if the old man was trying to be funny. He got his answer when his father said, "Don't be shy. It's tough to meet new people."

Right then Stallings realized he wouldn't be asking any hard questions of his father tonight.

Lynn concentrated on the accounting program Thomas Brothers Supply had apparently purchased before there were actual computers. Although it was frustratingly slow, she couldn't say she did not understand the software or how it worked. The company made a great profit and the Thomas family had become wealthy and well-known in the area. They had used some of their money to start a private school in the northern part of Duval County. It had started out as a place to send their own children and friends to get a good education, but, as is always the case, the rich get richer. Now the school cost more than thirty thousand dollars a year in tuition and had a waiting list to get in.

She felt a presence in the doorway as what little sunlight filtered in was blocked by the giant form of one of the loading dock supervisors. Dale Moffitt never tucked in his gray uniform shirt, instead wearing it like a muumuu. It was hard for her to get a fix on his age, but he probably wasn't much more than thirty, which was sad because he was obese, balding, and most troubling of all, obnoxious.

Dale smiled, revealing the stained teeth of a chewing tobacco user. "Hey there, good looking. What you got going on tonight?"

"Work." She didn't even look up, not wanting to encourage any extra conversation.

"Here or at the other place?"

"Dr. Ferrero's office."

"Shit, old man Thomas doesn't pay you enough? You control the finances around this place, why don't you just funnel some to yourself?" He gave a hearty chuckle to emphasize that it was just a joke.

"Just two nights a week. Never hurts to have extra cash coming in."

"What's a doctor need a bookkeeper for anyway?"

Lynn felt a headache coming on, and talking to this moron wouldn't help things. She ignored him for a moment while she picked up her purse and rummaged through it for Tylenol.

Dale stepped closer and set down the paperwork he had in his hand; then he said, "Damn, girl. You gonna party tonight or what?"

When she gave him a puzzled look he reached across the desk and plucked a Baggie full of loose prescription pills out of her purse without her permission.

She snatched them back and tried to control herself so he wouldn't get the idea they were that important. "These are all the loose pills I found at my house and my parent's house. I'm going with my mom to see if any of the prescriptions need to be refilled." She played with the bag, looking at the assortment of Ambien, homemade ecstasy and anything else she could buy on the street easily. Then she glared up at Dale to put an end to the conversation by saying, "If it's any of your damn business anyway."

* * *

John Stallings tried to hide his frustration about waiting until eleven o'clock to talk to this fucking slug. They were at the fraternity house of Tau Upsilon, where the brothers at the beach hotel had told them they could find Connor Tate. When Patty called Mr. Tate, he'd informed her that he rarely saw visitors before eleven. Stallings had assumed that it meant he had class, but now he realized the slacker stayed in bed until almost lunchtime. He controlled himself because, according to the other fraternity brothers, Conner and Zach Halston were very close.

Patty had dazzled the hungover, red-eyed moron with her brilliant smile and perky attitude. Even though she was twenty-seven, she looked a lot more like a college coed, only prettier. Connor responded by inviting them in and even turning on the overhead light and ceiling fan. Stallings would've thought he'd make an attempt to hide the bongs, knowing the cops were coming to talk to him. But that was not the case.

Stallings knew he had to play it cool in front of Patty and not mention what he was really interested in about Zach Halston. He let Patty start off by asking the general questions and getting a list of all the fraternity brothers and their contact information. She went through the standard questions about girlfriends and enemies but got the standard answers that he had no steady girlfriend and no known enemies. Connor and Zach were among a dozen seniors in the fraternity house and he knew Zach kept a separate apartment. The University of North Florida was too small to have on-campus fraternity houses so they had an arrangement with an apartment complex to have two-bedroom apartments and a separate building for the clubhouse. Zach's parents paid for this apartment and visited quite often. That explained the crash pad.

Patty looked over the list of brothers and said, "You guys all stay in pretty close touch even after you graduate?"

"Try to." His voice was scratchy and hoarse. "We have a couple of parties a year where the alumni come back and even brothers from other schools come over."

Patty said, "Is there a chance Zach is hanging out with one of the alumni somewhere? Was he close to any of them?"

A cloud passed over Connor's face as he looked down and said, "He and Alan Cole are good friends, but Alan was in a car accident yesterday down in Daytona and is in the hospital. I know Zach isn't with him."

Stallings looked over at Patty and gave a slight head nod. They'd worked together as partners enough for her to know his signals and he knew hers. She was getting frustrated with the diffident attitude of this stereotypical asshole fraternity boy. She cleared her throat and said, "I'm gonna take a look around. You boys can chat."

Connor tried to stay cool and show he didn't care if she poked around the apartment. Stallings gave him his best shot at a warm smile and eased over to the couch and sat down next to the young man. He purposely waited until Patty moved off to another room of the apartment. His heart was starting to race like he was on a search warrant instead of an interview. There was even a slight tremor in his hand as he opened his notepad and pulled out the photograph. He had to ask questions about the photograph before Patty walked back in the room because he couldn't even tell her what he had found and what it might lead to.

He just held up the photo for a few seconds until dipshit got the idea to stare at it. Finally Stallings said, "Do you recognize her, Connor?"

The buff young man shrugged his muscular shoulders, ruffled his long, surfer hair, and studied the photo. "She's pretty, isn't she?"

"Yes, she is. Do you recognize her?"

"Yeah, I recognize her, but I don't remember much about her." He turned to look at Stallings and said, "You know how it is, man. Zach scores well with the ladies. Know what I mean?"

The father in Stallings wanted to pop his kid's head like a pimple. He felt a fury start to rise in him that scared him back to reality. He had not felt a murderous rage like that since the last time he caught a middle-aged man trying to meet a teenage girl. He took a moment to breathe deeply and clear his head. While he was working through the exercises the psychologist had given him to manage his anger, Connor said the one phrase that probably saved his life.

"I think I remember her now."

"All right, Connor, what has penetrated that petrified brain of yours?"

The dazed student gave Stallings a sly look, signaling he liked the idea a cop could joke about his marijuana use. "She hung out with Zach about two years ago. Nice girl. I think she lived in some really cheap apartment close by. She didn't have a car or anything. Her name was real common."

"Jeanie?"

"Nope."

"Are you sure?" Stallings was careful to not let the kid pick up on the true nature of his questions.

"I'm sure her name wasn't Jeanie, but I can't remember what it was. I know we didn't have a nickname for her like we do for a lot of the chicks that hang out here." He scratched his head and mumbled, "Really cute, that's all I remember."

Just then Patty walked back into the room and Stallings shifted gears quickly and smoothly. "And you are certain no one has heard from Zach in the last week?"

"I'll ask around again, but I haven't heard anyone mention it. Should I be worried, dude?"

"We should all be worried until he's home safe. You keep checking with the other brothers and get back to us."

As they walked out of the apartment, Stallings wondered if he sobered this kid up whether he'd have a clearer memory of Jeanie. He might even remember something important about Zach.

SIX

It was late afternoon and John Stallings found himself once again roaming the streets of Jacksonville considering what he'd just discovered and if he should tell anyone else. As a cop and a resident, the streets were utterly familiar to him. He liked to call them the mean streets of Jacksonville, even though he knew some big-city people might scoff at the idea. But the South had an edgy toughness to it that no one truly understood. It wasn't just number of firearms on the street compared to New York or Philadelphia; it was a multi-generational attitude that people just didn't want to take any shit. Ironically, that was also one of the reasons people were generally more polite. To avoid confrontation.

Stallings searched every face that passed him on the busy sidewalk wondering if one day he would stumble across Jeanie walking casually to a job. Why not? He apparently could've done it just a couple years ago. That was what bothered him now. Maybe if he had looked just a little bit harder and been more alert he might have seen her walking along the street to a job or to meet a boy or to go to a party at the fraternity house near one of the universities. The whole idea made him feel sick.

He did sometimes feel sorry for himself. Especially when he saw young families with their kids laughing at the table at a restaurant or at a park. That was all he ever wanted and he really didn't think it was too much to ask.

The photograph of Jeanie and Zach Halston was neatly tucked in his shirt pocket just above his heart with his light jacket covering the pocket for safety. But the photograph weighed on him like a heavy burden he was not able to hand off or even tell anyone about. It was Maria who really concerned him. How would she take news like this? It might be the one thing to push her over the edge.

It was also times like this when the only thing in his head was Jeanie that he wondered if, even for the briefest moment, he'd done something wrong to drive her off. All parents of runaways thought the same thing. It's almost like the stages of dying ending in acceptance. The parents of kids who end up being serious drug users have a similar guilt that leads to doubts. Was there something else they could've done? Had they missed some sort of clue? The whole issue was far too complex for easy answers. Sometimes Stallings wondered if an extra sport here or more attention there might steer a kid away from a bad influence. Who knew what intricate formula went into making a happy, successful child? Maybe it was just luck. Whatever the reason, a well-adjusted kid was a precious commodity. Beyond all cost.

Stallings realized sometimes he spent too much time roaming the streets hoping to recapture what he'd lost. But now, for the first time in a long time, he wondered if his Jeanie might come back on her own.

Once she was back at her desk, Patty felt at home with a stack of leads that would keep her busy and occupy her mind. This was an ideal pace for her because she had no downtime, but there wasn't the stress associated with the usual homicides that seemed to roll in to the office far too often.

She'd been very impressed by the way her partner had handled the young stoner over near the university. For some reason she'd had the feeling Stallings wanted to clobber young Connor Tate, but instead, he had sat down like a father and chatted with him while she looked through the rest of the apartment. They had a few names and addresses to run down but nothing that pointed to any foul play. Patty had learned early on in her career in the crimes/persons unit to never jump to conclusions. More missing people turned up safe than turned up dead. More murderers turned out to be friends or relatives of the victim than strangers. It was nothing like TV and she was glad of it.

She was also happy to see Stallings visit his estranged wife more often. She knew the stress of losing Jeanie had torn the family apart, but Stallings had also had to deal with reuniting with his father, then learning the old man had Alzheimer's. It was enough to break anyone's spirit, but no one could tell Stallings had any personal issues at all. The guy just seemed to go and go and go without ever wearing down. He had lost some of his Joe Friday look, tending to wear more casual, long-sleeved shirts and leave them untucked to cover his gun. It made it easier for them to get into a lot of places in Jacksonville. Stallings had a charm with women that he didn't even realize. His easygoing manner coupled with his rugged, natural good looks, which made him look like an intellectual athlete or a doctor who had played sports in college, made it easy for him to deal with females. But sometimes a shortcut to dealing with men involved a fist or an elbow in places no one wanted a bruise.

Patty stepped back from her chair and stretched her legs, trying to assess how much her back hurt. She had to admit she felt pretty good overall and probably wouldn't be using any painkillers tonight and hadn't worried about the Xanax since yesterday. Part of it might've been that her mind had been occupied as she thought about the runner named Ken she had met the other night. He'd made a couple of cracks in a self-deprecating way that had made her laugh. But there was no doubt the guy was a full-on athlete. She liked that. A lot.

She pulled out a sheet of paper where she had scrawled his cell phone number and wondered what would happen if she gave athletic Ken a call tonight.

All of a sudden she felt like she might need the Xanax.

* * *

After a quiet few days, Lynn liked the loud music. Friday nights were made for loud music. The throbbing bass reminded her of a place she used to go to in Tallahassee right off Tennessee Street, almost across from the university. Back when she had a much more carefree life, when her biggest concern was passing business accounting or making sure her parents didn't find out that she was drinking underage. She was the smartest of all her siblings because she'd moved away from her hometown of Jacksonville for school. The others had always lived with their parents or had to worry about them dropping in on them. The East Coast was too close together. It didn't matter what school you attended, you were never more than a few hours away from her parents. They weren't opposed to the kids moving out or getting their own apartment and if one of her siblings was going to a local school, like any parent, they showed up unannounced on a number of occasions. But never in Tallahassee. That long drive along I-10 was too much to risk without a phone call first.

The beat of the bass tickled her stomach as her eyes scanned the crowded room. Finally she saw the guy she was searching for at the far end of the bar, leaning back like he was a manager watching the crowd. He was a few inches taller than anyone around him; his blond hair picked up the light over the bar. Lynn waited patiently while he started to check out everyone at the bar, skipping past single men and most couples. Finally his eyes fell on her and stayed. She felt a little thrill and didn't mind the compliment. She wasn't Nostradamus about men, but she had predicted he would work his way down the bar shortly after he assessed her. He strolled, casually nodding to a few of the men because everyone knew this was his usual hangout.

Before she knew it, he eased up to the bar right next to her, smiled, and said, "May I buy you a drink?"

She gave him a subdued smile, not wanting him to think she would fall all over him like most women probably did. She shrugged and said, "Sure, why not?"

He leaned down to place his elbows on the bar so he could look her right in the eye. "Has anyone ever said you have the prettiest eyes in the whole world?"

When she smiled at his comment, the inevitable follow-up came out.

"And the prettiest smile to go with those beautiful eyes."

This guy was smooth. Sometimes when they looked as good as him they didn't worry about their flirting A-game. He was the exception.

He gazed at her for a few seconds too long. It started to feel awkward when he said, "You look awfully familiar. What's your name?"

"Lynn."

He straightened up so she could see exactly how tall he was and had his shoulders back so she would notice his broad, muscular chest. He understood the instinctual cues women looked at in men. Like the Discovery Channel shows that talked about the basics of finding a mate and how both men and women subconsciously evaluate each other about traits they would like to pass on to their children. DNA had a much stronger role in our lives than anyone realized. Lynn figured it was DNA that was pushing her to do what she had been doing.

She looked up into the young man's eyes and said, "What's your name?"

He smiled and said, "Connor Tate."

SEVEN

John Stallings sat in the living room of his former house, in his traditional spot on their long, leather couch. He'd already spent more than an hour kicking the soccer ball back and forth with his seven-year-old son, Charlie. He spent an additional thirty to fifty seconds conversing with his fourteen-year-old daughter, Lauren. Now both the kids were upstairs. He wondered why Lauren wasn't going out on Friday night. On the other hand, neither was he.

He sat in awkward silence with his wife, Maria. More and more of his friends at work referred to her as his "ex-wife," but, in fact, they were merely separated. He still held out hope they could patch up their nineteen-year marriage. He had done much of what she asked about putting family first and not working long hours at the sheriff's office. The only problem was he had not been working as many hours because there had not been nearly as many cases. It was just a slow time, like all police units experience. It seemed like it was either feast or famine. He didn't mind the lack of missing persons or the apparent absence of homicidal morons, but he had not found the satisfaction he'd been hoping for in his marriage either.

Now he sat, agonizing about showing Maria the photograph he had found of Jeanie with Zach Halston. On one hand he'd like to get her to verify this was a photograph of their missing daughter. On the other hand, with no information to support his discovery, the photograph would do nothing but rip open old wounds. So he just stared across the couch at her beautiful face. The daughter of Cuban immigrants, raised in Miami, she still had the exotic and fresh face of a twenty-year-old.

Maria said, "I'm glad you had so much fun with Charlie this evening."

"What else am I gonna do on a Friday night?"

"You could come with me to one of Brother Ellis's services."

Stallings had been to one of the long Baptist services. It was a small price to pay to be around Maria for a couple of hours. But he considered himself a Catholic and thought she did too until she had fallen under the spell of the dynamic evangelical preacher. So far, the kids had not warmed up to their mother's new-found fervor for religion sparked by the revivalist named Frank Ellis.

Maria said, "Brother Ellis is the one that says we must all forgive. It's a message worth hearing. I talk to him a lot about my problems."

"I'm just not one for the Holy Rollers."

"Don't try to denigrate what he does. He had fifty thousand people watch at the football stadium and he fills the giant church out near Blanding Boulevard every Sunday. Tonight is just a fellowship."

Stallings raised his hands in surrender, having no interest in starting a fight. But her dark look told him this was not the time to show her the photograph of Jeanie.

"Sure, I'll go."

Connor Tate played it cool as he drove slowly so the chick he'd met at the Wildside bar could keep up with him in his slick new Chevy Camaro. The throwback car was shit on mileage and slightly uncomfortable, but it looked really, really good. He was glad this girl had her own car so he wouldn't have to worry about giving her a ride home or calling a cab later. She'd claimed they didn't know each other and had never met, but this girl, Lynn, seemed awfully familiar to him. Even though he was trying to concentrate on the road with a blood alcohol content that had to be at least twice the legal limit, Connor was still pulling up bits and pieces about this girl from his memory. He just couldn't place exactly where he knew her from or who she was.

He was hoping none of the brothers were hanging around outside the clubhouse so he and Lynn could slip quietly into his apartment. The nice thing about not having Zach around was the privacy. This spunky chick was a prize and he wasn't interested in sharing just yet.

The fraternity had a game all of the brothers participated called *Score a Skank,* or *SAS* for short. It was an elaborate point system for scoring with women. The most points were awarded for simply bringing a chick home and banging her. There were a number of ways to verify this, but the most common was a cell phone camera photo. More points were awarded in special categories like older women and really good-looking women. The extra points were on a sliding scale from one to ten, and if you got the right photo of a girl, she might be worth as much as eight extra points. There had only been one instance of a brother winning an extra ten points—when one of the guys in the house banged a drunken cheerleader from the University of Florida. In uniform. He deserved the points. And the herpes he got from her too.

Connor parked directly in front of his apartment building and was relieved to see the walkway to his apartment was clear. He paused while she pulled her spiffy Toyota into the slot next to his. She seemed even happier than he was that no one was around. In fact, she was so nervous he wondered if she wasn't stepping out on her husband or boyfriend. That was a question better left unasked. He slipped an arm around her shoulder and gave her a friendly squeeze as they wobbled to his apartment. They'd been drinking a lot and he felt himself swerving on the sidewalk, but for a petite chick she seemed pretty sober and helped steady him until they got inside.

The world really started to spin once he was through the front door. All he could focus on was his soft couch, where he had spent most nights stoned and watching Jimmy Kimmel and Jimmy Fallon. But he wanted to show this girl he wasn't too drunk and took a second, staring into her eyes, then leaned down and gave her a deep kiss. He loved those innocent eyes and the expression on her face. It might have been fear because he was so much taller than her and she probably figured he was anatomically correct. In fact, most women were disappointed in his size once they were alone and naked. The last woman he'd banged here in the apartment had even asked him when he was gonna get completely hard. He'd had to admit it was as long as it got. He intended to make this girl happy that it was long as it was. He was going to go all out.

She didn't respond to the kiss quite the way he thought she would, but she did help him to the couch, then let him plop down and stretch out.

The girl—her name was getting hazy, but he thought it was Lynn—said, "Where do you keep your alcohol, big boy?"

He couldn't believe she was ready for more. Connor mumbled, "Cabinet next to the fridge." He was wasted and needed to clear his head if he wanted to score any legitimate points for the contest. That's why sometimes Zach was good to have around because he could surreptitiously film an encounter that might earn him extra points.

Connor could hear the girl rustling around in his kitchen, so he took the time to struggle with his shoes and slip off his jeans.

This was going to be one great night.

Tony Mazzetti had enjoyed his dinner with the cute assistant medical examiner, Lisa Kurtz. He'd known she was interested in him for some time when she'd invited him to work out with her at the JSO gym. She always took extra time with him, explaining anything she found during his investigations and slipping in obvious hints about the lack of datable men in the Jacksonville area. She'd moved down from upstate New York, where she had gone to Syracuse. Somehow she felt like that was a connection between them. He didn't mention to her his opinion of upstate New Yorkers was no better than it was of Southerners. Basically, if they weren't from one of the five boroughs or maybe Long Island, they were just a bunch of rednecks who were lucky if they knew how to read. It wasn't that bad, but sometimes he really did feel like it was. He knew a lot of the native Floridians resented this attitude that many New Yorkers held. He couldn't have given a shit. These backwoods morons never failed to remind him that he was living in a state that used to be a swamp. He didn't care about his partner Sparky Taylor's assertion that the average Floridian had a higher level of education than the average New Yorker who moved to the state. He didn't care about the embarrassing things that went on in New York City because he could explain it away as an anomaly. He didn't care what people down here said about New York. His role as the top homicide investigator in the entire sheriff's office, maybe the whole state, backed him up on his attitude about Southerners.

He had sat quietly and listened while Lisa prattled on about her numerous romances and challenges in medical school and how she had become interested in being a coroner or medical examiner after a class on the subject. Her career decision had horrified her gynecologist father and psychiatrist mother, but she loved her work and apparently loved talking about herself too.

Mazzetti didn't mind as he stretched and leaned back in his chair at the chain seafood restaurant on the second floor of Jacksonville Landing. Even though he enjoyed being with this pretty girl, he'd seen too much crazy shit in this tourist trap to not keep his eyes moving over the restaurant and the people walking along the river. Not too long ago the body of a woman stabbed through the heart had been found in her car parked in the parking garage. They never figured out who killed her and there was a second set of blood drops in the car that were never identified. Jacksonville, not the place to let your guard down.

The whole time Lisa talked about her brothers and sisters and experiences in college, Mazzetti couldn't help but think about Patty Levine and feel a pang of guilt. Even though it was she who had broken off the romance, he felt like he should've given her a heads-up he was going on a date. The first one since they had broken up. He decided maybe he'd just have a nice sit-down with her Monday morning.

As Lisa droned on about some class she'd taken, Mazzetti caught the waiter's eye and signaled for another Jack and Coke. Then he held up two fingers to make sure he got a double.

Maybe a walk along the river would quiet her down.

Lynn stood on her tiptoes to make Connor believe she was interested in kissing him. He tended to ignore the way she swiped his hand away from her breast and broke the kiss off early. She had a burning desire, but it wasn't the same as his. This loathsome, drunken creep was a stereotype of what she had expected. He was tall and handsome and his parents no doubt had money, and because of all that he expected women to do everything he wanted. Just like he'd expected Lynn to drink with him at the bar. But he had not noticed how she would slide her nearly full glasses down the bar. He hadn't noticed her encouraging and cheering him when he threw down shot after shot of tequila. It was a fine line to get this moron plastered but not so plastered he called attention to them at the bar. She had been careful to allow him to walk out to the car, excusing herself to the ladies' room, then meeting him in the parking lot. There was no way she would be identified as leaving the bar with him.

The only guilt she felt so far was letting him drive while still hammered. Her fear was he would plow into a car of innocent people. Shattering their lives like her family had been shattered. It was still early and she wondered if Connor and his friends did this kind of drinking every night. If he did, she hardly needed to intervene. But she had a plan and knew it would work.

In his small kitchen she took the cleanest-looking glass and grabbed a half-empty plastic bottle of water from the refrigerator. She filled the glass halfway, dug in her purse and recovered the Baggie filled with mixed and matched pills, and started the final phase of tonight's mission. She pulled out two homemade ecstasy tablets one of her neighbors had stashed in his apartment. They had a logo that said J2A. She didn't know what it meant, but she had been assured they were powerful. She crushed them both up and slipped them into the drink. Then she took three sleeping pills her doctor had prescribed her mother several years ago. She did the same with them. She poured some red Gatorade from the refrigerator into the glass and stirred it. The half-and-half mixture was a light red.

As she walked back to the living room, Lynn forced a smile.

Connor sat up on the couch, his jeans tossed on the floor, tighty-whities visible under his shirt. He grinned and said, "Whatcha got there, cutie?"

She avoided a shudder. "You need to drink this to stay up with me and to keep from getting a hangover."

"Right on" was all he said as he eagerly reached for the glass. He gulped it down, spilling a few drops on his shirt. He patted the couch next to him.

Lynn's eyes darted around the room until they fell on a long bong in the corner. She pointed to it and said, "Fire one up while I use the ladies' room." She made a show of wiggling her butt to motivate him before the drugs all hit him at once.

Inside the tiny, disgusting bathroom she waited until she smelled the unmistakable aroma of pot. She'd tried it a couple of times in college and never saw the appeal. She heard him call out to her twice, the second time nearly incomprehensible.

This was too easy.

EIGHT

Patty Levine couldn't remember the last time she'd smiled so much in the evening. After a moment of reflection she realized it was her last real date with Tony Mazzetti. She had been supposed to meet him at a swanky Italian place named Gi-Gi's. Instead, she'd thought she'd surprise him by stopping by a construction site where he was conducting interviews. She'd walked into the middle of a fight Tony was losing badly against several burly construction workers. It had been her quick work with her ASP, cracking some of the construction workers in the leg, that had saved Tony at least a few punches and certainly some embarrassment. By then she'd known there was something wrong with the relationship anyway. She realized it was mostly her fault, but the fact that they were both cops and there was always some work issue breaking into their personal life had been what really broke them apart.

Tonight she had eaten sushi, drank a really big twenty-two-ounce Ichiban beer, and even tried some sake with Ken, the runner she'd met in the park. It was their first date, which was always special, unless the guy was a

dud. Ken was no dud. He was a podiatrist who special-
ized in sports injuries and was a consultant to the Jacksonville Jaguars. He was laid-back and funny, with
interests other than police work. He was exactly what
Patty needed tonight.

She often worried that Tony Mazzetti would scurry
back into his cave of isolation when they broke up. It
was her biggest concern about the relationship. Tony
was a great guy and deserved more credit than he gave
himself when dealing with women. If she believed
everything he'd told her, Tony had not had a date in
years before they hooked up. But she couldn't understand why. He was handsome and intelligent, and once
you got past his façade of arrogance, he was actually a
very sweet and pleasant guy. He lived to impress his
mom and sister in New York and felt the only way he
could do that was to either publish the ultimate book
on history—a passion of his—or maintain the best
clearance rate for homicides in the country. Patty knew
he had written a lot of articles on history and maybe
his goal was to write a book, but there was no doubt
Tony Mazzetti took his clearance rate for homicides
seriously.

Her concerns for Tony skipped to the back of her
head as she listened to Ken tell her about growing up in
Brownsville, Texas, and going to Temple University for
the school of podiatric medicine. She liked the laugh
lines that filled out on his face when he talked about
being a fish out of water.

"It took a while to get used to a big city like
Philadelphia. I must've run up twenty different flights
of stairs to imitate Rocky before I finally got the right

set. I swear every building looks like an architectural work of art even if it just houses the public works department." He smiled and gazed across the table directly into her eyes.

Patty took the final swig of her Ichiban, then reached over and took hold of his right hand. "Which do you like better, Jacksonville or Philadelphia?"

"If you would've asked me two weeks ago, I would've said Philadelphia, but now definitely Jacksonville."

She beamed and thought about leaning across the small table and laying a kiss on him. This was a great first date.

A walk along the river would be the perfect piece of the puzzle.

John Stallings tried to hide how uncomfortable he was in the brightly lit fellowship hall next to the giant Baptist church. The preacher with a giant, cartoon head gave a quick opening prayer; then everyone started to chat over nonalcoholic punch and tables full of homemade cookies. Maria seemed to know a lot of people, which surprised Stallings. She was generally on the shy and reserved side, but this place had brought her out of her shell.

She introduced Stallings by name, never saying he was her husband. She seemed perfectly at ease among these people. There was no music, but it still felt like a party.

The preacher, Frank Ellis, approached them, greeting couples on the way.

He gave Maria a hug and looked at Stallings, saying, "Don't tell me this is John."

Stallings shook his offered hand, shocked Maria had talked about him to the preacher. He made his cop's quick assessment. The guy was about his age, on the soft side, but wore expensive shoes and had a manicure. Could be harmless or on the make. Immediately Stallings didn't trust him.

Brother Ellis said, "I feel like I know you. I'm so glad you came to our friendly gathering."

"Maria can be quite persuasive."

Brother Ellis shared a quick glance with Maria and said, "That's not what she tells me. I hear she can't persuade you to leave police work and spend more time with the family."

He was about to snap back with an answer when he saw this guy's game. He was trying to bait him. Stallings took a breath and said, "We do the best we can, don't we, Father?"

"I'm a reverend, not a father."

"Sorry."

Brother Ellis held his smile, but probably knew his cover was blown. "What is it about your work that's so compelling?"

Stallings gave it some thought. "Helping people."

"What about your coworkers? Do you like them?"

"Most."

"How about your partner, Patty? I hear she's quite the looker."

That caught Stallings by surprise. What the fuck? If the preacher thought that, he must have gotten it from

Maria. Stallings steadied himself and said, "She's a great cop." He felt the urge to punch this prick rise in him. A shot to his giant noggin would knock him off his perch.

The preacher's instincts told him it was time to move on to another couple. All Stallings could do was turn and stare at Maria.

Patty Levine reached down and took Ken's hand as they strolled west along the St. Johns River in front of Jacksonville Landing. It seemed natural the way he interlocked his fingers in hers. Neither said anything as they passed other couples out on a walk. It was still relatively early and the dinner crowd was pouring out of all the restaurants in the big tourist mall.

After a few minutes Ken asked, "What are you thinking about?"

She didn't know. For the first time she could remember she wasn't thinking about some horrible crime from work or worried about a personal problem. She blurted out, "How nice this is."

He stopped, took her arms in his hands, and was about to lean down when Patty noticed a couple approaching from the right. Her eyes darted that way out of instinct and it stopped Ken in his tracks. Then Patty saw who it was and stepped away from Ken as she turned. What were the chances?

Patty threw on a forced smile and said, "What are you guys doing down here?"

NINE

The room was a gray haze of marijuana smoke when Lynn stepped out of the bathroom. She'd considered taking off her top to keep Connor interested in the scam, but then thought she'd rather avoid it altogether and just hoped he'd sunk deeper and deeper into a drug-induced coma. To her surprise, when she stepped through the cluttered living room and into his bedroom, he was sitting upright and puffing on the giant bong she'd noticed earlier. What the hell? Had life in a fraternity made him build up immunity to all drugs and alcohol? By her reckoning he had ingested four sleeping pills, two ecstasy tablets, a couple generic prescription-strength painkillers, six shots of tequila, a few beers, and now this pot. She hated to abandon her plan to make this death look like an accident, but she did have a knife in her purse if she had to use it. She was not leaving this apartment while Connor Tate was still breathing.

She sat down next to him on the edge of the bed. He automatically handed her the bong, which she politely refused. When she saw his eyes, Lynn realized how far gone he really was. His eyes didn't focus in any way and his pupils looked like giant hollow black caves. They were something out of a nightmare.

Connor slurred, "What's your name again?"

Instead of answering, she patted him on the shoulder, then guided him down onto the bed and made him comfortable with a pillow fluffed around his giant head. She rubbed his forehead, trying to get him to calm down and let the drugs kick in.

He mumbled, "That's nice."

She had learned not to listen to these arrogant frat pricks. If she did, she'd back out of every one of the murders. But in this case he did sound like a lost eight-year-old boy, and she wondered if she'd have the nerve to stick the knife in his throat if the drugs didn't work. Her purse was at the foot of the bed and she leaned across Connor's feet to look into it and grabbed the four-inch folding Buck knife one of the loading dock workers at Thomas Supply had given her. She took it in her left hand and sat back up to continue to rub Connor's head.

Just as she thought he was drifting off, he said, "When you're done with my head, play with my dick."

There it was. That's the kind of conversation she'd expected to have with this immature brat. She smiled and said, "Just relax for a few minutes and we'll see what happens." She heard a satisfied moan and could feel him relax under her touch. She looked over at her left hand and the knife that was still closed. It would be messy, suspicious, and dangerous, but she was starting to think she had no choice. She reached across and fumbled with the blade until it opened. Connor turned his head slightly, his eyes opened but unfocused.

He mumbled something three times before Lynn realized he was saying, "What do you got there?"

Her stomach tightened and she took a very deep breath. Her yoga instructor would be very proud of her. The knife was open and seated in her right hand as she looked over at Connor, his head lulled in the opposite direction. His entire neck was exposed and she could see a blue vein running down it like a river marked on a map. She had to wonder if it was a sign. She didn't much believe in omens, but this seemed awfully obvious.

Her hand tightened on the knife as she built her courage.

Then she heard something that made her pause.

Patty was nearly speechless as she regained her composure and scooted back to Ken. She didn't want him to feel awkward with people he had never met.

Patty smiled and said, "Ken, this is John Stallings and his—" She wasn't sure what to say. Then she blurted, "Maria." She watched as Stallings shook Ken's hand and looked him in the eye. In that instant, with a feeling of pride blossoming inside, Patty realized how much John's approval meant to her. He was her authority figure. He was so much more than just a partner. But the look on Maria's face was harder to read. She looked antsy and uncomfortable, not able to hold Patty's gaze.

Stallings said, "Where did you two meet?"

Patty sensed something odd about him as well as

Maria. He stayed close to Maria, away from Patty. His body language was not the usual confident, busy John Stallings. She wondered if the lull in cases had affected him by throwing off his normal rhythms. Maybe he needed the stress and thrived on the chaos.

Stallings said, "Well?"

"Well, what?"

"Where did you two meet?"

Patty said, "In the park by my house. Ken's a runner too."

Maria now looked like she was appraising the couple. Still she remained silent.

Patty said, "I'm surprised to run into you two out here."

"We were at a . . ." He paused, then said, "gathering. I suggested we take a walk. I've only been over here on business. At least in the last ten years. Wanted to see what all the fuss was about."

"Did you eat at the Landing?"

"No, we thought we'd get some dessert or something. The only place we saw was Sal's Smoothie Shack up the street."

Patty just said, "Oh." She knew Stallings was thinking the same thing about Sal's. They had worked on a homicide where one of the victims, a bright girl named Lexie, was an employee of Sal's and met her killer there late one Friday night. There were places that gave her the willies like that all over the city.

Patty sensed it was time to move on and let the Stallingses go about their business. John Stallings gave her an abrupt nod good night, never moving from

Maria's side. She wondered what she had interrupted as she took Ken's hand and led him on down the river walkway.

Lynn lay on the bed next to the long, silent form of Connor Tate. His snoring had caused her to wait before plunging the knife into his exposed neck. It seemed to have worked out well. She had waited patiently until she hadn't heard another sound for more than five minutes. She'd been comfortable as she lay with the knife still open in her right hand resting across her stomach. If he had showed any signs of consciousness she had been prepared to drive the knife down with tremendous force. But over the past forty-five minutes, Connor had gone from a light snore to a wheeze, to now nothing at all.

Lynn checked his pulse and thought she'd felt a slight beat so she decided to wait a few more minutes. She looked down at Connor's exposed, muscular legs, his defined abs under his hiked-up shirt, and the child-like expression on his handsome face. It didn't make her feel guilty. If anything this was fitting, if not very satisfying. After her first murder, Lynn realized she loved the sound of the victim's scream. Boy, did he scream as he sat trapped in the fire. It was a great, bloodcurdling cry. But not perfect. The sound of the fire and the fact he had pulled a pillow over his face in a useless attempt to save himself made the acoustics questionable and muffled.

Her next victim just talked and cried. It wasn't until

she'd pulled the trigger that she'd realized what she was looking for. It was the absence of a scream that made her understand that was what she was hoping for.

Alan Cole had made a decent yelp, but the impact of the fast-moving Suburban had been too much and cut off any real chance she had at hearing a gruesome scream.

Now big, dopey Connor had simply faded away without a sound.

On the bright side, no one could link four deaths with such different scenarios. Two would certainly be considered accidents. The other two were in different cities and had no connection. Other than her.

A smile slid over her face as she realized how cunning she'd become. Maybe she should do something more in the business world than be a bookkeeper. She'd work in her father's fading business, but he abhorred aggressive business practices. He just wanted to transport.

Lynn reached down and placed two fingers along the side of Connor's neck. Nothing. Now she could figure who was next and how he was going to die.

TEN

Dennis Switeck hated working Saturdays in the fall.
One of his true passions in life was college football,
and living in Florida gave him a firsthand look at three
of the perpetually best teams in the country. In the last
twenty-five years, the University of Florida, Florida
State, or the University of Miami had been in the national championship game nineteen times. That was as-
tounding. He loved the fact that people from Texas
talked about what a football state Texas was and how
they bragged about it constantly. Whereas Florida didn't
have TV shows made about high school football or
have to shout to the world how it was a great football
state, but went on to dominate college football year in
and year out.

Dennis's job as an assistant medical examiner in
Duval County meant that he had to work every third
Saturday. He could still catch most of the games on the
TV at the office, but it wasn't the same as partying with
his buddies at one of the sports bars or in someone's
party room. Today had been slow football-wise because
everyone was gearing up for the annual Florida–Florida

State game next Saturday, the weekend after Thanksgiving. It was almost like a state holiday when the two titans of college football met. Even though Dennis had gone to Michigan, he still got fired up for the rivalry game. It wasn't Michigan–Ohio State, and Floridians would never understand the intensity of that rivalry on every level, academic as well as sports wise. But it was still a great game and a fun weekend. That's why he had switched with Lisa Kurtz, who didn't give a shit about college football. Why would a Syracuse graduate care about sports anyway? She was happy to change weekends because she had some big date with the hotshot homicide guy from JSO.

Dennis got a call about 1:30 from a detective saying he was on the scene of what appeared to be an accidental overdose at one of the fraternity apartment houses near the University of North Florida. Now, two hours later, he was about to do the autopsy on the young man who'd been found in his own bed. He was anxious to get started and cleaned up so he could head out to catch the night games, but the detective on the case, Luis Martinez, had been in the bathroom for what seemed like half an hour.

Finally the short, intense detective came into the procedure room, clapped his hands, and said, "Okay, Dennis, let's get this show on the road."

Dennis had to chuckle because Martinez was one of the funniest detectives he knew. But he still had a lot of questions. Martinez explained that the young man's body had been found in the late morning when one of his fraternity brothers had had to enter his apartment to get the key to their clubhouse. It wasn't unusual for the young man to sleep late, but when they hadn't been able to find the key they'd had to try and wake him up.

Dennis said, "You got the notes I needed?"

Martinez handed him a clipboard that started with the decedent's name, Connor Tate.

Martinez said, "My guess is a mixture of dope and alcohol. We didn't rush through the scene and we bagged his clothes and the blanket he was lying on. It didn't appear that anyone else had been in the apartment. None of his buddies saw him last night. He's a big drinker and is not opposed to using all kinds of pharmaceuticals. Plus his fucking apartment reeked of weed. I mean like every single crevice and carpet fiber smelled like pot."

Dennis shrugged his shoulders and said, "None of them listen to the public service announcements. We must get ten of these a year from the different universities." He had already figured out what he would say in the official report even before he started his circular saw and cut the top of Connor Tate's skull off.

John Stallings was frustrated the week flew by so quickly. A workweek with a holiday in it threw off his schedule. The occasional Monday holiday like Labor Day or Presidents Day didn't bother him too much, but Thanksgiving, falling in the middle of the week and using up both a Thursday and Friday, put a cramp in his investigations. It also threw off any support he hoped to get. Analysts took the whole week off; even Patty was leaving soon and wouldn't be back until Monday.

Stallings had kept himself busy by interviewing a

dozen different frat boys who were all friends of Zach Halston. Patty had focused more on other aspects of finding the missing young man. She spent a lot of time with the computer techs going through his computer and working with the analysts scouring phone records. Stallings didn't mind because he showed the photograph he'd found of Jeanie and Zach to everyone he talked to. It made it easier to hide what he was really doing from Patty. Some of the fraternity boys vaguely remembered Jeanie, but no one recalled her name. Stallings could feel the pressure building inside him to find Zach Halston and get some answers.

He heard from one of the brothers about the death of Connor Tate. Stallings checked with Luis Martinez, who'd been assigned the unattended death. Martinez was satisfied it was just a simple overdose. Everything pointed in that direction. Connor had a history of recreational drug use, was a heavy drinker, and wasn't afraid to mix his pharmaceuticals. The autopsy had shown that he was healthy and suffered no trauma. The medical examiner's office was still waiting on the toxicology reports, but Martinez had said there were pills in the apartment, half-empty bottles of alcohol everywhere, and the apartment reeked of pot. It sounded like the time Stallings had visited.

The Tau Upsilon fraternity overall didn't seem like a bad bunch of kids; most were focused business majors and some of the alumni had decent jobs. The gaudy, multicolor tattoos on the inside of their right ankles were the only thing they all had in common. All the tattoos were identical and showed the fraternity Greek letters set in palm trees in the back of a red pickup truck. Stallings liked the sense of Florida and the boys' sense of humor.

But here it was the day before Thanksgiving and he was no closer to finding Zach Halston than he had been last week. He'd made a dozen copies of the photograph of Zach and Jeanie and given them to a couple of the boys. He'd been very specific about them only showing it to other fraternity brothers and only telling him of the results. No one else.

Stallings started to sketch out some plans to talk to fraternity brothers outside the area when Patty walked up to his desk.

She had a bright smile when she said, "Whatcha working on?"

"Figuring out who we might need to talk to next week. What about you?"

"I used my feminine wiles to get the computer guys to rush the review of Zach Halston's computer." She plunked down a pile of paper on his desk. "List of what appears to be his customers. The list of all the fraternity brothers. Some unknown telephone numbers that look like they might be associated with his partners in the pot business and a half a dozen credit card numbers that he and other brothers were using to buy stuff online. All the cards are under other people's names and the two people I checked with didn't know that they had credit cards under their name. So it looks like Mr. Halston, in addition to being a college student, is a pot dealer, identity thief, and probably at the top of many people's hit lists."

Stallings patted the paper and said, "Does it bother you to go outside of guidelines to have some computer nerd rush your request?"

"You scare people, I tease people. We each have our skills, and as long as we don't abuse them, it's no problem. For instance, you haven't punched anyone in front of me for several weeks. I think you're using your scary skills reasonably. I made no promises to any of the computer nerds, but I'll admit I unbuttoned my shirt one button and leaned in while I was talking to them. If that makes me a bad cop then I'm guilty."

Stallings let out a laugh and said, "You're not a good cop, you're great cop, and don't forget it."

"Does that mean you won't think less of me if I cut out early this afternoon and head down to my parents' house?"

"That where you're having Thanksgiving dinner?"

"Yep, what about you?"

"I signed on for the whole deal tomorrow afternoon at my mom's house. It's supposed to be my dad, my kids, and Maria. My mom says my sister may even make a guest appearance, which would make it the first time we were all in the same room together in more than twenty years."

"It was nice seeing you and Maria out last Friday night."

"There wasn't much to it, I'm afraid. But I'm working on it." Stallings paused and smiled and said, "Your date looked like a nice young man."

"You think anyone that isn't Tony Mazzetti is the perfect match for me."

Stallings started to argue the point, then held up his hands. "I'm just saying, Ken seemed very nice."

"I thought about asking him to my parents' for Thanksgiving dinner, but I didn't want to scare him off. I hope to hook this fish more securely before I decide to reel him in."

Stallings looked up and said, "Enjoy your time off and we'll crank up again on Monday."

Patty gave him a dazzling smile and a quick wave and was on her way.

Tony Mazzetti returned Patty's wave as she hustled out the door. All morning he'd been hoping she might sit down and chat with him at his desk. He didn't need much, just a quick whiff of her perfume or an up-close look at that beautiful smile. He knew they weren't getting back together, but he wished she'd spend more time with him in the office.

His cell phone rang as he watched Patty disappear out the door. He dug the phone out of his pocket and whipped it open to see Lisa Kurtz's office number on it. He felt guilty not answering it. It had nothing to do with how he felt about Patty. He just couldn't face the pretty Syracuse grad explaining why she was the most fascinating and intelligent woman in the world.

She may not have been all that bad. Mazzetti had to recognize he liked being the center of attention himself and it may be that she was just too close a reflection of himself. Regardless, he had no intention of spending his Thanksgiving with her, nor did he really want to explain to her why he wouldn't be. The easiest solution seemed to be to avoid her at all costs.

The medical examiner and the homicide squad worked hand-in-hand, and she would know he wasn't too busy right now. Just the thought of the tall, red-haired assistant medical examiner surprising him in the office caused him to gather up his stuff and scurry for the door right after Patty.

Lynn gripped the Buck knife with the blade facing away from her hand. She swept past her target and then drove it in with a hammer fist. She did it two more times and watched the holes open. She stepped back switched grips, plunging the knife three times quickly into the center mass of her target. She stepped back, breathing heavy, watching the sand drip out of the large burlap bag she had strung up in a tree behind her duplex. She had studied knife fighting through YouTube videos and two books she checked out from the library. She realized she wasn't big enough to carry a lot of power behind her strikes so she had to focus on targets. The only target everyone agreed on was a victim's throat. She could slash it or gouge it and cause enough trauma to kill the victim.

The first few days she had practiced so hard with a knife that her hand had bled in several places. Lately she had started to realize how tough she was. A few scratches or blisters on her hand weren't going to keep her from completing her mission. When she'd first started dealing out her own kind of justice, she'd been a mild-mannered bookkeeper no one took seriously. But she had proven herself to be dangerous and, over the course of her mission, grown confident and efficient. If she had regretted any of her actions, that was behind her now. She looked forward to dealing with her next obstacle. It made her feel like she mattered. She wasn't a mousy coed. She was in charge. She was in charge of life and death. Justice had failed her and her family, and it made her feel sort of like a superhero to be handling matters herself.

Her next plan was more complicated than the others. It involved waiting for one of the creeps near his parents' house in Orlando. College kids always headed home for Thanksgiving dinner. That was a no-brainer. She also knew none of these fraternity assholes could resist going to a bar at night. That's where she'd make her move. By doing it in Orlando she added one more jurisdiction that wouldn't be able to figure out why a nice young man had been killed for no apparent reason.

She closed her sharp Buck knife and took one more look at the sad and ripped burlap bag in front of her. This was a skill that could last for her whole life.

John Stallings had a list of nine phone numbers in the Jacksonville area from Zach Halston's computer. Usually Patty handled jobs like this. It wasn't that he was anti-technology or unable to figure out how to track down information, but everyone recognized Stallings's strength lay in talking to people. And that was the strength he was going to use right now. He thought about what Patty had said earlier. She really could get

help from people in the building who barely acknowledged his existence. So now he swallowed hard and
thought about Jeanie as he approached one of the
squad analysts. She was the last analyst on duty before
the Thanksgiving break. Alice, the analyst, had made it
clear to Stallings on several occasions that she'd like to
take him out for dinner and possibly other things
whenever he felt he was past the breakup of his marriage. It didn't matter how many times he explained to
Alice that he was only separated and hoping to reconcile with Maria, she still probed and questioned him
about when they might meet after work.

Stallings approached her with a single sheet of
paper in his hand. He had handwritten the nine different phone numbers, four with 904 area codes, two with
386 area codes, and two more with 850 area codes. All
the numbers were either in Central or North Florida
and they had all been called by Zach Halston within
five days of his disappearance. The phone records that
Patty had retrieved on his cell phone had not shown
any calls since the last day anyone had seen him almost
three weeks before.

Before he had even reached her workstation, Alice
glanced up and a smile spread across her pretty face.
She brushed her bleach-blond hair out of her eyes and
turned to meet Stallings, who slipped into the chair on
the other side of her desk.

Alice said, "Does this mean you've finally come to
your senses?"

Normally, at this point, Stallings would set her absolutely straight. Instead, he tried to work it, handing
her the sheet of paper and saying, "I'm sorry, Alice.

I've just got too much going on right now to think about my private life."

"Even with the long weekend coming up?" She winked at him. Alice was in her mid-thirties and very attractive. She was not known as a flirt around the sheriff's office and Stallings couldn't understand why she was fixated on him.

"*Especially* with the long weekend coming up. I need to get a fix on these numbers as soon as possible. Any ideas?" He leaned in and gave her the best smile he could come up with. He had to think about Charlie and him kicking the soccer ball and Lauren laughing at one of his stupid jokes.

Alice looked at the numbers and said, "Wait right there and I'll run these through our intelligence database and see if it ever came up in any other investigations. Otherwise we'll have to get a subpoena from the state attorney to figure out who owns the phones." She didn't wait for a reply; instead she used her mouse to click through a few screens on her computer and then typed furiously for about thirty seconds. Then she looked back up at Stallings, making sure her eyes met his. "One of these numbers in the 386 area code came up in a narcotics case earlier in the year."

"Can you see what it was about and who owns the number?"

After a minute of typing and reading, Alice said, "Looks like it's a number from northwestern Volusia County. All it says here is that it belongs to a J. L. Winter, who was supplying pot to a couple of low-level dealers here in Jacksonville."

"That's it!" Stallings didn't mean to shout, but it

came out a little too loud. His intuition told him this was the guy supplying Zach Halston with the pot he, in turn, supplied to the youth of Jacksonville. He was so happy he wanted to jump up and kiss Alice, but the look on her face told him she might not let it stop at that. He understood what Patty was talking about. It was fun to use every possible skill to get the job done. He stood and said, "Alice, you're a lifesaver." Because he didn't feel right about leading anyone on, he said, "I couldn't do my job without you."

Now he had a lead.

ELEVEN

John Stallings drove slowly down US 17 near the town of Seville, Florida. He had lived in North Florida his entire life and he'd never been to Seville. The town literally had one stoplight and three Baptist churches. About three miles north of the town limits, a mailbox without a name or number sat in front of an entrance to a farm. It was a familiar enough sight in rural North Florida. Except Stallings paid attention to details. Most cops did. The first hint was high corn blocking a view to any part of the farm. Corn? Really? Florida could grow so many profitable crops. The demand for citrus grew annually. Nebraska could grow corn. Ohio could grow corn. But only Florida and California grew much citrus.

The next clue was the motorized, chain-link gate that was reinforced and spotless. A security gate like that cost at least ten grand. That was a lot of fucking corn. In addition, two security cameras scanned the entrance from concealed boxes on either side of the gate. Stallings couldn't believe an industrious sheriff's deputy hadn't looked into the suspicious farm yet. But he wasn't here to bust pot growers; he had much more important questions on his mind.

He pulled his car to the far side of the road a third of a mile from the entrance to the farm. He waited there fifteen minutes to get a feel for the traffic at ten o'clock in the morning on Thanksgiving Day. There wasn't much visiting going on in this part of the state today. In the back of his mind he was cognizant of his need to make the hour-and-fifteen-minute ride back to Jacksonville in time to be at his mother's by two o'clock. He had assured Maria last night he would not be late for dinner. He knew she was uncomfortable waiting at his mother's house without him. It felt as if he was on thin ice since the short conversation with Brother Frank Ellis and then the awkward meeting with Patty Levine and her new boyfriend. Stallings had hoped that seeing Patty with a good-looking, younger man would eliminate any fears Maria had about the relationship between Stallings and Patty. Instead, once again, Maria had turned inward and silent. So far it had been a shitty week.

Stallings slipped out of his Impala, crossed the empty two-lane road, and walked along the edge of the property until he found where the chain-link fence stopped and turned inward at a right angle. The property next door to the farm was abandoned and easy to access to follow the fence protecting the priceless corn. Stallings worked his way through the tree stumps and lawn trash until he was about a hundred yards off the road and facing the six-foot-high chain-link fence. Experience had taught him a number of things. One was that it was always easier to go under a chain-link fence than over. Even in his jeans and heavy flannel shirt with his Glock tucked in his waistband, Stallings knew he could sneak under the fence easily.

He made sure his gun was secure, put his cell phone on silent, and stuffed it in his lower left shirt pocket. This shirt had the two cargo pockets low that held a bunch of stuff. He liked the style. Too bad there were only a few days he could wear a shirt like this. Then he got to work.

First, he made sure there were no motion-sensor devices or tripwires run through the fence. Then he pulled a pair of heavy wire cutters from his shirt's lower pocket. He kneeled down next to the nearest metal support pole and snapped the wire straps holding the fence to it. Then it was just a matter of pushing the fence away from the post and rolling underneath. He stepped into the corn and within ten feet found his first row of four-foot-high marijuana plants. At least these weren't stupid rednecks. Since most of the marijuana eradication efforts by the state and federal government were done through helicopter survey of wide areas, it was smart to hide the pot within the rows of corn. Stallings could tell by the way the corn drooped over the lower pot plants that they'd be very difficult to see from the air. Every three or four rows of corn another row of pot sprang up.

Finally he found the inner row, with three trailers set up corner to corner to form a U with the driveway in front of them. He could see the driveway was built in a series of twists so no one from the road could look down the driveway and see anything but corn. Again, a bright move. Now that Stallings was here he didn't want to startle anyone. He had to make it clear all he wanted to know was where Zach Halston was and if anyone here recognized the girl from the photo.

Stallings was hoping he'd see someone walk from one trailer to another. But the longer he sat there the more he wondered if anyone was even present. There was a new Ford F-150 in front of the center trailer and a beat-up, older Chevy pickup on the side of the far trailer. It was a cool morning so it didn't surprise him that none of the air conditioners were running.

As he stepped back farther into the corn to move around closer to the trailers, Stallings bumped his head on something metallic. When he turned he was looking into the barrel of a shotgun and the angry face of a young man behind it, who said, "You better start talking quick and hope I don't have a reason to pull the trigger."

Tony Mazzetti sat in front of his fifty-two-inch Samsung flat-screen TV in the most comfortable La-Z-Boy recliner ever made with a Swanson's extra-large, microwavable turkey dinner with peas and yellow corn. He never took moments like this for granted. This was a guy's nirvana. On the giant TV, the CBS pregame show appeared on screen, with Dan Marino giving insights as to how the Detroit Lions were going to blow another Thanksgiving Day game.

He had already made the obligatory call to his mom and his sister. They were both insisting he start using the computer for video calls. Jesus Christ, it wasn't like he was eight years old. He was thirty-nine and his looks didn't change that much between visits back to Brooklyn. His sister didn't make the trip from Westchester County down to see his mother much more often than he made the flight up to see her. Sure, his sister was a judge and had a family and claimed that her time was already tight. But she was only thirty miles from the house they had both grown up in. Besides, his mother loved seeing her grandchildren. He understood that. He also understood that she expected him to start producing his own crop of children soon. That was one of the reasons he had yet to tell her that he'd broken up with Patty. He wouldn't lie to her, but he avoided the subject. Today when she'd asked about Patty, Mazzetti had mumbled something about her eating at her parents' house down in Ocala. As far as he knew that was true.

There was a rap at his front door. It was strong and steady, almost like an official police knock. He sighed and carefully set the plate full of food on the arm of his La-Z-Boy. He padded through the living room, glancing out the window to see if he noticed a car in the driveway. He had no idea who'd be knocking on his door in the middle of the day on Thanksgiving.

He twisted the dead bolts and opened the door and was surprised to see Lisa Kurtz standing there with her arms folded and her red hair in a ponytail flipped over her shoulder and running down to her chest. She had on an all-weather coat that went all the way to her knees, almost like a trench coat. She was tapping her right foot impatiently.

Mazzetti stared at her silently for a moment, then said, "Ah, Lisa, um, everything okay?"

"Are you trying to avoid me?"

He thought about his policy of not lying to people and decided silence was the best choice in this case.

Lisa didn't wait for an answer anyway. "Do you like me?"

"Of course I like you."

"Are you certain you like me?"

He wasn't lying. He did like her. He just wasn't sure he liked being around her. But he didn't feel like getting into this right now. Not before an afternoon football game. He said, "I think you're terrific."

A broad smile spread across her face. She opened her coat to reveal nothing but some very sheer lingerie, silk stockings, and lacy garters. Before Mazzetti could say anything or react, she stepped inside and enveloped him so quickly with her arms and legs that it felt like she was an octopus and he was the octopus's next meal, but somehow he didn't mind one bit.

One of the first things Stallings learned in the police academy was *never give up your gun*. No matter what. He looked up the barrel of a shotgun and tried to assess the young man behind it. This was no stoner. This was a businessman protecting his merchandise.

Stallings did his best to keep calm and said, "Don't get worked up, son. I'm not here to cause any trouble."

"You're on private property, which is completely surrounded by a six-foot-high fence, and you just walked through a million bucks of marijuana. I think you are here to cause trouble and I can't let that happen."

"I guess this is the wrong time to mention I'm a cop, huh?"

This caught the man by surprise and he took a second to swivel his head in each direction to make sure Stallings was alone. "You got a warrant, cop?"

"I don't need a warrant. I'm not here to arrest you or disrupt your business in any way. I just want to ask you about a young man who's missing in Jacksonville."

"Bullshit."

"Come on, you're not an idiot. Why would I make something like that up? Of everything I've just said, what sounds like a lie? I just want to talk."

"Who's the boy you're looking for?" Stallings could see the young man's finger slip off the trigger slightly.

"Zach Halston." The effect on the man was immediate. He knew Zach.

"What made you come here to ask about Zach?"

"His cell phone records showed he made a call here not long before he disappeared. I figured out the number he called belonged to J. L. Winter. Can I assume you're J.L.?"

The man stepped away from Stallings and motioned with the shotgun for him to step out into the open driveway. "Raise both of your hands and if I see either drop to your waist, I pull this trigger and all the buckshot rounds will pass right through you. Understand?"

"Like God himself were explaining it to me." He stepped out of the corn and into the driveway.

The man said, "Over towards the F-150."

Stallings wasn't in the mood to push the surly man with a shotgun. He started to walk quickly toward the new pickup truck with his hands up and out so there would be no mistake he was listening to commands.

He paused at the pickup truck and the man barked, "Walk up to the trailer."

Stallings complied and paused at the foot of the stairs leading to the clean double-wide, professionally set up on four-foot-high supports.

The young man shouted, "J.L., I found someone trespassing. He wants to talk to you."

Stallings watched as a curtain moved at the front window. A few moments later the door to the trailer opened and a woman about thirty, in jeans that accentuated her perfect curves and a low top that showed off her other assets, stepped onto the wooden stairs. She had a beautiful face with long, straight black hair. Her dark eyes looked from Stallings to the man with the shotgun.

The woman said, "Who are you?"

Stallings was so stunned all he could say was, "Are you J. L. Winter?"

"I am. And if you don't tell me your name I'm going to have Junior here blow your motherfucking balls off."

He couldn't say it fast enough. "John Stallings. Nice to meet you."

TWELVE

It was early afternoon when Lynn sat down to Thanksgiving dinner with her entire family, including her father's two brothers, who were in business with him, and their five children. It was quite a crowd, but her mother's silent toil over two gigantic turkeys kept her from feeling too festive.

Before dinner she noticed her father calling her cousins by the wrong names and forgetting where he had placed his scotch and water. Considering the high-pressure business he had spent a lifetime building, it was hard to imagine that he had become absentminded. Lynn had been so concerned that she and her older brother had taken him to a neurologist. The diagnosis was simply stress and exhaustion. There wasn't even a hint of Alzheimer's or some other neurological disease. As soon as she heard the young doctor explain it was stress and exhaustion, Lynn understood exactly how it could happen.

Her mother had taken another track. She was not nearly as expressive and vivacious as she had been Lynn's whole life. Her mom had been the den mother

for Cub Scouts, the team mom for soccer, and the orga-
nizer for Lynn's twirling team, as well as being involved in the Chamber of Commerce and City
Council. Now she seemed to read a lot and cook ex-
travagant meals that she and Lynn's father just picked
at.

Her father's lack of drive had caused the business to
suffer greatly. She suspected that was one of the reasons her uncles had come to Thanksgiving dinner. Neither of them had her father's international vision or
genius for transportation, but they had supported two
families riding on his coattails.

Of her own siblings only her younger brother Josh
had shown any interest at all in her father's business.
And he didn't have the contacts to complete the transportation needs if her father could no longer do it. Josh
was a salesman. He didn't think globally, he only
thought locally. He liked being close to Mom. He'd
even gone to the University of North Florida so that he
could still be within arm's reach of Mom.

Even thinking about Josh focused her attention on
the task ahead of her. Tomorrow afternoon she'd leave
for Orlando.

Stallings sat on the nice leather couch next to the
beautiful J. L. Winter in the double-wide trailer that felt
more like a luxury suite at the Four Seasons on the inside. A big-screen TV with a dozen speakers placed
around the room sat at one end and a wet bar stocked
with every imaginable high-end alcohol sat at the

other. He noticed two safes bolted to the floor next to the wet bar. He wondered why someone would go to the trouble of securing expensive, heavy safes to the floor of a building that could be driven away. A love-seat was tipped backwards and designed to sit over the safes, hiding them from view. Stallings wondered if J.L. had tried to stash something in the safes when he walked up. It didn't matter now. The moron with the shotgun had been sent away and he still had his gun and badge. If they were going to pull any shit, they would've pulled it by now.

Junior popped his head in the door and asked in his heavy, North Florida twang, "This old man behaving himself, J.L.?"

J.L. let a sly smile slide across her face. Her teeth, jawline, and cheekbones were flawless. She had a twinkle in her brown eyes as she slowly turned her head to her associate and said, "No man who looks like this would harm a woman who looks like me."

It wasn't a boast. Not the way she said it. Or the way she looked. It was a fact. The only word Stallings could come up with was *stunning*. He had a million questions about how she'd ended up running a marijuana farm in the middle of fucking nowhere. They were obviously turning a profit and she wasn't ashamed of her occupation.

J.L. turned and looked him directly in the eye, leaned in close, placed a hand on his knee, and said, "Your eyes tell me you really are looking for someone. I can see the truth in people's eyes. That's my gift. It's one of the reasons I'm successful in a business like this." She let her hand linger. Finally she said, "How can I help you, John?"

Stallings tried to act casual as he reached into the breast pocket of his flannel shirt and pulled out one of the photographs of Jeanie and Zach Halston. He handed it to J.L., who took her time examining the photo. She looked back at him and said, "Are you looking for Zach or the girl?"

Just the way she said it cut through Stallings like a knife. She was damn near psychic. He cleared his throat and said, "Both."

J.L. nodded and said, "Of course I know Zach. You know I know Zach. But I've never seen this girl. We always met Zach up around Blanding Boulevard and handed off a couple of pounds of product at a time. He was just a small-time distributor for us, but he didn't argue or steal, so we kept a pleasant arrangement with him for about two years." Now she leaned back, crossed her legs, and said, "You didn't think I would be this open and honest, did you?"

"Not on my drive down. Once I met you I knew that you were a model citizen who wouldn't try and hide things from the police."

She smiled at his deadpan comment. "Will my honesty keep you from informing the local cops about my little business venture?"

"You give me something that helps me find Zach Halston and I'll forget I ever came south of Flagler Beach."

"What if I gave you something you might enjoy more than information?"

"I doubt my wife would enjoy me enjoying anything other than information."

J.L. let out a chuckle and said, "A married cop who doesn't wear a wedding ring. Your eyes tell me there's more going on in your marriage than you care to admit."

"Then why would I admit it?"

"Well played."

"Do you have any idea where Zach might be?"

"He called Junior a few weeks ago and said he was in trouble with some other dealers. We're purely a production facility and don't know anything about disputes between distributors or street justice. Junior told him it had nothing to do with us. We haven't heard anything else from any of our distributors about a problem. But Zach hasn't called us back. He hasn't been answering his phone either. If he was in that much trouble with another dealer someone would've heard about it and told us. That's why we never took him seriously. We just figured it was amateur jitters. These kids like the extra money, but they get paranoid about other dealers and cops."

Stallings wrote down a few quick notes.

J.L. leaned forward again and said, "Do you think he's all right?"

"To tell you the truth, I don't know. But I'm trying as hard as I can to find someone who knows what happened to him."

"I'm surprised a cop is out working on Thanksgiving."

"You guys are working on Thanksgiving."

"The pot business never takes a break."

"Neither does crime."

J.L. started to laugh. When she had finished and wiped her eyes with her French manicured fingertips she said, "Zach used a couple of his fraternity brothers to help him. I met two of them when I delivered some product. One was his roommate named Connor. The other kid was younger and very thin as I recall. His name was Kyle something and he was from Orlando. He was cute as a button and very preppy. Did you talk to him yet?"

Stallings shook his head as he scribbled down the name and description. He decided not to mention Connor's unfortunate overdose. He looked up to see J.L. staring at him. Stallings said, "I appreciate the help. Can I call you if I need more information?"

"You can call me for any reason at all, sweetheart."

John Stallings had rifled his desk like he was on a search warrant until he found a printout he and Patty had compiled of all of the Tau Upsilon fraternity brothers. He had to put on his reading glasses to follow the names as he placed his index finger at the top of the page and worked his way down. Finally he found an entry with the first name of Kyle. It was Kyle Lee and his cell phone number had a 407 area code. Jackpot. That was Orlando. Stallings even considered calling the boy right now but had to wonder about the wisdom of asking someone about unlawful marijuana sales and meeting other pot dealers over the phone. There was also the issue of the photograph. When all was said and done, Stallings was anxious to talk to this boy about the photograph of Jeanie, not about the missing, pot-dealing, fraternity brother.

Then another thought entered Stallings's mind. It was really the first time he had thought about it on this case. What if Zach Halston was dead? Aside from the fact that it would be a homicide, it would, more important, be a dead end to Stallings's inquiry about the photograph of Jeanie. He didn't know what he'd do if that happened. It was the main reason he hadn't even seriously considered telling Maria about the photograph.

The more Stallings pondered Zach Halston's missing persons case, the more he had to believe the young man was dead. Often a missing young person would not contact his family, but he would call friends. Sometimes a person goes missing on purpose to avoid an uncomfortable relationship or business dealings. That was still possible with Zach, but the fact that he had not called anyone in three weeks made it seem more likely that he was *unable* to call anyone.

Stallings had to assume Kyle Lee had gone home for Thanksgiving, but he would check the fraternity house first. He was about to bring up a map of Florida on his computer and see how long a quick ride to Orlando would take when he took the page with Kyle Lee's phone number and tucked it into his shirt pocket. He felt something in his pocket. His phone. He normally didn't wear heavy, flannel shirts with pockets in odd places, so he had forgotten about his phone altogether. When he flipped it open he saw there were six messages waiting for him. What the hell?

Then he noticed the time on the face of the phone. It was 3:30. He felt sick to his stomach for just a moment. Where had the time gone? He was an hour and a half late for Thanksgiving dinner with his entire family.

Thirteen

Stallings entered his mother's house without knock-ing. He'd made it from downtown at the Police Memorial Building in just under eleven minutes at great risk to his and other people's lives. He thought it was best to face his family in person rather than call and give them a chance to build up their aggravation with him.

As soon as he entered the living room he caught a quick look at Maria's murderous glare. His mother was much more direct when she said, "Look what the cat dragged in. Where the hell have you been?"

But it was the sight of his sister, Helen, chatting with his father at the edge of the living room sofa that shocked him. He stood there, ignoring Maria and his mother, staring at his sister. How could this be? Helen had always credited their father with driving her out of the house at fourteen. She'd run away and been missing for two years. When she came back she was never the same Helen. In fact, she had never moved out of the house again, aside from a brief stint living with Maria and the kids. She still lived with their mother. And she worried about every possible aspect of life. One of her biggest concerns was that somehow her running away had affected Jeanie's disappearance. Almost like it was in their genetic code to flee their families.

Helen had disliked their father so much and for so long that when she found out he was still in their mother's life, she would leave the house every time he came over. Now, his attractive, older sister sat in a church-style dress with her back straight and hands in her lap, talking earnestly with the father who had been gone for almost twenty years.

Stallings's mother walked up and gave him a hug, whispering into his ear, "I know how you feel. I'm just as amazed as you are. It really is a miracle."

Stallings just nodded. He didn't want to interrupt their conversation. Instead, he turned just in time to catch Charlie as he barreled into him for a hug. He looked over the boy's shoulder for Lauren and saw her in the dining room, reading a book at the already set dining table.

When Charlie wandered back over toward the TV, Maria stepped up to him and said, "What were you doing that was so important you kept us all waiting almost two hours?"

Stallings hated to lie, so he had to say, "Something came up at work." He knew how she felt about him putting work first. This would be a prime example that she could talk over with Brother Frank Ellis about how inconsistent Stallings was with his promises.

Maria said, "Were you working with Patty?"

"No. She's in Ocala at her parents' house. I was on my own today." As soon as he finished saying the words he realized the implications of what Maria was saying. She really was jealous of Patty. But if he said anything too strongly now it would look suspicious. He reached into his pocket and felt the photograph of Jeanie and Zach Halston. He wanted to show her so badly. He wanted to change the focus of her rage. It'd be the easy way to get out of the situation he found himself in right now. It might change her entire opinion about him.

Or it might break her all to pieces.

He removed his hand from his pocket and left the photograph.

This was going to be one long Thanksgiving dinner.

FOURTEEN

The Friday after Thanksgiving had always been somewhat of a letdown for John Stallings. When he was a child he looked forward to Thanksgiving as a chance to spend time with his mother's family, who would drive down from South Carolina to visit for the long weekend. He felt like a grown-up, watching football with the men in the living room, either waiting for or recovering from a giant meal. But by the next day, he was relegated to entertaining his younger cousins and once again ignored by his father. In the past few years it had been an empty holiday, giving him more time to think about his missing daughter and less time to work on finding her or other kids. This year, being separated from his wife and living in a lonely house over in Lakewood, Stallings had no intention of spending the day at home, alone and brooding.

He had waited until midday, having made a few phone calls to make certain the people he needed to talk to were where he thought they'd be. In the case of Kyle Lee, friend and fraternity brother to the missing Zach Halston, Stallings had been able to scare one of the other fraternity brothers into silence after he told Stallings Kyle was at his parents' house in Winter Park, a quiet, upscale suburb of Orlando.

Now Stallings found himself pulling into Gainesville after slightly more than an hour through the back roads of North Florida from Jacksonville. Stallings had always liked the atmosphere of the college town. Although the Gainesville cops told horror stories about what went on with the students at the University of Florida, the town itself always seemed pleasant and friendly. Stallings figured that any school as big as the University of Florida had problems that would scare the average parent of an incoming freshman. More and more he understood the value of a smaller school like the University of North Florida or Jacksonville University.

He pulled into a string of buildings that looked like they were part of the university even though they weren't specifically on-campus. Part of the university's School of Art and Art History, these offices held university personnel who didn't officially teach classes. They were tech people and former movie business employees who knew how to work cameras and create special effects. It seemed to be the perfect haven for the artist sick of show business but still in love with his craft. It was here that Stallings had cultivated one of the oddest and most rewarding relationships of his professional career.

He saw the older Toyota Tercel, covered in bumper stickers to hide scratches and holes, directly in front of the main entrance to the last building. It was the only vehicle in the entire lot. A smile spread across Stallings's face. He could relate to being the only one who worked on a holiday. The front door was unlocked and he knew his way down the long hallway to the small office crammed with old photographs and newspapers that had to be digitized, examined, and sometimes disseminated. To Stallings this was a very special place.

He paused at the open door and gazed in at the woman, in her early sixties, who peered through thick eyeglasses at a photo that looked like it was from the 1940s. She sat forward in her chair almost like it was a stool as a way to help support the massive weight of her hips.

After a moment her eyes moved from the photo to Stallings and a broad smile stretched across her pretty face. "You should call before you come over. How did you even know I'd come in today?"

Stallings smiled and shook his head, saying, "I could tell you I was psychic because I know you really like that kind of stuff. But actually I called the house and Louise told me you had some project you're working on here at the office."

The woman held up a stack of old photographs and said, "I promised the dean I'd preserve the photographs of his parents' wedding. I put it off for more than three months and it's their anniversary on Sunday. Besides, if I had to sit around and listen to Louise bitch about the cats or why we're stuck in a shitty little town like Gainesville, I'd have to call you to come over and shoot me." She set down the photographs and pulled off her magnifying eyeglasses. "Come over here and give Sonia a hug." She held out her hands like a baby asking to be plucked out of her crib.

Stallings crossed the small room and gave his friend a long, comfortable embrace. He sat on a stool next to her desk as they caught up with each other's lives from the past eight months. Sonia had a talent for identifying people from photographs and enhancing the photographs to get the best results when the photos were published in public. Her work had been recognized across the country when missing children, as well as ailing elderly people who had disappeared, were recognized from photos she prepared for publication. More than once she'd helped Stallings on his quiet quest to find his daughter. She'd used university resources without documenting what they were used for and she had never asked for anything in return.

She was the model of a good friend.

After they had chatted for almost an hour, Sonia said, "I know you didn't come by to listen to an old lesbian's complaints about living in a Bible Belt college town. Now what you got for me?"

Stallings slowly pulled the photograph of Zach Halston and Jeanie from his notebook. This was the original photo he'd taken off the missing boy's wall. As he handed it over to Sonia, he saw the tremor in his hand exaggerated by the photograph.

Sonia carefully took the photo, laid it flat on her desk, picked up her glasses, and adjusted the lamp on her desk. She studied the photo for a full minute without saying a word.

Then she sat up straight, took off her glasses, and faced Stallings. "I know who the girl is in the photo. Who is the boy?"

Stallings took a moment to gather his thoughts and

said, "He's the focus of my missing persons investigation. I just happened to find this photo while searching his apartment."

"This was taken after Jeanie disappeared, wasn't it?"

"Yes, it was."

"My, my, that's a twist. What did you want from me, exactly?"

"First, I wanted someone to verify that I was actually looking at a photograph of my daughter. Second, I was wondering, with your connections in the missing child world, if you could circulate her photograph. If the photo came from me, my bosses might take me off the case altogether."

"I think they would have to take you off the case. Ethically speaking."

Stallings stomach tightened as he wondered if he had overstepped the bounds of their friendship and forced her to make a choice between ethics and helping a friend. He tried to get a fix on her until she said, "Luckily, since I am not a member of the law enforcement community directly, I have no ethical issue. I'm assuming you don't want me to bill JSO for any of this?" She smiled and suddenly Stallings felt a tremendous wave of relief.

Sonia said, "If all guys were like you, decent, funny, and cute, I probably would've given men more of a chance when I was younger. But as you know, most men are pigs. So I'm quite happy with my life. I would dearly love to see you happy with yours."

Without even realizing he was saying it, Stallings mumbled, "Me too."

*   *   *

Tony Mazzetti had never stayed in bed past noon in his entire life. When he was a kid, his mom would yell at him to be up before eight o'clock even on the weekends. After years of shift work and investigations, he had made it a habit, even if he worked all night, to be up by eleven. But somehow lying naked under his cool sheets with Lisa Kurtz giggling next to him, he didn't feel like he was wasting a day off.

Aside from a couple of trips to the bathroom and grabbing all the fresh fruit and orange juice in his kitchen, he had not left his bed since yesterday afternoon. The way they had been going he wondered if he might need to invest in a heart rate monitor if he intended to continue dating the assistant medical examiner. She was all energy, enthusiasm, wavy red hair, and soft white skin. It was a cliché, but this thirty-year-old made him feel young too.

She snuggled in next to him and he wrapped his arm around her shoulder. She said, "I wish you had a TV in here so we could watch the college football games on today."

"There's no decent games the day after Thanksgiving. But there's Florida–Florida State tomorrow."

"Are you planning for us to stay in bed until tomorrow?"

"I could plan it, but I wouldn't survive it."

Lisa giggled. She turned her head and stared up at the ceiling and said, "Practically all I watch on TV anymore is sports and comedies. God, those TV police shows . . ."

"I know what you mean. If our CSI guys talked to

me like that I'd have to crack one of their heads open with my ASP."

"I know, right? I love how the crime scene guys get in more shoot-outs than the narcotics guys on that show."

Mazzetti realized that even though Patty Levine was a couple of years younger than Lisa, she was more mature in her attitude and speech. Lisa sounded like a college student more than a college grad. But right now, when she wasn't yakking about medical school or the medical examiner's office, and he felt her warm, soft body against his, he didn't care one bit. Maybe she wasn't too bad. He couldn't compare everyone to Patty Levine. If he did, he was afraid he'd be disappointed the rest of his life.

They lay there comfortably for a few more minutes before Lisa said, "I forgot I traded weekends and have to work tomorrow anyway. As slow as it's been, it's not going to be a big deal."

"That's the way it is in homicide. It's like a roller-coaster ride with a lot of ups and a few downs. We call it the feast-or-famine syndrome and we're definitely in a famine right now. That's why I'm so frustrated I still can't solve the shooting of the auto parts manager from a few months ago."

"I'm sure something will break on it soon. I saw something that reminded me of the victim earlier in the week."

"What's that?"

"We had an UNF student who died of an overdose over the weekend."

"The one Luis Martinez is working?"

"Yeah. It looks like a simple overdose. The kid was a known drug user and big drinker. We're just waiting for toxicology. Anyway, he had the same funky tattoo on his right ankle as the victim from your shooting."

"The one with the Greek letters from a fraternity in the bed of a red pickup truck?"

"The exact same one."

"No shit?" He started to calculate the odds of two fraternity brothers dying, when he was distracted by Lisa starting to kiss his chest, then his stomach.

Lisa said, "Now I think I need some more protein."

Mazzetti felt himself respond but not like he had yesterday. He might need some protein himself. If this kept up he might need a regimen of vitamins.

Or something stronger.

FIFTEEN

A quiet, rational conversation with a woman like Sonia always put Stallings in a positive frame of mind. He felt like he had accomplished something and he was doing his best to find his daughter and piece his life back together. He knew it was a tremendous long shot, but it was better than brooding at home.

Now he raced down Interstate 75 toward Orlando and his surprise interview with Kyle Lee of Winter Park. As he came through Ocala, Stallings had to pull off to grab something to eat. He slipped into a Firehouse Subs shop and ordered the first thing on the menu board with a Coke and took the whole meal out to his car. He ate the sandwich as he continued south on the interstate. His car looked like it had been attacked by terrorists. This was not like him. He liked order and cleanliness. There were food receipts and discarded wrappers across the passenger seat and floor. He started to wonder if he was losing his grip on reality. Maybe Maria was right and he had his priorities all mixed up. He didn't want to worry about it right now;

instead, he wanted to get down to Kyle Lee's house and find out what the University of North Florida student knew about Zach Halston's disappearance and if he recognized Jeanie from the photograph.

He found the house easily enough. It was an up-scale, two-story house in an upscale neighborhood of an upscale town. Winter Park had essentially been established by a wealthy northern industrialist as a southern getaway more than a century ago. Now it had a nice, calm, artsy feel to it.

Grabbing his notebook and keeping his ID visible, Stallings walked past a new pickup truck in the drive-way and knocked on the front door. A pleasant-looking, plump woman in her early fifties answered the door. Her eyes popped slightly at the sight of his badge, a common response of suburbanites dealing with law enforcement officers.

The woman said, "Oh my, is everything all right, officer?"

Stallings smiled in that flat, unemotional way Patty had taught him. "Yes, ma'am, everything is fine. My name is John Stallings and I'm with the Jacksonville Sheriff's Office. I was wondering if I could have a few words with Kyle if he was home."

The woman's eyes cut over her left shoulder and then back to Stallings. The instinct to protect your child cut across all social barriers and cultures. He could see her calculating the risk of hiding her son from a police officer. She said, "Why'd you want to talk to Kyle?"

"I am working on a missing-persons investigation.

Zach Halston, one of Kyle's fraternity brothers, is missing and I wanted to ask Kyle a few simple questions."

The woman looked visibly relieved and called over her shoulder, "Kyle, there's someone here to see you." She invited Stallings inside.

He did quick assessment of the house and its furnishings. He made her husband as an upscale accountant or money manager of some kind. There was no real reason for this rush to judgment, nor did it mean anything, but it ran through his head just the same.

A teenage girl walked through the living room and gave Stallings a fleeting smile. She reminded him a little bit of Jeanie, but nowadays almost every young woman reminded him of his missing daughter.

A thin, average-looking young man padded in from the family room and paused for a moment when he saw Stallings and his badge. Stallings noted the apprehension about talking to a cop.

After they had exchanged introductions and Mrs. Lee had left them alone, they sat on the ornamental couch in the living room and Kyle answered the standard questions Stallings would ask about any missing person. He had not heard from Zach, but hadn't really been worried either. Zach was known to go on short vacations and not show up for a few weeks at a time.

Then Stallings started getting serious with Kyle. "You knew about Zach's off-campus apartment, right?"

Kyle nodded. "I've been there a few times."

"Did you know how he afforded to live off-campus?"

"I, ur, um, I thought his parents paid for it."

Now Stallings had the young man where he wanted him. He had caught him in a clear lie and realized this boy was concerned about something more than a missing friend. Stallings let his hard look sink in on the boy for a few moments before he said, "You think his parents didn't mind paying for an on-campus and off-campus apartment? Cut the shit, Kyle. There's something going on here I don't understand and you're going to explain it to me." He leaned forward and grasped Kyle's forearm and said quietly, "And I mean you're going to explain it to me right, fucking, now."

Kyle swallowed hard, his Adam's apple bouncing up and down in his scrawny neck.

Stallings added, "This is not the time to lie to me either, Kyle." He could tell by the look in the boy's eyes that he was about to hear the truth. Maybe for the first time in this case.

Lynn pulled her black Nissan Sentra to the curb at the end of the street where Kyle Lee's parents' house sat. She was confident no one would notice a young woman sitting in a nondescript car in a suburban neighborhood. She felt sort of like a spy watching the house of a target after finding the address through several public records websites. She recognized his Dodge Dakota pickup truck. Clearly it was another upper-middle-class white kid trying to fit into the culture of Jacksonville. The easiest way was to buy a pickup truck. She'd seen the same truck around the fraternity apartment complex several times so she knew this was the right house.

She had arrived earlier than she had intended. It was still midafternoon, but she could always go and get something to eat and putter around downtown Winter Park. She wondered how cops were able to sit on stake-outs. She'd have to leave to pee at least once an hour, but somehow cops seem to get their job done. At least on TV. That was the extent of her involvement with the police.

She felt a twitch of excitement in her stomach and she dug into her purse for the Buck knife she intended to use on Kyle Lee. She had changed so much since this had started. She had gone from being terrified to now being excited by the prospect of taking someone's life. She could see how serial killers got started and couldn't stop. The idea of using a new instrument of death, like this knife, added another element to her excitement. Until recently she had never killed anything. She wouldn't even fish with her father. The idea of harming innocent animals repulsed her. But these were not innocent animals. Just animals.

Lynn had never thought of herself as cunning, but her plan to commit the murders in different jurisdictions and using different methods struck her as extremely cunning. She knew no one had a clue. So far it looked like even the fraternity members thought it was just a string of bad luck. She'd still have to head back to Daytona and handle Alan Cole. From what she had heard he was in a coma at Fish Memorial Hospital. There wasn't much information available other than he'd been struck by a hit-and-run driver in a large, blue SUV. Perfect.

Lynn considered how she might employ the knife when she finally met up with Kyle. She was searching for the perfect scream that had eluded her so far. A scream that would justify her actions and give her some satisfaction.

The only problem was she'd trained to strike him in the throat. Many of the knife-fighting references on the Web said the throat was the best target. The heart was protected by the sternum and was a relatively small target after the blade plunged through skin and cartilage. The throat stood out there exposed, begging to be slashed and stabbed. At least that's how one website described it. If Lynn followed this formula she forfeited her chance to hear Kyle scream. Scream in terror and sorrow. That's what she wanted to hear.

Stallings kept staring at Kyle until the young man looked up at him with a quick nod.

Stallings said, "You know how Zach made his extra money?"

Kyle just nodded.

"Is he missing because of that?"

"I don't think so. Like I said earlier, he's really unpredictable. He could've made some extra money with his pot business and taken off to Hawaii with some new girlfriend. That's the way Zach is."

Stallings assessed the young man and decided he was telling the truth even though he seemed somewhat evasive. Stallings pulled the photograph of Zach and Jeanie from his notebook and handed it to Kyle.

The young man took it in his hand and studied it for several seconds.

Finally Stallings said, "Do you know the girl?"

Kyle nodded his head slowly. "I think her name was Kelly. She was around for a couple of weeks maybe two years ago. I know she was gone by the time we had our big blowout that got the fraternity on probation. Everyone remembers that party and where they were and what they were doing before and after. It's like nine-eleven. I was only in elementary school, but I can remember the days leading up to it and after the attack. This party was just like that. And I know Zach had moved on to another girl by the time of the party."

Stallings's heart raced at the first news he had heard about Jeanie from an eyewitness in three years. He wasn't sure he could count his father, with his failing memory, as a reliable witness. But the fact that this boy remembered her as Kelly jibed with what his father had said. Stallings looked at Kyle and said, "What else can you tell me about this girl?"

"Why? There's no reason she'd know where Zach was."

Stallings contained his temper, but still felt like he was about to growl. "Never mind why. Just tell me what you know about her?"

"I don't know. She was nice and quiet. I think she worked at one of the old shops along University. You know, the secondhand shops that sell all kinds of funky stuff." He scratched his head and looked at the photo again. "She might have lived in an apartment close by too. I don't think she had a car."

"Do you have any other information on her?"

"No." He shook his head, more open to talking about the photo than he was about his friend's occupation. "Do you want to talk to her about Zach?"

"No, she's missing too."

SIXTEEN

It was just getting dark outside when Kyle started to settle down after talking to the big, scary-looking cop. He was glad Detective Stallings had come all the way down here to talk instead of at the fraternity house. Kyle was more comfortable here. He was always more comfortable at home. Unlike the other brothers, he wasn't cocky and sure he could score with women or ace a test. That wasn't in his personality.

It wasn't like him to get involved in drugs and heavy alcohol use either. He felt like a stick in the mud when the other fraternity brothers really got cranking. Look where it had gotten them. Zach was missing and Connor was dead. He wished Zach would call someone and tell them he was okay.

But Kyle had to wonder if this cop who'd come all the way down from Jacksonville was really just looking for Zach or if he was looking for something more. No one in the fraternity really thought it was just a simple missing-persons case. Not with all the shit Zach did. The whole encounter with the cop had shaken

Kyle and made him want to just stay home and watch a movie with his folks.

He wished he hadn't promised to meet some buddies from the University of Central Florida at a bar just outside Winter Park called The Knight's Tower. He was forced to go out most nights in Jacksonville. Tonight he really wanted to see his friends and the only place he could see them was at the bar.

Tomorrow night he planned to stay home and help his little sister with a school project she was doing on Florida water resources. Every time he looked at her he shuddered to think what his fraternity brothers would try if he ever let her come up and visit him in Jacksonville. Sometimes they acted like animals.

John Stallings hustled out of the Lee house, checking his watch and looking up at the sky. He calculated the route home, cutting up I-4 to I-95, in his head. With some luck he could miss rush hour and maybe be home in time to take the kids out for a surprise dinner. He was pretty sure Maria still wasn't speaking to him after his late arrival at Thanksgiving dinner.

He backed out of the driveway and pulled down the street, wondering what it would be like to be a cop in a town like this. The only person he saw out on the street was a young woman in her Nissan Sentra, parked at the curb. No hustlers, no dealers, no domestics, and no frantic cops trying to keep a lid on things. He settled in behind the wheel and headed northeast.

Stallings felt old and tired on the drive back to Jacksonville. He'd slipped past Daytona before rush hour and was now outside Jacksonville. It really had not been a hard day for him, but he was exhausted. It didn't seem that long ago when he could work all day and night and not notice the first sign of fatigue. Was forty really that much of a turning point in a cop's life?

He was starting to take the Zach Halston case more seriously. Aside from the fact that he wanted to ask Zach about the photograph, he no longer viewed him as just a spoiled, missing college student. He considered the possibility that Zach's marijuana business may have played a role in his disappearance.

As he passed the exit to Flagler Beach, Stallings's phone rang. He was surprised to see his old home number on the screen. It was Maria.

"Where are you?" she asked.

"Working."

"I figured as much. I went by your house and you weren't there. I thought you had today off work."

"Something came up."

"Something always does."

Stallings paused and then said, "I already apologized for yesterday. I really meant it too."

"You're right. That's why I wanted to talk to you. Would you consider coming to another fellowship tonight?"

"With Brother Frank Ellis?"

"He'll be there, but I thought you could go with me."

He felt a goofy grin on his face as he said, "I'll pick you up in an hour." Suddenly he didn't feel quite as old or tired.

* * *

Not long after Lynn had parked her car down the street from Kyle's house, she saw a nice-looking man who was in his late thirties or maybe forty get into the Impala in the driveway and pull down the street. She noticed him looking in each direction and their eyes met very briefly. She didn't think it was Kyle's father, and she was intrigued by all the possibilities that ran through her head. It was a little game to pass the time. But as she continued to wait there was no more activity from the Lee house.

One of the sneaky or cunning things she had done was to create a fake Facebook page and use the photograph of a tall, female volleyball player from Florida State. She knew no fraternity boy would pass up being friends with someone like this girl and Kyle accepted her immediately. In his profile he'd mentioned a bar near his house called The Knight's Tower where he would meet his friends who'd stayed in town to go to the University of Central Florida. She had already driven past the bar a few miles away and had an idea that's where Kyle would be heading tonight.

She had to be careful not to be seen with him by too many people. She had slipped on a low-cut top and tight jeans, knowing that you catch more flies with honey. This had already worked for her with these fraternity brats and she didn't mind giving it another chance at the bar. She still wasn't sure where she'd make her move. Lynn had no illusions about how messy it'd be. She had a change of clothes in her car and intended to discard her jeans and top as soon as she was done practicing her knife skills on Kyle Lee.

* * *

Maria stepped off the porch before Stallings even came to a complete stop. As usual, she wore no make-up and no fancy clothes. Just jeans and a nice top. And she was still one of the most beautiful woman Stallings had ever seen. She had a certain grace, even walking down the two steps from the porch. She flashed him a smile as she approached the car and he grabbed the larger pieces of trash on the floorboard of the passenger side of the car and tossed them into the backseat. It'd been so long since anyone had ridden with him that he hadn't even considered the mess.

She slipped into the passenger seat, turned, and said, "What'd you do today?"

What'd she say? Friendly chatter. He couldn't remember the last time she had talked to him in that tone. He couldn't believe how much a simple sentence like that meant to him.

He shrugged. "Just looking for a missing fraternity boy from UNF." He pulled away from the curb slowly. "Any trouble getting Lauren to babysit?"

"Nope. She'd do anything for us to spend time together."

Stallings thought, *I better raise that girl's allowance.* He drove along in pleasant silence as opposed to the usual strained silence.

Maria dug some paper from between the seat and console. He noticed her glance at each scrap as she crumpled them up and tossed them on the floor. Then she kept one and studied it.

Maria said, "This is from today."

"Yeah, I ate in the car."

"Firehouse Subs."

"Yep."

"In Ocala?"

He wondered where this was going.

Then Maria said, "Isn't Patty in Ocala? Is that the kind of work you were doing?" She turned and gave him the kind of look he'd use to wither a suspect's resolve. "This is why you worked on a holiday?"

Before he could answer she had sunk back into her seat with her arms folded. "Just drop me off" were the only other words she spoke.

Lynn couldn't believe how accurate she was predicting what Kyle would do. She'd left her spot near his house three times. One of the times was to eat dinner at a trendy, upscale sandwich shop, where she legitimately took a few minutes to contemplate what she was doing and if she should stop this crazy mission right now. But something wouldn't let her. Some force or power inside her kept pushing.

Now she found herself following Kyle as he pulled into the half-full parking lot of The Knight's Tower. The sports bar had a mix of low-class, cheap student vehicles and moderately well-maintained everyday cars. The building was long and sturdy, made up to look more festive than it really was. Basically, it was a long, concrete block structure with square windows, on which someone had painted a decorative black and gold mural depicting the mediocre accomplishments of the University of Central Florida Golden Knights football team. The two players that were highlighted in

tenth-grade-level artwork were former NFL quarter-
back Daunte Culpepper and NFL receiver Brandon
Marshall, easily the two most notable grads of the
sprawling Orlando-based university.

Inside, Lynn found the bar laid out like many sports-
oriented establishments. A long, walnut-colored bar
led to an open bay area with the required sixty-inch
flat-screen TV against one wall that featured whatever
the main game was for the day. Tonight a giant sign
underneath it read FLORIDA–FLORIDA STATE TOMORROW
AT 3:30. In Florida all other college games paled in
comparison to the titanic struggle between the archri-
vals. It didn't matter if either school was in the hunt for
the National Championship or not; the game had taken
on epic mythology with every Southern football fan.

She eased onto the stool closest to the entryway and
ordered a chardonnay. She was able to see Kyle clearly
as he sat at almost the opposite end of the bar and
turned around to face the big TV showing highlights of
the pro and college football games from the last two
days.

The walls of the bar were decorated with memora-
bilia from the University of Central Florida with a few
shirts from Rollins College, a local, high-end private
school. There was an unwritten code that none of the
big three football schools would be acknowledged in a
place like this. There was no FSU garnet and gold. No
University of Florida blue and orange. And no green
and white of the University of Miami. Over the years
the University of Central Florida had eclipsed all three
schools in sheer size but had never accomplished anything close to the athletic glory each of the other Flor-

ida schools enjoyed. No one wanted to be reminded they were mediocre.

Lynn was patient, waiting to make sure there was no one inside the place who Kyle was going to meet. Once she was certain he didn't know anyone in the main room she started to build up the nerve to approach him. Her goal was to get him outside before anyone realized he'd been here. She still wasn't sure what she was prepared to do to accomplish this goal, but in this sexy getup with her best lipstick and eyeliner on she was hoping it wouldn't take too much.

Just as she was about to stand up and make her way toward Kyle, she felt a tap on her shoulder that made her jump. Lynn turned to see a young man, about her age, with a big grin on his face. He had a cute, preppy look to him and dark eyes.

He said, "Hey. I've never seen you in here before."

This was the first kink in her plan.

SEVENTEEN

John Stallings had been stunned by Maria's tirade after finding the receipt from Firehouse Subs in Ocala. Stallings had not taken Brother Rick Ellis seriously when he'd suggested Stallings and Patty had a romantic connection. Obviously this was a real concern for Maria and nothing he'd said had calmed her down in the least. She had demanded he take her back to the house immediately and had even threatened to jump out of the car and walk home.

Stallings saw the futility of his position and agreed to take Maria back to the house. His heart broke a little as he watched her march away from his car and up the stairs to her porch without even glancing behind her one time. He sat there like a doofus in front of his former house for more than five minutes before he realized he needed to do something. Anything.

Stallings started to drive, and before he realized it he was in front of the soup kitchen where his father worked most Friday nights. Stallings was careful to park more than a block away so his unmarked police car didn't spook any of the patrons of the soup kitchen. The chief volunteer, a lovely woman named Grace Jackson, who was a local teacher recognized often in the paper for her community spirit, had once told him never to park any vehicle that could be interpreted as a police car in front of the place.

As soon as he walked through the door he saw that most of the patrons had been served and the cleanup was almost completed. At the far end of the room his father sat at a round table eating a fried chicken leg and chatting. As he walked across the room a real fear rose in Stallings that his father might not recognize him immediately. His memory bounced around from perfect to almost blank without reason or schedule. Stallings often worried this man he'd just gotten to know again after more than twenty years would eventually forget him altogether. It made Stallings feel like he didn't exist at all if his own father had no memory of him. But on his good days he rationalized that it was better to have made amends with his father even if it meant only a short time together than to have remembered him as the bitter, drunken bully he had been for most of Stallings's childhood.

At the table next to his father sat Grace. She was younger than Stallings, perhaps thirty-five, with a pretty face and a perfect, chocolate complexion. The last time he had seen her, several months earlier, she had told him how much his father meant to her. Now, as he saw them smiling and talking, he felt a pang of guilt over not establishing a relationship with his estranged father sooner.

Stallings felt this tension release when Grace gave him a bright smile. His father turned and Stallings's heart stopped for a second until the older man smiled too.

James Stallings said, "Hello, Johnny. What brings you over here tonight?"

Stallings couldn't believe how happy he was to see his father's smile and hear his lucid words. It was almost enough to wash away the lingering feelings about Maria's fit.

James Stallings turned to Grace Jackson and said, "This is my son, Johnny. He's a big-shot detective with JSO."

Grace smiled. Her teeth were bright and straight and beautiful. She said, "I've met your son." Then she surprised Stallings by standing up and greeting him with a big hug. She was shorter than him, around five foot two, and a little plump, but he definitely sensed something extra in their lingering hug.

Stallings liked the way she held on to his hands as she released her hug and just stared at him for a moment. The last time he had seen her she was in an apron and had been working behind the kitchen counter for hours. There was something about her that looked fresh and invigorated. She had the most alluring dark eyes set in a pretty face, so Stallings just enjoyed the moment.

They all sat together at the round table and chatted about different things. Stallings felt comfortable enough with Grace to pull out the newly found photo of Jeanie and slide it in front of his father.

James Stallings took the photo and stared at it for a

moment. He looked up at his son and said, "Today it's crystal clear in my mind. I can even remember the sound of her voice."

Stallings said, "You once said she went by a different name too. Do you remember?"

The older man nodded his head and said, "Kelly."

It was all coming together. Between what Kyle had said and now his father, he was sure Jeanie was alive. He was about to ask his father another question—then, without warning or reason, James Stallings started to sob.

Lynn was polite but firm. She didn't want to have anything to do with this preppy pest. But his cheerful smile gave no indication that he understood what she was talking about. He just kept nodding and insisting he wanted to buy her a tequila shooter.

Finally she had to say to him, "Is English your first language?"

The pest giggled and nodded his head. "You are just too cute. There is no way you're leaving here without me getting a number."

Lynn would've almost thought it was funny except for the fact that Kyle was getting ready to move from the bar. She still wanted to catch him before he met with his friends. But the pest was insistent.

He asked, "Are you meeting someone?"

She didn't want to say yes, then have him see her with Kyle and possibly describe her later.

When she didn't answer, he said, "C'mon, just one drink."

She nodded her head reluctantly. "Okay, just the one. Then you have to leave me alone."

He smiled and she appreciated how cute he really was.

He said, "I can wear anyone down eventually." He ordered a Grey Goose on the rocks and she was able to talk him out of a shot of tequila and into another chardonnay for her.

The bartender caught Lynn's eye in a subtle way. She understood he was silently asking her if this guy was bothering her. She smiled and shook her head, not wanting to draw attention to herself, but she realized she was losing an opportunity. They sat and sipped their drinks while the pest told her he was a stockbroker in Orlando and had attended UCF. She was surprised how few questions he asked about her so she didn't have to be evasive.

Then she saw Kyle stand up and greet a burly young man in a tight-fitting UCF football jersey. The window had closed. She realized there was nothing to do now but step back.

Lynn looked at the pest and said, "I'm sorry, I'm running late. I really have to be leaving." Before the young man could put up any argument she grabbed her purse from the stool and immediately started to hustle through the door. She made it all the way to her car, then started to feel an odd sensation. A letdown. Lynn realized she'd been looking forward to using the knife on Kyle. It scared her to have feelings like this.

Lynn looked down the aisle of vehicles and saw Kyle's truck. She wondered what would happen if she simply waited in the parking lot and caught him as he tried to get into the truck. She reached into her pocket and felt the solid outline of the Buck knife. Then, from behind her, she heard the pest yell, "Hey, cutie, I didn't even get your number."

Something came over her in an instant as she watched the young man jog toward her. She visualized plunging the knife into his neck. Then she rationalized that she could use the practice. Lynn said out loud, with almost no thought, "Why don't you follow me down the street while I run an errand? Then we'll see what happens."

The broad smile on the young man's face was all the answer she needed.

Patty Levine laid on the gas a little hard in her personal Jeep Liberty. She liked the way the small SUV handled and the zip it had on the street. She occasionally got stopped by troopers on the interstate but rarely had to go so far as to play the fellow police officer card. A pleasant smile or giggle was enough to make the big bad Florida state troopers tell her it was "okay, just bring it down a few miles from now on." She was sorry she was leaving her family's home in Ocala. The Saturday after Thanksgiving was always a lot of fun. They would watch the UF–FSU game and she'd play touch football with her brothers in the backyard. They would all drink a lot of beer and she'd forget her problems.

There were no grandkids in the family yet, so there was no need to be responsible and watch the kids. The brother a year younger than her had a tremendous fear of commitment. He'd be unattached well into his thirties. And her youngest brother was probably gay, but he hadn't come out of the closet and no one pushed too hard to find out for sure. Patty didn't understand his reticence because no one in her family had ever shown any bias against gay people. But it was hard to predict how people want to be viewed. It wasn't like they were Catholics. They were Methodists, the ostriches of the faith community. What they didn't know and didn't see, they didn't care about.

Patty was pushing her blue Jeep hard because she wanted to surprise Ken. It was probably a little early in a relationship for her to show up unannounced on Friday night, but it was a risk she was willing to take. She wanted to know if he was a player. Something told her he was more interested in one woman at a time.

Patty pulled off the exit just past the Flagler County line and found his condo, sitting on a river. Ken had already told her he wanted to find a house closer to the ocean, but that this condo was very comfortable. He said he had a weakness for comfort.

She hesitated in the parking lot, wondering if she should give him a quick call on her cell phone. But as she approached the front door a man was coming out and held it for her. It was a sign, as far as she was concerned.

She paused again as the elevator opened on the fourth floor and she stepped out into the hallway. Ken's apartment was at the end on the right. Patty swallowed hard and started walking at a steady pace as the door got closer and closer. Before she could talk herself out of it, she pushed the doorbell and heard the chime on the inside. Immediately she could hear someone moving inside.

She held her breath, wondering if this was a bad idea. How she would explain herself? What would she say if there was someone in the apartment with him?

The door opened. Patty looked in and had to take a moment to assess what she was seeing. Without meaning to, she said out loud, "What the hell is this?"

It wasn't hard for Lynn to convince the little stockbroker pest to follow her in his Mustang. She had no real plan where she was going but knew if she wanted to do anything at all it could not be in the parking lot of The Knight's Tower. A real thrill rushed through her and she visualized how she might best utilize the knife. It seemed like such a good idea but also a huge risk.

The streets of Winter Park were very quiet as she drove north on one of the main highways. The pest was still directly behind her. She saw a large parking lot with only a very few cars in it. It was an off-brand supermarket that had taken over the shell of a departed Kmart. She pulled to the far corner where burned-out lights caused huge shadows.

She was out of the car with the Buck knife in her hand before the red Mustang had pulled to a stop. Lynn liked the weight of the sturdy knife in her hand. She hadn't opened it yet. Staring down at it made her heart rate increase and she felt an odd surge of power.

The pest hopped out of his Mustang and scurried back to her like a kid ready to open a Christmas present. He all but rubbed his hands in nervous anticipation.

As he came closer, Lynn felt like she was snapped back to reality. What was she thinking? This is exactly what she did not want to become. A random killer. Not only would it divert her from her real mission, it would eat away at her from the inside out. This was not who she was or how she'd been raised.

She still had the empty, unsatisfied feeling of allowing Kyle Lee to escape. And it was pretty much this idiot's fault. As he stumbled to a stop right in front of her, Lynn looked at him and without thinking swung her hand with the closed knife in it. She struck him across the temple and watched him drop to the ground like a sack of rice. He lay there, stunned and disoriented, while she stood above him trying to gather some of the excitement she had lost when Kyle Lee walked out of the bar.

It clearly wasn't as exciting as plunging a knife into someone's throat. But she knew this was a better option. Lynn looked down at the stunned man and said, "Have you learned your lesson?"

The pest still couldn't speak. He was able to cut his eyes up at her as blood dripped down from the gash on the side of his head.

"When a woman tells you to leave her alone, you leave her alone. Do you understand that?"

In addition to being hurt, the young man now started to tremble uncontrollably. He struggled to simply nod his head.

Now Lynn was experiencing some of the high she'd missed. The young man's shaking body and blood satisfied her need to feel important. It was not as effective a practice run as using the blade of the knife, but she figured if she could knock a healthy, adult male off his feet by slapping him in the head with a closed knife, an open one would be even more effective.

She left him whimpering in the dirty parking lot. Maybe he wouldn't bother women anymore.

EIGHTEEN

Patty stood at the door speechless. She had considered a number of possibilities as she took the elevator up, but this was not one of them. Though she had meant to surprise Ken, she now found she was the one who'd been surprised. This had been a test. She'd prepared herself for the fact that it could destroy their fledgling relationship. But she'd thought it was better to know things now rather than wait and invest months with someone she couldn't trust.

However, this was different.

Ken stared at her and could only manage a "Hey."

"Hey." Her voice seemed small and shaky.

"I didn't expect any company."

"Obviously."

"Would you like to come in?"

She couldn't believe how cool he was being.

Ken said, "I thought you'd be in Ocala and I needed a night like this." He lifted his hands above his head and swept them down his body. He wore a clear plastic shower cap with some type of cream conditioner in his hair. His face had avocado mask smeared over it. He had mitts over his hands. A dark silk robe ran the length of his body and his toes were separated by cotton balls. All he could say was "I needed a night of beauty."

Then Patty started to laugh uncontrollably.

It took a while for Stallings to pinpoint what was bothering him. Or at least what was bothering him more than usual. It had been the sight of his father breaking down and sobbing. He'd never seen his father lose control like that before. When Stallings was a child, his father had seemed like the biggest, toughest man who ever lived. Now he realized his father's distance and drinking had kept him from any broad emotional displays. But now the older, frailer version of James Stallings cried for more than twenty minutes about God knew what, taking Stallings by surprise.

His father wasn't able to put his finger on it, but he felt it was a combination of his fading memory and his inability to help her son find Jeanie. Grace was wonderful as she sat there quietly and offered the occasional hug. She even volunteered to come with Stallings when he left in case he needed something, but he knew right now he needed to be alone. After dropping his father off at the rooming house where he lived, Stallings headed toward his own house in Lakewood.

Having a few minutes to think, he wondered if it would be a good time to take a leave of absence from the sheriff's office. An extended leave from work, so he could do nothing but concentrate on finding Jeanie. But immediately he saw the error in his plan. He would limit his resources if he wasn't at the sheriff's office.

The other issue was Zach Halston. The fraternity brother had gotten under his skin and no matter what, with or without Jeanie, he still needed to find out what had happened to Zach Halston. Some people called it the gift of curiosity and the building block of what made a good cop, but Stallings looked at it more as a curse. Once something got in his head, there was almost no way to move on until he resolved the issue entirely. It was that attitude in homicide that drove him to spend so much time on each case he lost track of his own family. He couldn't live with the idea of a killer getting away with a murder. It kept him awake at night. To this day he still kept track of the few cold-case homicides he couldn't solve. That's what he did and who he was. You could never escape responsibility. Responsibility to your kids at home, or your parents as they got older, or your work if you took it seriously.

One bright spot in the evening was getting to know someone like Grace Jackson, who was just the kind of example he needed to keep moving forward and not lose hope.

It was a long drive back to Jacksonville, and it gave Lynn time to think. She could not deny the immense satisfaction she'd felt slapping the knife across the stockbroker's face. The power that surged through her was not quite as exhilarating as killing someone, but it was a temporary remedy.

She didn't want to be like the killers she'd read about. She didn't want to be driven by only one thing. She had a life. A family. Lynn still wanted to have a family of her own. Now she was determined more than ever to finish this and move on with her life.

She'd get to Kyle Lee next week, then follow her schedule to be done with all of this by the New Year. Then she could pursue the life she had intended. No regrets and no more anger.

NINETEEN

John Stallings had driven the length of University Boulevard, which ran through the entire city from Lakewood. He rented this tiny house all the way north where it ended in Charter Point. The road got its name from Jacksonville University or, as virtually everyone in the city called it, JU. It was a smaller, private university known for its basketball and baseball teams. The argument could be made that the much larger public university, the University of North Florida, was also close to University Boulevard, but in reality it was farther east, off Kernan Boulevard near J. Turner Butler Boulevard. The large apartment complex that served as the hub for fraternity houses was closer to UNF on Bean Boulevard.

Right now the fraternity house and the missing Zach Halston were not the primary ideas occupying his mind. Armed with the photograph of Zach Halston and Jeanie, Stallings intended to question the owners of all the small, independent shops that lined the road in different areas. Kyle Lee had said that he thought Jeanie worked in one of the shops. Stallings intended to find out if that was true.

Stallings felt guilty about not inviting Patty. But he couldn't let her know what he was really looking into. He rationalized it by thinking it was more efficient for Patty to look at other elements of the investigation anyway. He'd told her he was going to be checking with snitches, which he intended to do, and they were skittish around more than one cop at a time. Patty had met a couple of his informants over the years and knew this was true.

Stallings pulled to the curb in front of an antique clothing shop. He recognized this was the first time he'd ever taken an active step in interviewing a potential witness about his missing daughter. Sure, he had his regular routine. He called around on Thursdays to missing persons detectives all across the country and on Saturdays he sent emails to even more. The National Center for Missing and Exploited Children knew Stallings's name better than any other law enforcement officer in the country. His daughter had more cops looking for her than any missing teen in history. But until today he could look his bosses in the eye and say that he, personally, had never investigated his daughter's disappearance.

He sat in the car for a moment looking into the plate-glass window at the elegant, frilly long dresses and took a deep breath. Then he said in a clear voice, "Is today the day that changes the rest of my life?"

* * *

Kyle Lee wasted no time calling together the inner circle of Tau Upsilon. He had waited until most of the guys had gotten out of their morning classes. Many of them took classes as a group so they could study together, or get ahold of an old test and use it as the ultimate study guide. Kyle had skipped class this morning; he was too worried to concentrate. The weekend had been brutal, isolated at his parents' house, unable to talk to the people he needed to talk to. He'd barely paid attention to the Florida State–Florida game. He had just sat at a party, going over all the possibilities in his head.

But now, in front of his eight most trusted friends, he felt more confident. Kyle looked around the room and said, "We all know that a cop has been looking for Zach Halston."

One of the brothers from the back of the room said, "You mean the two cops who came out to the hotel on the beach? One of them was a really cute chick."

"And the other one's name was John Stallings. He is not cute and he is not a chick. I did some research online and found out he is one of their top homicide detectives. He caught the crazy guy that was strangling women. He also caught the Bag Man last year. He is a big shot at JSO. Why do you think he's looking for Zach?"

Kyle waited while the group huddled in close for a serious discussion. Finally, Elroy looked up and said, "You think he's more interested in things that might've happened over the last few years?"

Kyle shrugged. "I don't think he's working in narcotics. And I don't believe he's only in missing persons and worried about Zach's well-being. That means he's interested in things we don't want to talk about." He looked around the room, making sure he had everyone's attention. "It's more important now than ever before that we stick together. No one talks to the cops about anything unless we hear from Zach. If he calls or contacts any of us, we need to let the cop know."

Elroy raised a long, skinny arm. The odd, birdlike young man said, "Do you think Zach is a victim of the curse?"

"There is no curse, Big Bird. The fraternity has just seen some bad luck."

"It seems like a missing brother, one dead from an overdose, and one killed in a robbery is more than a coincidence."

That caused a stir among the crowd and Kyle knew he needed for them to focus. He raised his voice and said, "You're talking about stuff that's happened over a year and a half. We have a lot of members and shit happens. Think about how many members we have who did good things over the same time. Think about how many got a decent job, or got married, or graduated with honors. A few accidents don't make a curse. You guys all know what I'm talking about and why we need to keep quiet. Either way we don't say anything to this cop, Stallings. I don't care how big and scary he is." He let his eyes scan the room until everyone nodded in agreement; then Kyle let his gaze fall on Elroy, or as most of the brothers called him, Big Bird. He was worried the business accounting major might not have the nerve for this kind of thing. Kyle was worried about him from the beginning, but Zach said they needed his

head for numbers. He made sure Elroy caught his gaze
and understood what it meant.

Patty had spent most of the morning going over phone
records supplied by Zach Halston's family. There had
been no calls on his cell phone for nearly two weeks,
and she had yet to find a pattern of calls that indicated
he had a girlfriend or someone he might stay with for
an extended period.

She was so used to spending her days with John
Stallings that it felt odd to be working quietly by herself in the office. Tony Mazzetti had been unusually
quiet sitting across the squad bay. She had caught a
couple of odd, furtive glances, and other than saying
hello he hadn't spoken to her all morning.

Sergeant Zuni popped out of her office just before
lunch and wandered over to Patty's desk. The sergeant
had proved to be outstanding. She stood up for her people when they needed it and pushed the lazier detectives to do their best on every assignment. She was a
particularly good role model to Patty, who saw that
when you were tough, but fair, no one could really
complain. Her exotic good looks and petite frame didn't
seem to matter one bit in this profession dominated by
men. Patty had seen more than one detective wither
under her hard stare. But with things slowing down
around the squad the sergeant had seemed a little lost.

She eased into the chair next to Patty's desk, then let
her green eyes scan the room. When she felt comfortable that they were alone, Sergeant Zuni said, "Anything new on the missing fraternity brother?"

"It's like he just disappeared. John is out checking with informants and a lead he had about businesses on University Boulevard and I'm going back to his phone records."

The sergeant nodded, then looked over her shoulder at Tony Mazzetti working quietly at his desk. She leaned in closer to Patty and said quietly, "Just between us girls, what's going on between you and Tony? I know I wasn't supposed to sanction a relationship between two of my detectives, but you guys weren't causing any problems."

"It's all over. He's even started dating one of the assistant medical examiners."

"Lisa Kurtz?"

"How'd you know that?"

"She's the only one over there that's smaller and less hairy than Tony."

Patty had to laugh at the only joke she'd ever heard her sergeant tell.

Sergeant Zuni placed her hand on Patty's arm and said, "Are you doing okay?"

Patty nodded her head. "It is what it is. I just don't think the stress from a job like this helps a relationship."

"Stress from anywhere is tough on a relationship. But I'm very impressed you guys handled it so quietly. That shows maturity and common sense. One thing a detective bureau does not need is extra drama."

"I appreciated it."

"Now that we've got that out of the way, go find Zach Halston for me so my boss will get off my ass."

*   *   *

Lynn sat at her desk working on the accounts receivable for the Thomas Brothers supply company. She was surprised how well she could concentrate after the events of Friday night. Spending the weekend with her family had helped calm her down, but she still got a little charge thinking about slapping the pest in the face with the closed knife. But the pace here at the supply company could be hectic and cause her to stress. The whole day was planned from money coming in during the morning to money going out in the afternoon. She'd have no break before she headed directly to Dr. Ferrero's office to handle his payroll and pay the bills for the month. He made more money selling supplements for animals than actually tending to them medically. He had two employees who did nothing but sell and deliver special food.

She liked the young doctor's easygoing manner and the way the office always seemed calm and efficient. There was never anyone shouting obscenities over the noise of a forklift. No one in the office smoked. That was so nice. Lynn liked it so much she had even considered going back to school and earning a degree in the medical field. The practical side of her said that not all offices would be like Dr. Ferrero's. No matter what she did, at least she'd avoided the family business and all the associated pitfalls. Besides, Dr. Ferrero was a veterinarian and only a few could afford to hire professional help like him. Most of the poor vet techs Lynn had met barely made enough money to live.

As Lynn sat at her desk reviewing the pile of accounts receivable, a huge shadow fell over her like an eclipse. She knew without lifting her head who was standing in her doorway. She mumbled, while keeping her eyes on her work, "Hey, Dale, what can I help you with?"

She heard the deep, creepy chuckle, then looked up to see the sweat-soaked T-shirt of Dale Moffitt.

"You have a good Thanksgiving?"

"I did. What about you?"

"We had a fine time. And we had a cookout for the Florida–Florida State game. Maybe you'd like to come to one of my cookouts sometime." The way he looked down as he said the last comment made her smile.

Lynn gave him a noncommittal nod, waited, then said, "Is there something I can do for you, Dale?"

The big man stepped into the office and ran his hands down his dirty T-shirt like he was trying to spruce up. "Well, that was kind of it. I was wondering if you would like to come over for a cookout or have a drink sometime."

"I appreciate the offer, Dale, but between both my jobs and all that's gone with my family, I'm short on time."

"You short on time or you just don't want to go out with my kind?"

Lynn caught the edge to his comment and noticed him step in closer and lean toward her desk.

The loading dock foreman said, "We can't all have a fancy Florida State degree. I know I'm just a working-man, but I make a fine living and I haven't seen you going out on the town much."

"How would you know anything about that, Dale? I keep my private life very private."

"I bet I know a little bit more about your private life than you suspect. You forget I was raised around here and I know your older brother."

"So?"

"So I probably know a few family secrets. I also know you returned the company Suburban with front-end damage."

Lynn's face flushed as she said, "I don't know what you're talking about."

"Yes, you do, but you don't got nothing to worry about. When the tubby Mexican fella that washes the cars showed it to me, I told him I'd take care of it. I scrubbed it really good and straightened the grille the best I could. It's hard to get blood all the way off a car grille."

Lynn just stared at him and saw that he was enjoying his little game. She was trying to calculate if he was smart enough to track down a hit-and-run all the way in Daytona. When she had finished her calculation she looked up at him and said, "When would you like to get together, Dale?"

It was after four when John Stallings decided he had shown the photograph of Jeanie and Zach Halston to enough store clerks along University Boulevard. Of the fourteen stores he'd visited, no one recognized either of the young people. He used the photograph with Zach because if he was questioned by any bosses, he could make it sound like he was only looking for Zach. Only the lieutenant and Patty and a few others at the sheriff's office would recognize the girl as his missing daughter.

Now he was in downtown Jacksonville, an area he was more familiar with, looking for his most reliable informant: Peep Moran. Peep was a local drug seller who moved between marijuana and pharmaceutical sales as the profits dictated. He had earned his unusual nickname through his habit of watching women urinate in public. The general population didn't realize how often homeless women had no access to a bathroom and found ways to relieve themselves nonchalantly without anyone noticing. But Peep noticed. He was on the lookout all the time. It was his experience on the street that allowed him the ability to know where to catch the best view.

Stallings waited at a set of bushes where Peep often hung out and sometimes hid his product. It was only a few minutes before he noticed the diminutive man in his late thirties walking up the street dressed like any street vendor in relatively clean jeans and a pullover shirt. When Peep's eyes met Stallings it looked like the scrawny dope dealer was about to turn and run—a common occurrence when the two of them met. Instead, he continued on his same track and walked directly to Stallings.

Peep said, "Do I bother you at your job?"

"As a matter of fact, you do. This is my job. A second ago it looked like you were going to run from me. Why?"

"Just the sight of you usually startles me. And I thought I was holding when I saw you. It took me a second to realize I ran out of product midday today. With all the students back in town, demand is way up."

Stallings appreciated an honest answer like that,

even if Peep was admitting to a felony. He held out the photograph and said, "Do you recognize either of these two kids?"

Peep stared at the photo for a second, then nodded his head. "I know the boy. He's been trying to creep into my territory for a long time. As if I don't have enough trouble with the black guys from Arlington, now I have snotty-nosed college kids thinking they're Scarface and can sell pot easier than me."

"When's the last time you saw him?"

"I don't know. At least a month. I remember him because couple of years ago he and another college kid had a big hassle out on the street about who should be selling pot. I guess it was just a college thing. It went on for a couple of weeks. I saw the two of them get in a shouting match once. I heard about one or two other encounters between them. They were friends and knew each other, but apparently they didn't work well together."

Stallings assessed his informant, then said, "If you see either this boy or this girl in the photo you need to get ahold of me immediately."

"What's it worth to you?"

"If it's information that helps me find them, you can write your own ticket."

"Stall, you never said that before."

"I never needed to find anyone this bad before."

TWENTY

The smell of salt water and the sound of the boats passing by on their way out to sea had a calming effect on Kyle Lee. He was shaken by the cop coming down to Winter Park and he didn't like having to call a meeting of the brothers who may be affected. But here, on the jetty, next to the dock, waiting for the deep-sea fishing boats that docked about this time, he felt the most relaxed he had all weekend.

There was just something about the dock, whether it had fishermen on it or not. Tonight he was all alone, but that wasn't uncommon for a Monday. He knew later on, the older guys who had families or jobs that kept them a late would show up and try to hook a snapper but settle for perch.

Kyle had first discovered this marina, east of the city, along the St. Johns, when he'd come here with Zach Halston to sell pot to some of the fishermen on Friday and Saturday nights. They'd done great until an off-duty Gainesville police officer took offense at their offer of cheap pot and chased them a half a mile. Zach had been smart enough to split up, double back, grab their car, and pick up Kyle before the cop was able to catch him. It had been a wild night that Zach had thought was great but that had made Kyle vomit as soon as they were a few miles away.

He didn't miss going out with Zach as he made his rounds, but he would like to hear from his friend. That was one of the reasons he'd decided to come down here and throw a line in the water for an hour or two. He was waiting for the deep-sea fishing boat called the *Catch 'Em All* to arrive from its regular afternoon outing. He loved to see what fishermen had caught a few miles off the coast and enjoyed chatting with the first mate.

He caught the first glimpse of the professional fishing boat coming up the river and started to reel in his line. A thrill rushed through him like he was a little kid. The sun had just set, the temperature was very mild, and, for a change, it wasn't raining. This was a good night.

Lynn finished payroll in record time. She'd been afraid she'd be distracted by the comments Dale had made until she realized he was just a big, dumb redneck who wouldn't be able to figure anything out anyway. She had agreed to have a drink with him later in the week just to make sure she was right.

She'd not seen Dr. Ferrero in the afternoon when she stopped by to reconcile his accounts. He sometimes left early to go for a run before it got dark and this time of year the days were getting shorter and shorter. By Christmastime he'd have to leave around 4:30 to finish his run before dark and that was only if wasn't raining. But it always seemed to rain in Jacksonville.

The work she'd been doing to plan everything so well involved following Kyle and the fraternity brothers around at different times. She knew that Kyle Lee often fished from the dock of a public marina out toward the beach. She didn't know why he kept going to the same place because it didn't seem like he'd ever catch anything. All she could figure was he was selling pot to the fishermen. She knew that was how Zach had started.

She didn't push her Nissan Sentra too hard because the last thing she needed was a smart cop to see she got a ticket near the site of a murder. Lynn drove past the marina one time, then turned around and pulled into the lot. Kyle's truck was parked in front near the water. A few other vehicles were scattered across the lot. It looked quiet enough for her to do what she had to do.

It was early for Patty to eat dinner, just after six. She'd grown used to the weird hours for everything— eating, sleeping, living. That was one of the major factors in her drug use and she'd been disappointed that a "normal" relationship with someone outside police work had not lessened her dependence on the various prescriptions she used. She also worried that Ken, being a podiatrist, and able to write prescriptions, might notice her pop a Xanax or painkiller. They'd yet to spend the night together so she wasn't worried about him picking up on her Ambien use. In the months she was with Tony Mazzetti, he'd never had a clue. At least she didn't think he had a clue about her drug use.

Ken met her at the restaurant, a slightly stuffy, high-end natural food place. He nodded to the waitress like he knew her and the manager came by and said hello. Ken looked fresh, like he had just showered after a workout.

Ken said, "Sorry, my appointment ran late."

"Did you have to give someone an examination?"

"No, manicure and pedicure."

Patty tried to hide her astonishment. "You got a mani-pedi?"

"As a podiatrist, I know how important nail care is. Besides, it makes me feel good."

"You didn't get nail polish too, did you?" She let a snicker slip out.

"Just a coat of clear on my toenails." He was completely serious.

Patty wondered if she should worry about who the man in the relationship was. This was definitely a conversation she would've never had with Tony Mazzetti.

Lynn left her car to stalk Kyle like a wildcat. After she had learned about Zach and Kyle's business venture in the marina, she'd seen Kyle twice during the semester fishing here. Both times it was on a Monday night. She thought it had something to do with the fishing boat schedule. She seemed to know one of the boat workers and they talked after the *Catch 'Em All* docked.

Being an organized, numbers person, she had a checklist that she often went through before taking action. First, she had to make sure he didn't notice her. She wanted complete surprise and shock on her side. Second, no one else in the near-empty marina should notice her so she could slip away without the police getting a description. Third, and most important, she had to get her timing just right. She'd wait for the few deep-sea-fishing customers to wander out to their cars, then move in quick. She felt butterflies in her stomach at the thought of using the knife for the first time. The familiar thrill and satisfaction once it was done excited her, but there were also a few nerves.

Lynn watched as he gathered up his tackle box and rod and stood as the forty-foot fishing vessel rumbled up toward the dock. She had the knife tucked in her front pocket. It would be nothing to flick it open, but then the question became, neck or kidney? Whatever she did she'd have to be quick and it would be out in the open. She intended to strike and move.

John Stallings was drained. The excitement he'd felt earlier in the day looking for Jeanie himself had turned to disappointment and frustration that seem to sap him of all his energy. But now, all he wanted to do was get back to his rented house and collapse in bed. Instead, he found himself at the community center where his father volunteered.

Lately, Stallings couldn't fall asleep easily without knowing his father was safe. He supposed it was a common enough feeling for children of parents with Alzheimer's, but it was odd considering how little time he'd spent with his father in the past twenty years. But he felt a wave of relief as soon as he saw his father working with a group of older, homeless men at a large round table in the corner of the giant room.

Stallings didn't really need to talk to his dad; he just wanted to ensure the old man was safe. But as he was about to turn and leave he heard a voice behind him say, "I thought I might find you here."

Grace Jackson stood behind him in a sundress that brought out her beautiful, dark complexion and bright smile.

Suddenly he didn't feel so tired.

Kyle watched in fascination as the forty-two-foot-long fishing trawler revved its twin diesel motors, causing water to churn like the inside of a blender. Even though he'd seen it a hundred times before, he could barely take his eyes from the frothy water. Maybe it was being raised in landlocked Winter Park, or maybe it was because he needed to work on the ocean. That mix of salt air and diesel made Kyle feel like he was at an amusement park. The smell alone was almost enough to make him drop out of UNF and sign on as a mate.

There were only a few customers on the boat as it powered into its berth at the dock. He'd noticed a trend toward empty boats but didn't know whether to attribute it to fewer fish or fewer tourists.

He waited anxiously for the first mate to acknowledge him.

*   *   *

Lynn watched Kyle in silence from the far end of the marina. He looked like a little kid fascinated by the big boat. He stood motionless on the dock slightly behind the banged-up fishing trawler. But she was committed to her goals no matter how innocent he seemed, now that Lynn had already made the judgment. She'd proved her restraint by not killing the pest Friday night. It had left her with a slightly hollow weekend, but it had to do while Kyle Lee was still away.

The familiar thrill started to creep through her and she imagined approaching the unsuspecting fraternity brother. She craved the satisfaction of completing the task and knowing she was that much closer to a normal life. Sometimes Lynn wondered what exactly a normal life was. Did it mean getting married and having children? Did it mean working at Thomas Brothers Supply the rest of her life? She felt like she had developed a real skill and wondered if there was a chance to apply it for the greater good of society.

She decided to let the big, philosophical questions rest for a while and focus on what she had to do. There was no way she'd let Kyle Lee get away. Not tonight.

John Stallings felt very comfortable in the corner of the cavernous community room, sharing a cup of coffee with Grace Jackson. While he got to spend time with this lovely woman, he was also able to observe his father from a distance and feel more confident about the older man's ability to function, despite his diagnosis of Alzheimer's disease.

He was so relaxed he found himself telling Grace

about personal problems he wouldn't even discuss with Patty Levine. He told her about his marriage and the disappearance of Jeanie and about Maria's drug use. He was careful never to blame Maria for the family's problems, because, as had become clear to him recently, he was more at fault than anyone else. He even told Grace about Brother Frank Ellis.

When he was finished, Grace said, "I hear what you're saying, John. But I don't understand why you think Frank Ellis is purposely trying to disrupt your family life. Could it be he was just trying to get you to pay attention to a problem that Maria had?"

Stallings thought about it for a few moments, frustrated by someone who was objective and trying to get him to look at a problem from all angles.

Then Grace said, "I wish my ex felt the same way about me that you feel about Maria. It's really very sweet. It's too bad she doesn't realize how rare it is to find a guy like you." She reached across the table casually and grasped both of his hands in her delicate but strong hands. "I do have to say that my ex-husband is trying to get his head on straight. He's been seeing the kids more and catching up on child support. But it has more to do with the kids than with me. He had another girlfriend even before we split up."

Stallings enjoyed her hands on his. "I don't know how you do it between a career, raising two kids, and all the volunteer work you do."

"My mom always taught me to be thankful for what I have and give back all I can. I'm trying to set a good example for my kids." She paused for a moment and glanced around the immediate area. "That's why I probably wouldn't say anything to them if you asked me out to dinner one evening."

"I'm in a crazy place right now, Grace, but I can't think of anything I would enjoy more than spending a pleasant evening with you."

Stallings flinched and yanked his hands away from Grace as his father walked up, saying a loud voice, "Two of my favorite people sitting at the same table. This calls for a drink."

Stallings turned his head and stared at his father in disbelief until the old man started to cackle and said, "For a cop, you're awful gullible."

Kyle spent a few minutes looking over the meager catch of the fishing boat. There were two wahoo, a snapper, and an amberjack that looked more like bait than a trophy fish. The customers must've agreed because none of them wanted to take the fish home with them. One of them was so shit-faced he wobbled across the dock and into the parking lot. Kyle was relieved to see he was only a passenger in a big pickup truck parked near the entrance.

He stood patiently while the first mate cleaned the snapper, cutting it into two small but equal fillets.

The mate looked up at Kyle and said, "You haven't been out with us in a while. What's wrong, school getting too tough?"

Kyle smiled and shook his head. "You know how it is during the holidays. I had to go home and visit my folks and school's been getting real busy."

"All Thanksgiving meant to me was an extra trip out

to sea in the morning. I couldn't believe how crowded we were. We did so well the captain even smiled for a few minutes on the way back."

Kyle said, "Looks like a couple of your customers had a little too much beer out in the boat."

The mate said, "Not my concern once they hit the cement. I don't care if they drive off the highway into one of the swamps." He moved fast to wrap up the fish and clean the table. Then he turned and jumped back onto the fishing boat as the captain revved the engine. The mate scurried around, untying lines as he yelled up to Kyle, "See you later, kid."

TWENTY-ONE

Lynn had slipped next to the dock without anyone ever noticing her. She had waited in the shadow under a burned-out streetlight while the three customers from the fishing boat shuffled toward their cars. One of them look like he had trouble walking until he opened the passenger door of a Dodge 1500 and was able to pull himself in easily.

She noticed Kyle chatting with the older, weather-beaten first mate while the tall, lean man cleaned some fish. Then the man made a graceful leap onto the boat, waving to Kyle as he landed.

She stepped onto the dock toward Kyle. This seemed right. No one was around and he was not paying the least bit of attention. The knife was in her front pocket. She reached down with her right hand and started digging.

Her heart picked up speed as she realized it was time.

Stallings liked Grace Jackson's idea of a quiet dinner together. The whole concept thrilled him and at the same time made him feel guilty. She was a very special woman, but he hadn't given up on Maria, who, in an entirely different way, was a very special woman. Still, he felt something was unresolved with Grace. It was a lighter problem than he usually faced, and it made him feel like a little time by himself, down by the beach, might help him get his head on straight. His father had made him laugh tonight with his joke about getting a drink, but mainly it meant he had at least some more time with the lucid James Stallings. The effect of Grace and his father had lifted his spirits more than he could have imagined.

As he headed east, away from the city, he thought about a park with the marina where he used to take Lauren and Jeanie fishing on the big commercial fishing boats. Charlie was too young and he so loved spending a few hours alone with his bright and beautiful daughters. The sharpest memory was how horrified Jeanie had been when she saw the first mate clean a snapper someone had caught. The fish twitched just as the knife cut in behind its gills, and Jeanie screamed in terror and started to cry, instinctively running to her father's arms and burying her face in his shoulder. She wouldn't eat fish for almost six months after the incident.

It was little memories like that that could make Stallings appreciate the life he had experienced so far. It was still early and he thought he might get to see one of the boats dock.

That was exactly what he needed.

* * *

Tony Mazzetti wasn't sorry he'd passed up a dinner invitation from Lisa Kurtz. He'd seen her enough over the weekend. Thank God she'd had to work Saturday and left him a full day in peace. He tried to get started on a couple of writing projects, but his recent rejections had his mind wandering in a way that wasn't conducive to constructive creative writing. Instead, he read a couple of the magazines he normally submitted to, like *Civil War Times* and *History*.

He couldn't help but compare Lisa with Patty, and it made him wonder if Patty had been scarce during their relationship. Because it seemed to him like Lisa was in his face every minute. Was she too available? Should he say anything? The idea of being lonely again terrified the homicide detective. And Lisa certainly had some excellent qualities. She was very pretty, was great in the sack, didn't mind springing for dinner once in a while, and thought Tony was the greatest thing ever. On the downside, she'd only shut her mouth once while not eating during their entire relationship. And that was when she was focusing on a *New England Journal of Medicine* article.

Once Tony realized she focused hard on reading, he had supplied her with a number of back issues of magazines, two novels, and a textbook on police work that he told her was interesting. Anything to keep her engaged in reading as opposed to constant and irrelevant chatter.

Still, as he settled into a chair on his back porch and opened the magazine, he realized this was the kind of evening he would've loved spending quietly with Patty.

* * *

Kyle watched the froth at the rear of the boat again as the captain expertly revved and then slacked off the engines. He eased the beat-up fishing boat from the dock as the first mate raced to the front of the boat to untie the final line. Once again it was that mixture of smells and the sound of the engine that interested Kyle.

Out of the corner of his eye he caught a movement and started to turn toward the parking lot. Then he felt his world start to spin as he lost his balance and tumbled off the edge of the dock. He kicked his fishing rod as he slipped and saw it tumble to one side toward the water.

One second he saw the water, the next he saw the sky. He spun in midair until he saw the stern of the fishing boat and realized the water was the least of his concerns. He flailed his arms hoping to push himself off the stern away from the churning propellers. His heart fluttered in his chest, but he wasn't able to call for help. He needed to gulp some air. When he finally had oxygen in his lungs he used it to scream instead of call for help.

Just before he'd struck the water he'd caught a glimpse of someone standing on the dock where he had been. It was a woman. But that was the last rational thought he had as the two propellers spun relentlessly, one striking him just below the knee, the other in his lower back. He even noticed the red in the water and heard the engines sputter as the captain must've wondered what he'd struck.

Several things raced through his mind. Specifically the curse of the Tau Upsilon fraternity flashed in his consciousness before his entire world went black.

TWENTY-TWO

Lynn had already made it back to her car by the time she saw the captain and the first mate even bother to walk to the rear of the boat and peer down into the water. It looked like a scene from *Jaws*, with blood and body parts floating all around the vessel.

It had been a spur-of-the-moment decision to shove Kyle instead of sticking him with her knife. Now she could use the knife later. When she'd seen his precarious position and the blades of the propellers churning the water directly in front of him, it was almost an instinct for her to reach out and give him a little shove. She'd even been rewarded with a pretty good scream. Had water not filled his mouth and muffled his scream it might have even been perfect. But it would have to do for tonight.

She calmly drove out of the parking lot, checking her rearview mirror once as she pulled onto the main road. It didn't look like either the captain or the first mate had noticed her as she drove off.

Her Nissan picked up speed as she headed west toward town. A smile crept across her face as that satisfied feeling of accomplishment surged through her body. She was glad she never had to explain the feeling to anyone. She wasn't even sure what it meant to her. It wasn't exactly joy. It was more of a sense of power. A chance to prove how important she was. A chance to complete the mission she'd given herself.

About three miles from the marina a blue light started to flash in her rearview mirror. She looked over her shoulder to see a police car directly behind her as she swore silently and pulled onto the soft shoulder of the road.

As she heard the cop step out of his car, she reached into her front pocket and pulled out her knife. It wasn't an intentional act; it just seemed to happen.

Patty had politely refused Ken's offer for her to come back to his condo. It had been a lovely dinner and he was charming as always, but she just didn't feel like it tonight. After a quick drink and a few minutes lingering at the table, Patty and Ken had gone their separate ways and she found herself driving around Jacksonville in her Jeep Liberty. She never took a company car anywhere that she might have an alcoholic beverage. She usually refrained from alcohol because she didn't want any interaction with her prescription meds. But she'd made an exception tonight and shared a bottle of pinot noir with Ken. Of course he knew the exact vineyard and year the wine had been bottled. He sure could pick his wine and food.

As Patty drove near the St. Johns River she realized she was close to Tony Mazzetti's house. Her instinct was to drive by and say hello. Then she remembered Lisa and how unfair it would be to her if Patty showed up unannounced. Instead she headed back to her town house and her cat, Cornelia.

Tonight would be a two-Ambien night.

Officer Martin Haskell had been with the Jacksonville Sheriff's Office for nearly two years. He'd spent almost the whole time in traffic and rarely got an evening off other than his two rotating days off. To keep things more interesting at work, the twenty-five-year-old had made a bet with his roommate, who worked in the Tactical Anti-Crime (TAC) unit, to see who could get the most phone numbers from pretty girls in a three-month time period. So far Martin felt like he was lagging behind. The more glamorous assignment in TAC had to help his roommate. The TAC unit spent a lot of time near Jacksonville Landing, making sure the big shopping and eating attraction was safe for the tourists who'd made the mistake of coming to Jacksonville instead of going to Miami or Orlando. The TAC unit also dressed in plain clothes or slick T-shirts with a cool JSO logo. Their assignment could be anything from following suspected criminals to doing minor stings to catching scam artists who preyed on tourists.

As soon as Martin caught a glimpse of this girl's face in the rearview mirror of her Nissan Sentra, he realized he had to get her phone number. She had brown hair and an all-American, cheerleader look. He couldn't see what her body was like, but based on her neck and shoulders he wasn't worried. He didn't even bother to call out the vehicle stop on the radio. He had stopped her because she was going eleven miles over the speed limit, but he already knew he wouldn't write her. It was probably better he had no record of ever stopping her if he intended to ask her for her phone number.

He made sure his gig line was straight and she got a glimpse of his forearms that he worked so hard to make broad and muscular. He didn't bother to approach the car tactically like he normally would because his best features were his abs and forearms and he needed to face her directly to show them off properly.

Martin hesitated at the door as he leaned down and said, "You were going a little fast, weren't you, ma'am?" He was rewarded with a very beautiful smile. This was starting out to be a good night.

As he rolled down the highway, Stallings reflexively took his foot off the gas as soon as he saw the blue flashing lights of a JSO patrolman. As he eased past, he saw how the young patrolman leaned in to talk to a female driver and laughed out loud to himself. He knew the ploy uniformed cops used. He was already married by the time he joined JSO, but he had plenty of friends who'd met girlfriends or wives after stopping them for speeding.

Some of the other detectives would recall their time in patrol with fondness and even a certain degree of reverence, but Stallings was more practical. There was no doubt the patrol work could be fun, working with cops who were your friends and enjoyed doing something as interesting as police work. But that didn't change the fact that with each vehicle stop there was constant stress and the knowledge that a simple speeding ticket could turn into something much worse. Every time a cop stopped someone for a traffic infraction, the cop had no way of knowing if the driver was on his way to work or fleeing some horrible crime. More than a few patrol officers had been shot in the line of duty simply walking up to a window of the driver who had rolled through a stop sign or been going a few miles too fast.

Stallings was aware that patrol officers were often the only contact the general public had with police. Often the public's view of police work was shaped by TV and they couldn't understand when the officer who pulled him over was short or irritable, as if they weren't allowed to have a bad day. No one ever cut a surly patrol officer slack. And no one who was stopped speeding ever thought they deserved the ticket, only that they had been singled out.

After Stallings had passed the busy patrol officer he decided to skip the fishing docks and go directly to the ocean to fill his lungs with the clean, salt air. It was one of the few things he knew he didn't do enough. He lived a mere fifteen minutes from the ocean but saw it fewer than five times a year.

As he zipped east on the highway, a patrol car with its lights on roared past him, followed by two fire rescue vehicles. He briefly considered following them to see if he could help but realized they didn't need an older, plainclothes detective interfering with their duties.

Before he could even see the ocean, he rolled down the windows and felt the breeze and smelled the salt air.

This had not been a bad evening at all.

Lynn let her hand slip down around the handle of the knife as the patrolman walked along the side of the road from his car to hers. She wasn't sure exactly what she intended to do, but knew that it wasn't a good idea to get a ticket so close to the site of the murder. When the cop spoke to her, all she could do was give him a good smile and hope he leaned down closer.

What surprised her was the response to her simple smile. As soon as he leaned closer, showing off muscular arms and a handsome face, the young man returned her smile and somehow conveyed to her that she wasn't going to get a ticket. Instead he said, "You were going a little fast, weren't you, ma'am?"

Lynn nodded her head. "I'm sorry." She patted his hand, which was now resting on her car door.

The cop said, "That's okay, everyone makes mistakes sometimes." He looked up and down the highway. Then he smiled and said, "My name's Martin."

His friendly manner took her by surprise and she blurted out, "I'm Lynn."

"Well, Lynn, would you consider letting me take you out to dinner one night and explain the dangers of speeding to you? We could avoid a lot of messy court time."

He said it as a joke and not as any kind of threat. Lynn was stuck in a tricky position. Right now he didn't know her last name. But if she refused dinner there was no guarantee he wouldn't write her an official ticket or at least copy down her tag. She decided to give him her business card instead. All it had was the Thomas Brothers Supply number and not her personal cell.

The young cop looked at the card and said, "Thomas Brothers, that's a big operation."

"Biggest in Northeast Florida." She'd learned to recite the line after the eldest Thomas brother decided to start saying it whether it was true or not.

The young cop was about to say something else when his radio flared to life. Lynn could only catch a few words but recognized "marina" and "fatality."

The cop stood up and said, "I'll call you soon, but I've got to go to this accident. There's never a fireman around when you need one." He hustled back to his car and made a quick U-turn onto the road.

Lynn that let out a long sigh of relief as she saw his taillights fade into the darkness. Just from that brief encounter she knew that the cops already thought Kyle's death was an accident. She also saw how susceptible they were to flirting.

She would never be caught. Just the idea made her smile.

TWENTY-THREE

Tony Mazzetti felt antsy as he entered the small white administrative building of the Duval County Medical Examiner's Office. He still wasn't sure what he was going to say or how he would to say it. The last thing he wanted to do was to hurt Lisa Kurtz's feelings. That wasn't entirely accurate. The last thing he wanted to do was be lonely again, but the concept of having to hide from your girlfriend did not make for a particularly positive relationship. He realized it late Sunday night when his ears were ringing slightly from the constant chatter of his new girlfriend. That was reinforced last night when he'd spent the evening alone and decided he preferred it that way.

He nodded to a couple of the administrators and the operations officer, a tall gregarious fellow who never let an opportunity pass to tell Mazzetti he did not hold detectives in high esteem. Maybe that was because the lanky former investigator taught a class on what cops shouldn't do when they happen on to the scene of a homicide. He'd seen all the mistakes that could be made from trampling evidence to moving the body.

He'd even yelled at a young JSO patrolman for placing a blanket over a nude women's body in her own apartment, thinking that it was a sign of respect. The medical examiners' operations officer pointed out to him that she had lost her modesty and the most important thing was finding out who'd killed her and left her nude in the middle of her living room.

Mazzetti was certain the operations officer didn't like the prospect of a homicide detective dating one of the assistant medical examiners. He'd probably like it even less when he found out Mazzetti intended to break up with Lisa.

He followed the instructions of several assistants and administrative people who kept directing him farther back down the hall toward Lisa until he found himself in the procedure room at the back of the building. Things had been so slow around the squad that he had not been in the room for some time. He could remember when things were rocking and rolling in homicide, coming to the ME's office four times a week. In the last month he had come far more times on personal, social business than on official business. Hell, that's what this visit was all about.

As he entered the room he was glad he was still wearing his suit. The room was kept at a constant fifty-eight degrees and could be a little overwhelming if you weren't prepared for it. Lisa gave a quick wave and bright smile as she scurried around the room, placing instruments where she would need them for an autopsy.

She said, "What a nice surprise."

Mazzetti just grunted.

"I hope you don't mind if we chat while I work on an accident victim from last night."

"No, not at all." He waited while she walked to the rear of the room and rolled a gurney up into the position she had prepared with a bright overhead light and a recorder for her notes. Mazzetti could remember the first time he had seen a circular saw and drill laid out on the table and made the connection to what they would be used for. At that time, as a new homicide detective, it had made him queasy. He'd never admitted it to anyone, especially his partner at the time, but after they had left the procedure room and he'd claimed to have needed to use the bathroom, he'd thrown up instead of peeing. No one had ever found out, but he was sure they all suspected. Now the sight of the tools was as mundane as seeing a computer on someone's desk. Even the sight of the black plastic body bag on the gurney didn't cause him any concern.

Lisa fumbled with the awkward bag, always preferring to work by herself rather than with an assistant. She said, "This is the accident victim from the marina last night."

Mazzetti nodded, having seen a short story on the local news about a fisherman who fell into the blades of a deep-sea fishing boat. He said, "Bet I can tell you what killed him."

"Very funny." She slowly started to pull down the zipper of the body bag, saying, "This has a lot more to do with toxicology to see if drugs or alcohol played any role. We're starting to do more and more studies like that as long as the homicide rate has slowed down and we have time for it. This was the kind of stuff I expected to do when I graduated." She concentrated as she jerked the zipper the last foot of the bag, which was turned slightly on the side. The lower part of a leg, severed just below the knee, rolled out onto the table.

Mazzetti had become so jaded that the gruesome scene held no real interest for him. Until he noticed the familiar tattoo on the ankle. It was the local Tau Upsilon fraternity tattoo. He glanced up and saw Lisa had noticed it too.

She mumbled, "You don't have to say it. I think this is something you should look into a little more closely."

As Mazzetti stared at the severed leg he couldn't even remember why he had come over to the medical examiner's office, but it was a good thing he had.

Stallings burst through the door of the squad bay, annoyed that he'd been called in from checking with the businesses on University Boulevard. He had a clear plan of what he expected to complete today and yakking with the sergeant or lieutenant was not part of his agenda. But now that he was sitting in the conference room with Tony Mazzetti, Patty Levine, and Sparky Taylor, the sergeant had his complete and utter attention.

Sergeant Zuni stood in front of an easel with three sets of photographs. They were all of corpses at the medical examiner's with a tattoo of a red pickup truck with Greek letters in the back identifying the fraternity of Tau Upsilon. The sergeant said, "The first tattoo is from a shooting victim in Arlington. Tony's been working the case." She looked over at Mazzetti and said, "Anything new?"

Mazzetti looked down at the table and shook his head.

The sergeant continued, "Second photo is from an overdose over at the big apartment complex where the fraternities are housed. This kid's name was Connor Tate and I think Patty and Stall talked to him about their missing persons case." Her eyes cut over to Stallings and Patty, who were both nodding. "The last photo is from the young man who fell into the marina last night. His name was Kyle Lee. The folks at the marina and on the fishing boat said that he was a regular in the area and that they saw nothing unusual. But the fact that three young men from the same fraternity at a smaller school like the University of North Florida would end up dead in just a short amount of time makes me curious."

Stallings said, "How'd we make the connection between the three? Who recognized the tattoos?"

Sergeant said, "We can thank Detective Mazzetti for being sharp. I knew you and Patty had been talking with some of the fraternity members and my real fear is that Zach Halston is dead somewhere and we just don't know that yet."

Stallings mumbled, "That's my fear too."

"Do you have a rapport with the fraternity brothers?"

Stallings said, "I got rapport up the ass."

The sergeant let a slight smile creep across her pretty face. "Do you think you and Patty could go over and talk to some of the brothers to see if anything else has happened? I don't want to start a panic or put any ideas into anyone's head. I just want us to do our duty and protect the public if there's something other than clumsiness or drunkenness causing these deaths."

"We're on it."

The sergeant folded her arms and leveled a fierce glare at Stallings. "I don't want you to scare any of those boys. You understand me? No terror tactics."

Stallings was already standing when he said, "I understand perfectly."

Patty Levine considered intervening as John Stallings held Bobby Hollis by the collar of his Izod shirt, so close that Stallings's spit settled on the boy's cheek. They had not seen the young fraternity member since the first encounter at the beach that kicked off the whole investigation. Stallings rumbled, "Look, you little shit. I know you guys are hiding something."

The terrified young man shook his head furiously, saying, "No. No, sir." Stallings released his grip and the boy stumbled to one side and grasped a garbage can next to his couch and vomited.

Stallings backed off, saying, "Jesus, at least dopers don't get sick when you throw a little scare into them." He settled on a recliner and looked across at Bobby Hollis, who was now sitting on the beat-up leather sofa. Stallings said, "Look, son, I've talked to a couple boys in this fraternity and both of them ended up dying. I cannot believe that's a coincidence."

The young man shook his head again, his eyes cutting over to Patty for some kind of reassurance. She figured now was the time for her to move in as a good cop. Although sometimes Stallings went so far she could slap someone and still be considered the good cop.

"Bobby, all we're asking is if you heard about any other brothers that had been hurt or killed that we might not know about."

"You mean from our chapter?"

Patty had to think about that for a minute. "Your chapter or any chapters you guys are associated with in the area. Maybe as far south as UCF and as far north as Atlanta."

"I heard about a guy who graduated and had been by our chapter house a couple times. He was in some kind of a hit-and-run down in Daytona. I think he's still in the hospital."

Patty used an even voice to say, "You know his name?"

"Alan Cole."

"Anyone else?"

The boy seemed to hesitate, causing Stallings to lean forward and emit a low growl like a pit bull.

That spurred the boy to say quickly, "An upperclassman who graduated from UF before me died in a fire in Atlanta."

"Do you know his name?"

Bobby shook his head, but said he could get it.

Patty realized they had a lot of work to do.

Tony Mazzetti hadn't stopped hustling since the impromptu meeting a few hours earlier. He'd managed to send out an inquiry to law enforcement and medical examiners asking if they had seen any homicide or accidental death victims with tattoos similar to those on the dead fraternity brothers in Jacksonville. He'd been careful to list that it was just for information and no action should be taken.

Even as busy as he was, he had noticed Patty Levine stroll in and start working at her desk an hour before. When he needed a break, Mazzetti stood up and stretched and wandered over to her desk. He asked, "Where's Stall?"

"Still looking for Zach Halston. He's convinced the young man might hold the key to our investigation."

"Stall sure does get fixated."

"You have no idea. He's even worse on this case. He's been out at all hours showing photographs of young men to different businesses and witnesses along University Boulevard." She looked up at Mazzetti and said, "This is a great catch. I'm very impressed you noticed the tattoos and made the connection."

Mazzetti said, "I can't take all the credit." When he realized who he was talking to, he stopped short, but Patty had to ask, "Who else gets the credit?"

Mazzetti said, "Lisa Kurtz at the medical examiner's office picked up on it too."

Patty just said, "Oh." She almost looked disappointed.

Mazzetti said, "Sorry, I didn't want it to be awkward between us."

"It's not."

"Heard you've got a new boyfriend."

"Sort of."

"What's he like?"

"He's a doctor."

"Really?"

"Well, not really a doctor. A podiatrist."

"No shit. My foot has been bothering me lately. Should I go see him?"

Patty smiled and patted Mazzetti on hand. "You can see him, but he's not going to give you a discount."

Mazzetti mumbled, "Never mind." It would have been wrong to infringe on his former girlfriend's new squeeze anyway. He looked down at Patty's desk and said, "What's the chart you're working on?"

"It's a time line of the three fraternity brothers. How long they'd been at school. What people knew about them. Maybe we'll find some common factor." She looked back up at Mazzetti and said, "Don't worry, Tony. We'll figure this out together."

As Mazzetti walked back to his desk he couldn't believe how good a few words from the girl made him feel.

Lynn sat at her desk reading another online news story about Kyle Lee's unfortunate accident. The three stories she had read all said the same thing: he had accidentally fallen off the dock and was caught in the propellers of a large deep-sea fishing boat. The story made it sound so clean and antiseptic. She had been there and knew it was anything but neat and tidy. She didn't know if a reporter could ever describe the scene she'd caused. She'd dreamed about it vividly overnight but had awakened very refreshed and even relaxed.

It had worked out exactly as she had planned. Now she could figure out who else needed to be dealt with and move on. The whole episode had given her an enormous feeling of satisfaction and power.

She'd been able to focus like a laser this morning and completed balancing the gas receipts and mileage on the entire fleet of Thomas Brothers vehicles. That's why she had the time to scan the Internet for stories that didn't relate to either of her jobs.

Just before lunch, Dale, the loading dock manager who'd been pressuring her for a date, poked his head in the door. He said, "Hey, good looking."

Lynn cut her eyes up and casually and mumbled, "Hey, Dale."

The big man said, "Think you'll be ready for that drink soon?"

Lynn sighed, wondering if this might be an issue she'd have to deal with before she could complete her own mission. She said, "How about Saturday night?"

The big man whistled and clapped his beefy hands together.

John Stallings had to work hard not to fixate on the issues bubbling up at work. He was already focused on finding Zach Halston because he wanted to find out more about Jeanie. The young fraternity brother might also be the key to their larger case of looking into the deaths within the fraternity. All Stallings could do was think about Jeanie and the photo of her and Zach locked arm in arm.

But at this moment, playing a simple game of catch in the backyard with Charlie and Lauren, Stallings didn't want to focus on anything but the two kids laughing and telling him about their day. This was how he'd dreamed life would be when he was a child. But he'd never had a relationship with his father. Now, as the old man's memory faded, Stallings had the relationship he had always wanted. He was determined not to make the same mistakes with his own children. They seemed to enjoy having him around and looked forward to his daily visits. It had not surprised him that Maria had stayed hidden during his entire visit. He didn't know if she was still angry or if she was embarrassed by her allegation that he had traveled through Ocala to see his partner, Patty.

He had not even bothered to refute the ridiculous claim and hoped that the time and distance of the weekend might have caused Maria see how silly she'd acted and that was why she was avoiding him.

Looking at Lauren with her perfect smile and long, brown hair blowing in the late afternoon breeze, Stallings couldn't help but compare her to Jeanie. It was about this age, fourteen, that he'd felt his relationship with his missing daughter start to change. She'd become more distant and disappeared with her friends more often. He had assumed she and her mother were still communicating closely like they always had. It wasn't until later, after she disappeared, that he'd realized Maria had completely lost her grip on all aspects of family life. Apparently he had too. He had been so absorbed in homicide investigations he had lost sight of what was really important.

It was different with Lauren. He was involved in every aspect of her life and knew her habits and hobbies as well as she did. Lately, she'd been on a reading kick so he had bought her an Amazon Kindle and was gratified whenever he saw her curled up on the downstairs couch, reading the latest teen angst book. But she still liked to get outside and exercise. His fears about his middle child had eased somewhat since he'd caught her in a downtown bar with older girls less than a year ago. She had told Stallings she was going to study and it had broken his heart to realize his little girl had lied to him.

He didn't know why Lauren had backed away from her older group of friends but suspected it had something to do with her need to keep a closer eye on her mother. Since his sister, Helen, had transitioned out of the house, Lauren seemed to accept more and more responsibility.

After the game of catch was done and he made sure they had a reasonable dinner prepared, Stallings got ready to leave for his house over in Lakewood. He ached to tell Maria about the photograph he'd found of Jeanie, but he didn't know if he wanted to tell her because it was good news or because he thought it might get him out of the doghouse. He didn't want to do it for the wrong reasons and raise her hopes only for them to be crushed. He decided to wait.

Just as he had said good-bye to the kids and was about to open the front door he heard Maria clear her throat behind him and turned to see his wife standing halfway up the stairs. She wore a simple sundress and looked like she had either been sleeping or crying.

Maria opened her mouth, but all that came out was a very quiet, "Hey."

Stallings nodded and swallowed hard, trying not to say anything stupid. For some reason Grace Jackson's pretty face flashed in his head. Finally Stallings said, "You okay?"

Maria just kept looking at him with moist eyes.

Stallings said, "I didn't see Patty over Thanksgiving."

The statement was met by silence.

Stallings threw in, "But it looks like you have an issue with her."

Maria stepped down two more steps, then came all the way, opened the front door and pulled Stallings out onto the porch. She said, "Patty gets more of you than I ever did."

"That's not true. Patty and I have never been anything more than partners and good friends."

"I would've liked to be your friend. I didn't mind seeing you have coffee with the pretty woman downtown at the cafe. I knew there wasn't anything real between you. I could tell with one look. But Patty is different. She's important to you."

Stallings thought about it, nodded his head, and said, "I guess she is. But like a sister." Stallings looked at his wife's beautiful face and said, "How do you feel about Frank Ellis? Do you think about him as a brother?" He had to laugh at his own, unintentional Brother Frank Ellis pun. Maria's expression told him she didn't think it was that funny.

TWENTY-FOUR

It was awfully early in the morning, but Tony Mazzetti gritted his teeth and marched toward his partner's desk. The lull in homicides had kept him from having to spend too much time with the eccentric Sparky Taylor. Thank God for small favors. Now Mazzetti needed that giant brain of Sparky's to process some of the information they had and see if his odd perspective on life could tell him if the deaths related to Tau Upsilon fraternity were an accident or something much more sinister. As he approached the immaculate desk, his partner finished his last piece of wheat toast that he ate every morning, wiping his mouth after every bite with a new, clean napkin. Mazzetti cleared his throat.

"Hey, Spark. What's new?"

The rotund black man looked up at Mazzetti with those soft brown eyes and pleasant face—unlike almost any cop Mazzetti had ever met—and said, "I've been reading the files on the robbery victim, the overdose, and the accident victim from the marina to see if there was anything we might have to do on this case."

Mazzetti couldn't believe his partner was so far ahead of him, but he resisted saying something like *no shit*. Instead, he nodded calmly and said, "That's great. You come up with something?"

Sparky had a light Southern accent that Mazzetti assumed he had developed growing up in the Jacksonville area and honed during his four years at Georgia Tech. It was Sparky's engineering background and mind-set that gave him new ways of looking at the same old problems.

Sparky said, "I've taken the liberty of running a statistical analysis and boiled it down to its most basic components. I've come up with this formula. If you take into account the two-year span in education of the victims and you assume that the fraternity has an average of forty-two members plus or minus three each year with a turnover of ten to twelve members each year, you would have to assume that the fraternity had approximately sixty to seventy members from the time the shooting victim graduated until now. Three deaths among that number of young, relatively wealthy white men is out of the ordinary. That being said, there are always statistical anomalies."

Mazzetti looked at his partner and said, "Come on, Sparky, what the fuck does all that mean?"

As usual, Sparky didn't change his expression in any way. He simply said, "It means we have a problem that needs investigating and I suggest we jump on it with both feet."

* * *

Lisa Kurtz enjoyed being an assistant medical examiner and had aspirations to become the chief medical examiner of some jurisdiction, preferably in Florida. She liked the weather and the people. Although she found that most Floridians took college football far too seriously. She didn't worry about factoring her relationship with Tony Mazzetti into her career decisions. Those choices were at least two years down the road and she didn't get the sense that she and Tony would be together for too long. She enjoyed his company and his cute, simple tactics in the bedroom, but they didn't share many interests. What really fascinated her about Tony was his job. Although she had gone to medical school and considered herself part of the law enforcement community, she was not a detective and that's what really interested her. She read novels about detectives, she watched *Law and Order* almost every night, and she had read virtually every true crime book ever published. If it weren't for the hassle of the police academy she would consider becoming a cop herself.

The natural curiosity that made her think she'd be a great cop had led her to seek out the shirt that the overdose victim, Connor Tate, had worn the night he died. She knew she should take the shirt over to the sheriff's office crime lab or at least tell Tony what she was doing. Instead, she and one of the coroner techs, a former evidence custodian for Dade County, did their own forensic analysis of the shirt. They had scraped the residue from a stain that ran almost the length of the front of the filthy shirt. Now she would have to include the crime lab. She decided to deliver the tiny sample of scrapings herself and say it was part of an ongoing medical examiner's probe, which was true. They were always interested in overdose deaths and the prevalence of certain drugs in the community.

If anything came of it, she'd let Tony know. Until then she just would enjoy being a detective.

Stallings had been born and raised in North Florida, yet he had not spent much time on the campus of the University of Florida in Gainesville. He was glad Patty had been with him and able to guide them both around campus as well as using her status as a graduate to assist them in finding the fraternity house with little or no trouble. They wanted to branch out from the Jacksonville chapter of Tau Upsilon, which served several of the smaller universities in the area. Stallings had had a theory that perhaps other fraternities had suffered a recent spate of bad luck as well. Although he considered three deaths among such a small number of young men unusual, Stallings still wasn't convinced it was the work of some mastermind.

Now they were inside the house talking to a very nervous UF student who had been a member of the fraternity for his entire four-year career at the sprawling university. Stallings could tell by the look in this kid's eye that he was very uncomfortable talking to any law enforcement officer. Stallings let Patty start off the conversation smoothly and in her own style. There was no reason for this young man to be as shaky as he was acting.

Patty sat next to him on a long sofa and patted his

knee in an effort to calm the young man down. She said, "There's nothing for you to worry about. We're just curious if you know of any members of your fraternity who have died accidentally or otherwise in the past two years?"

The thin young man turned his pale eyes to Stallings, then back to Patty. He swallowed hard, his Adam's apple bobbing up and down like a fast elevator. "There's no one in the chapter that died for as long as we've existed. At least as far as I know."

Patty nodded like she was thinking, but Stallings knew she was trying to figure out what this boy's story was too. Finally she said, "What about any alumni?"

The boy physically winced and slowly nodded his head. "One of our brothers, Paul Smiley, died in some kind of fire in Atlanta last year."

Patty waited, thinking the boy might expand on his answer. When he didn't say anything else she said, "You sure that's it?"

"That's the only person who died that I know of."

There was something in his tone and delivery that made Patty say, "What about anyone seriously injured?"

The boy bit his lower lip and finally said, "Another one of our alumni, Alan Cole, is in the hospital in Daytona after he was hit by a car."

"Do you know any details about either incident?"

The boy shook his head. "I think whoever hit Alan drove away and hasn't been found."

Stallings scribbled down some notes but still had a sense the boy was hiding something. He cleared his throat until the young man looked up at him; then

Stallings said, "Did either of these guys spend much time at the chapter house in Jacksonville?"

Slowly the boy nodded his head. "They both had friends and other things that took them to Jacksonville. I think they usually stayed at the chapter house."

"Did they ever go together to Jacksonville?"

"I guess they did around Halloween."

"Why Halloween?"

"Because the North Florida chapter always hosts a kick-ass Halloween party."

Stallings exchanged a quick glance with Patty.

Yvonne Zuni prided herself on always being on top of homicides, drug cases, and missing children. But this latest wrinkle in the crimes/persons squad was different from anything she had ever had to deal with in her short career as a supervisor. She wasn't even sure a crime had occurred. They needed more proof than just a crazy theory about bad luck at a fraternity. She'd been told by Lieutenant Hester to keep things low key. But John Stallings and Tony Mazzetti were never low-key for long. Between the two of them something was going to be put on command staff's radar. Sergeant Zuni didn't mind; part of her job was running interference for her detectives. She just wished she understood the issue a little more clearly.

She wandered through the squad bay back toward her office, keeping a subtle eye on who was working at their desk and who was running their mouth at someone else's desk. There was usually too much work to allow much time for watercooler talk. But as effective as the squad had been the last few months she wasn't going to come down on anyone taking advantage of the lull in homicides or the precipitous drop in robberies over the past two months.

She noticed Tony Mazzetti at Sparky Taylor's desk working with the peculiar detective on something. She knew the two detectives weren't friends but had noted how they complemented each other so well. She had heard through the grapevine that Mazzetti's regular partner, Christina Hogrebe, was going to be promoted to sergeant before she finished her temporary assignment at the police academy. Zuni hadn't broken the news to Mazzetti yet but was gratified to see that he was working with Sparky on investigations instead of just treating him like an assistant.

She paused at John Stallings's cluttered desk and noticed a small stack of photographs. She moved aside a sheet of paper on top of them and pulled the first photograph off the desk. She noticed the other ten photographs were copies of this one showing a young man and a young woman smiling next to each other in a long hallway with festive lights strung behind them. It took her a moment to recognize the missing fraternity brother Zach Halston. She didn't know who the very pretty blond girl was. The sergeant assumed Stallings was using the photos to show different witnesses who might've come into contact with the missing fraternity brother.

She kept a photograph in her hand and set the piece of paper back over the remaining photographs on Stallings's desk. As she neared her office she heard her desk phone ring and hustled to catch it.

Sergeant Zuni absently set the photograph of Zach Halston and the girl down at the side of her desk as she picked up the receiver and simply said, "Sergeant Zuni, crimes/persons."

Dale squeezed into the tiny chair next to Lynn's desk. Since she had agreed to have a drink with him Saturday night he'd taken it to mean she wanted to see him more often during the workweek at Thomas Brothers Supply. Until she had a better idea of what he knew and what he planned to do with the information, she decided to stay on the large, smelly man's good side.

At the moment he was wolfing down a tuna salad sandwich, then gulping a twenty-ounce bottle of Mountain Dew. He repeatedly offered Lynn a bite of the sandwich or a drink from the bottle, which she politely refused.

Dale said, "What time do you want me to pick you up Saturday?"

Lynn said, "I'm going to meet you. I thought we might go over to Jacksonville Landing to sit at a bar along the river."

"Lady's choice. I'll take you wherever you to like to go. Maybe you could even bring some of your party pills if you want to have a real wild time."

"What are you talking about, Dale?"

"I'm talking about the Baggie of pills I found the other day in your purse." Now he cut his eyes slightly to the side and said, "Were you high the day you wrecked the Suburban?"

Lynn suddenly had a sickening feeling that Dale

was not the big dumb redneck he pretended to be. She wondered if she might not have a real problem sitting right in front of her.

Tony Mazzetti had given the matter a great deal of thought and had decided he fervently hoped that the deaths associated with the Tau Upsilon fraternity were a statistical anomaly. He could deal with one random robbery that resulted in homicide. Ultimately, perhaps after some luck and time, some street thug would be arrested for an unrelated crime and give up who shot the auto parts store manager. But three unsolved homicides meant that he had a severe blemish on his clearance rate. Two accidents were much easier to explain. Hell, half the kids in college today used pharmaceutical drugs recreationally. Mazzetti was surprised there weren't more overdoses. And the kid who had fallen into the river and been chewed to pieces by the fishing boat could have been anyone. He just happened to be a member of the fraternity.

The events that had attracted the attention of the sheriff's office had led Mazzetti to review the evidence on the auto parts manager's shooting. He went through a stack of DVDs from various security cameras, including one located inside the store. That was the only one with any faces that could be recognized. If the killer had walked into the store the night of the shooting, Mazzetti couldn't tell who pulled the trigger. In the four hours before the store closed there had been only a handful of customers. The man with three children, an older trucker, a guy in the yard service shirt who

Mazzetti and Sparky had tracked down and cleared of any suspicion, a middle-aged woman holding a broken windshield wiper, a young, cute woman who ended up not buying anything, and three young black males.

Using a still photo from the video Mazzetti had checked with all of his informants downtown and eventually found one of the three men. He had explained that they were looking for parts to restore a 1967 Mustang. Sparky and Mazzetti had visited the young man's apartment and seen the car, but more important, Mazzetti could tell the young man was not a thug.

He watched the soundless video once more over his desktop computer. The grainy images produced decent shots of each customer's face as long as they happened to glance up towards the camera. Right now he looked at the young woman he had never identified and noticed her look across the aisle at the manager, though she never appeared to speak to him. If it had been a male in the same circumstances Mazzetti would be killing himself to identify the man as a suspect.

Stallings had been anxious to get back to his canvass of businesses on University Boulevard. Patty was following up on information they got from the nerd at the University of Florida fraternity. Stallings had tried to hide his interest in returning to the seemingly mundane job of canvassing businesses for a missing person, but the trip to Gainesville had frustrated him greatly. He had lost an entire day. The drive over and back, as well as Patty's interest in showing him around the campus where she had spent four years on the gymnastics team, had killed any chance he had to talk to business owners the day before.

His mood yesterday had not been helped by the way Maria systematically ignored him when he'd come over to visit the kids. But today he had managed to squeeze in nine stores; unfortunately all of them but one were under new management and had no idea about who had worked there previously.

In the midafternoon Stallings found a vintage clothing store just on the south side of the river close to the University of North Florida. He took a moment to look in the windows noticing the expensive price tags on what he considered used clothing. When he was a kid they'd called them hand-me-downs. A bell tinkled as he stepped through the front door and a large woman with what appeared to be a tent covering her form glanced up from a copy of *In Touch* magazine.

Without looking up at Stallings, she said, "I already gave to the police athletic league and I don't give two shits about the Police Benevolent Association."

Stallings said, "I'm looking for someone."

"Who?"

Stallings laid down the photograph he'd taken from Zach Halston's apartment.

The woman glanced down at it, then said, "You're looking for Kelly?"

TWENTY-FIVE

Sparky Taylor had used his connections in Atlanta to get the details on the death of UF student and Tau Upsilon member Paul Smiley, which had occurred in the city a little over a year ago. It was death by fire, which in Sparky's mind was the worst way to go. He wasn't entirely sure he liked this assignment in homicide. They didn't seem to be as interested in following policy as he was. All his partner, Tony Mazzetti, ever thought about was ensuring his clearance rate on homicides was the best in the state. Mazzetti was a good detective, but he didn't always dig deep enough into the circumstances of a death. Sparky didn't think that was how the public expected a police department to work.

That was one of the reasons he had volunteered to track down any possible information on the death of a Tau Upsilon fraternity member who had graduated from the University of Florida the year before.

Sparky's call had been taken by one of his buddies who had attended Georgia Tech with him, and he was now speaking to a sergeant in narcotics. Sparky said, "Why aren't I speaking to someone in homicide?"

The gruff sergeant, who obviously wasn't happy about wasting time talking to some detective in a hick town like Jacksonville, said, "Homicide doesn't necessarily believe that death was anything but an accident. You know how they are about their clearance rates."

"I do know that."

"Anyway, the victim had two kilos of marijuana in his apartment and toxicology shows that he was stoned and had ketamine in his system. He was asphyxiated before he even realized there was a fire."

"Do you have a big ketamine problem in Atlanta?"

"Kids use it if they can get it. A few veterinarians have been burglarized and lost some, but it's not too bad."

"Is there any evidence or anything left to go through on the death?"

"There are few things in boxes in evidence, but it's just the bricks of marijuana and maybe some ID. I'm pretty sure the landlord never rented the apartment and there may be something over there. If you need more details or to come up here to look at the case I'll have to hand you off to one of the homicide guys."

Sparky scribbled a few notes while the sergeant read off the address and any other information he had on the case. Then the sergeant said, "Why would you guys be interested in something like this?"

"Because, like your police department, our homicide unit is more interested in clearance than in finding murderers. It's my job to make sure we do both."

The sergeant said, "You sound like a guy who could work for me any day of the week."

* * *

Yvonne Zuni sat in her office signing off to close cases regarding accidental or justifiable homicides. She had been very impressed with the work of several of the new detectives who had been brought on board in the last year. The one case she pulled out of the pile was Connor Tate, the overdose victim from the University of North Florida. In an effort to keep the inquiry into the Tau Upsilon fraternity quiet, the sergeant had opted not to tell the detective on the Tate case what was going on. As a result, Detective Luis Martinez had done his usual thorough job and turned in the case file with everything necessary to close it out permanently.

Right now the only ones who knew the cases could be related were the four detectives working the case and her lieutenant, Rita Hester. She expected the lieutenant at any time and had been cleaning up the files to get her signature on the closings. The lieutenant had not spent much time with the crimes/persons squad in the last six months while she helped convert the evidence computer system as well as work on the re-accreditation of the sheriff's office. On one hand it was a compliment to Sergeant Zuni and her abilities that no one interfered with how she ran the squad. On the other hand, it was a lot more work.

Sergeant Zuni recognized that Rita Hester had her eyes set on a position much higher up the ladder. Not only was she a good cop but she didn't shy away from the political angle of her job either. The sergeant recognized that Lieutenant Hester and John Stallings had been partners on the road years before and remained very close friends. She didn't think Stallings would ever go over her head to the lieutenant, but it was an important relationship to consider when dealing with politically sensitive cases.

She did recognize that although Stallings didn't go over her head, occasionally the lieutenant would use Stallings for her own needs. The lieutenant would allow Stallings to conduct investigations outside the lines of the normal policy with the subtle understanding that if he got in trouble no one would be there to help him. Sergeant Zuni considered this taking advantage of Stallings's natural tendency to fixate on a case and push to solve it no matter what the cost. That was why she would probably remain a sergeant for the rest of her career.

The lieutenant appeared at her door without a sound, like a genie. She gave a curt hello and immediately stepped around the desk to start signing off on the cases. After the lieutenant had completed the paperwork, as she stood up and stretched her large frame, she paused and reached down to pick up the photograph Sergeant Zuni had taken from John Stallings's desk.

The lieutenant asked, "Where did you get this?"

"From John Stallings. That's the missing fraternity boy he's looking for."

The lieutenant nodded but kept the photograph. She said, "Where's Stallings now?"

"Canvassing businesses on University Boulevard where someone had seen the young man before he disappeared."

The sergeant was surprised that all she got back from the lieutenant was a brief nod as she rushed out of the office with the photograph still in her hand.

It took John Stallings a moment to catch his breath, then say to the woman, "You know Kelly?"

The woman took her glasses off and allowed them to hang down around her neck by a rhinestone-studded strap. "Yes, she worked here for a couple of months a few years ago."

Stallings tried to keep his voice calm and even. "Have you been in touch with her since she left?"

"Why, has she done something wrong?"

"No. She's missing and her family is very, very concerned."

The woman looked at the photograph again and said, "I think the boy looks familiar too. I know she dated someone briefly while she worked here. It might have been him. I only met him one time."

"His name is Zach Halston."

"Yeah, that's him. There was something about him that Kelly didn't like. But I haven't talked to either of them since she quit."

Stallings pulled out his notebook ready to grill this woman until he had as much information as he could get on his missing daughter and Zach Halston.

TWENTY-SIX

Tony Mazzetti felt like a genius. After listening to his partner explain the conversation he'd had with the cop in Atlanta, Mazzetti came up with an idea that would solve two problems at once.

He looked at Sparky and said, "Why don't you take a ride up to Atlanta and look over the evidence yourself just to make sure everything's in order?"

"I don't know, Tony. That's a long ride up there and a long ride back. I wonder if talking to the medical examiner might not be more efficient."

"No, no, we're cops and we talk to other cops. Take a look at what they have and maybe we can conclude that it really was an accident and we're chasing shadows here."

"The victim isn't even from Jacksonville."

"Right now he's just an unlucky kid from Gainesville. But if we let people build this into a huge conspiracy they would consider him part of some kind of crazy cult or victim of a serial killer. He died in a fire that may or may not be suspicious. You look and see if there are any ties to Jacksonville or something that makes you think there's more to it."

Sparky Taylor nodded his head slowly, chewing his lip as he thought. "I guess it wouldn't hurt to get the sergeant's approval and spend the night up there. If this turns out to be more than bad luck it's something we have to do anyway."

Mazzetti patted him on the shoulder and said, "That's the way to look at it, Sparky."

Lynn was down in the parking lot of the Thomas Brothers supply company inspecting the grille of the Suburban she'd borrowed and used to run down Alan Cole. It had obviously been damaged and the grille repaired, and the entire truck had been cleaned thoroughly. When she had checked before she returned it, she'd only noticed a scrap of clothing, which she had pulled off the grille. Now she was concerned that Dale wasn't quite the blowhard or moron he pretended to be.

A tall man with sandy brown hair was washing one of the main delivery trucks when he noticed her and set down his hose. He stood out because he was the only non-Hispanic maintenance man and always seemed to be in a foul mood. Lynn didn't know his name even though she'd seen him around the facility over the past three months.

Dale drove up in the golf cart he used to shuttle from the loading dock to the far reaches of the lot. Before he even slowed down, he yelled at the man, "Leon, get your ass back to work. This ain't no charity." Then the big man softened and looked at Patty as he stopped the cart. "Look at you. You're as fine as the day is long." He was about to say something when his cell phone chirped. He looked down at the message and punched the gas on the cart. "Gotta go, beautiful." Without turning around, he called back to Leon, "Finish up and get to the loading dock."

The man shook his head. He looked at Lynn, apparently noticing the disgust on her face. The man said, "Not much for manners, is he?"

"Does he always treat you like that?"

The man just shrugged and mumbled, "I've had worse."

Lynn gave him a weak smile.

Then the man said, "I know who you are." His North Florida drawl was thicker than most of the other workers'. And that was saying something.

Lynn said, "I don't think we've met before."

"I've been by your parents' house and saw you there."

"I'm sorry, I don't remember you. How long ago were you there?"

"Since I just got out of prison three months ago it was probably about five years and three months since I've been over there."

"You must have me mistaken for someone else."

"Your daddy's name is Bill? And your uncle is Peter?"

Lynn immediately understood it was a business issue and she just shook her head. "My dad is retired now."

"Good for him. He's a fair man who treats people right. I owe him a lot." He stuck out his hand. "I'm Leon."

Lynn took his hand. "I'm Lynn."

"Lynn, you ever need anything, you let me know."

His eyes cut toward the loading dock where Dale was harassing one of the workers. "It's the least I could do for your dad. No one ever deserved a happy retirement more than him."

Lynn couldn't have agreed more and that was one of the reasons she'd undertaken her mission.

John Stallings had gained a lot of information from the woman at the vintage clothing store. He had several leads to follow up, including an address where Jeanie lived while she worked at the store. He was running the house through county records now to see who owned it and if they owned it three years ago when she worked at the store. He realized he was breathing quickly with excitement and took a moment to calm down. The rest of the squad bay was relatively quiet as he gathered up a notebook and several copies of the photo of Jeanie and Zach.

As he was about to leave, Sergeant Zuni stepped out of her office and said, "Stall, I'm glad you're here. The lieutenant wants to see us in her office right away."

"Really? Right now? I'm right in the middle of running down some leads."

The sergeant folded her arms and gave him a look. She'd been around too long to put up with a detective ignoring a direct order from the unit's lieutenant.

Ten minutes later, Stallings found himself sitting in the large, decorated office that housed the lieutenant for the entire detective bureau. He had no idea what Rita Hester needed to talk to them about, but he trusted his old partner and was always interested in her ideas.

Stallings sat quietly next to the sergeant for more than a minute before the lieutenant marched in from the outer office and eased into her chair before she said, "Detective Stallings, I'm glad you could find time in your schedule to chat with me."

Stallings immediately realized something was wrong from the tone of her voice and the fact that she'd addressed him by his title. Over the years he had realized that was her way of saying this was business and nothing but business. His personal friendship and longtime association with her was not a factor in whatever she wanted to discuss.

Lieutenant Hester said, "How is your search for the missing fraternity brother going?"

Stallings looked at Sergeant Zuni, then realized he was supposed to answer. "I'm following all leads that come my way, but so far we don't have anything concrete."

The lieutenant said, "I'm aware of the preliminary investigation into the deaths of three other members of the Tau Upsilon fraternity. I'm going to have to see more before I hit the panic button and draw attention to the city and especially the university. That's why I think it's so important that we find Zach Halston. Do you agree with that?"

Of course Stallings agreed, but he wasn't sure why the lieutenant had to ask the question. A rumble of acid rolled to his stomach as he considered a number of possibilities, but he was still unsure where this conversation was going.

The lieutenant retrieved something from her middle desk drawer and leaned forward as she slid it across her immaculate desk. Sergeant Zuni leaned forward to look at the photo, but Stallings knew what it was immediately.

The lieutenant said, "Does this look familiar?"

Sergeant Zuni immediately said, "That's the fraternity brother Stallings is looking for."

Lieutenant said, "Do you recognize the girl?"

The sergeant shook her head.

"Do you want to fill her in, Stall, or should I?"

Stallings didn't say anything.

The lieutenant waited a few moments, then said, "The young lady in the photo is Detective Stallings's missing daughter, Jeanie. I knew Jeanie most of her life and recognized her immediately. I am also thrilled to see that there is evidence she's alive. What does not thrill me is that Detective Stallings would abandon his assigned duties to investigate something to do with his own daughter instead of handing it off to the detectives responsible. It bothers me that he would intentionally mislead you or me about his activities or intentions." Her voice rose ever so slightly with each sentence. "It bothers me that he would put the mission of your squad at risk for his own personal investigation. And it bothers me"—she looked directly at Stallings—"that you don't think enough of me to tell me what's going on."

Stallings had no answer for any of her rational and legitimate concerns.

It was obvious Sergeant Zuni had been stunned into silence.

The lieutenant said, "As of this moment, Detective Stallings is no longer working on this missing persons case. I am getting tremendous pressure from above to find out what happened to Zach Halston. It would've been nice to have one of my senior detectives on that. But you are to stand down. I don't care what you do. You can organize the pencils on your desk. But you will not be working this case." She leveled her dark, intense eyes at Stallings. "Is this clearly understood?"

All Stallings could do was nod.

TWENTY-SEVEN

John Stallings sat on a picnic table in the shadow of a giant condominium across the street from the PMB. The security guard at the condominium was a retired New York City cop and left the picnic table accessible to any JSO officer who needed to get away from the office for a few minutes. It was on a manicured lawn and looked out over the St. Johns River. This time of day it was usually a refuge for a worried detective having an argument with his girlfriend that he didn't want his wife to find out about. Patty even joked that the picnic table should be called Tiger Woods Stadium.

But Stallings liked the peaceful retreat to consider cases and, in this instance, consider his career. He was angry, but not at Rita Hester. He could see from her point of view it was the only thing to do. She was a boss now and had to make decisions that were favorable to the Jacksonville Sheriff's Office, not just her friends. But that didn't change the fact that he was a father with a missing daughter. Like most fathers in that position, he would do anything to find her.

He had considered resigning. Although quitting would give him some level of satisfaction it would not make the job of looking for Jeanie any easier. Even if he got his private investigator's license, that gave him no more access to police files than anyone else. It might also mean less help from the cops across the country who were doing what they could now. In general, cops viewed private investigators as a joke.

Stallings prided himself on being decisive, but at this moment he had no idea what to do. None. He knew that Zach Halston was the key not only to finding Jeanie but also to shedding light on the deaths of the other fraternity brothers. Stallings had some information from the owner of the store where Jeanie had worked, and he didn't care what his status was with the sheriff's office. He needed to follow up. He had an address of an apartment near the store and he intended to talk to the owner. But his overwhelming issue right now was how to clear his head and do the right thing.

He had no idea who to talk to. Maria wasn't an option in her fragile state. He didn't want to put Patty between him and administration. She had her own issues and someone needed to work the case with a clear head. His mom was focused on his father's worsening Alzheimer's and didn't understand the politics of a large police department. Then he realized everyone he trusted in the world, everyone that he wanted to talk to about a personal problem, was female. Could that have something to do with the relationship he had with his father? Or were women just that much smarter than men?

Suddenly he realized who he could call. He dug his cell phone out of his front pocket and found the name that might be able to set him straight.

Patty could tell by the sergeant's demeanor that this was not the time to ask questions. The sergeant simply said, "Stall has been reassigned. You'll be working with Tony and Sparky. See if you can get a lead on a missing kid, Zach Halston. Otherwise, whatever Tony needs, help him out."

Patty had to say, "John's not in trouble, is he?" Usually the answer to that would be yes, but she would've heard about it by now.

Sergeant Zuni shook her head and mumbled, "He's not suspended or anything like that. I'm sure he'll tell you what's going on if he wants to."

Patty was used to the mysterious workings of the Jacksonville Sheriff's Office and didn't worry about how things happened, only about how to work around glitches like this. She ran through her head the encounters Stallings had had with different people over the last week and couldn't think of one where he had stepped out of line. Certainly he hadn't punched anyone.

Patty reached for her cell phone, then hesitated, figuring that Stallings would call her if he needed to tell her what was going on. He kept very little from her and she appreciated him all the more for it.

She was worried about John, but the idea of working closely with Tony Mazzetti held some excitement.

* * *

Stallings sat along the small tributary that ran from the St. Johns River. The cozy café was built out over the water and featured fresh seafood as well as other local favorites with a strong influence of southern cooking. That usually meant everything was sautéed in butter or fried.

As soon as she entered the front door he couldn't help but smile. She was still dressed for work but radiated warmth that affected everyone she came in contact with. Even the snooty hostess smiled and pointed to where Stallings was waiting.

He stood as she approached like you would for any woman. Those were the manners his mother had drilled into him as a child. But it was awkward as she came closer because he wasn't sure if he should offer a hand or a hug.

Grace solved the awkward dilemma by embracing him warmly, then kissing him on the cheek. Stallings held her chair and sat across from her with a stupid grin still on his face.

They chatted for almost a half an hour, learning more about each other's families and the sadness they'd felt as their marriages disintegrated. Grace was the one in her relationship who had taken decisive action and cut her husband loose. That gave Stallings a different perspective from which to view his own situation.

He finally explained what had happened when Lieutenant Hester had found the photograph of Jeanie with Zach Halston and how he was now in a dilemma about what to do next.

Grace calmly looked at him and said, "Do you tell the sheriff's office everything you do while off duty?"

"No, of course not."

"It sounds like you just added another task to your busy personal life. Don't forget you've got two kids at home."

It was pretty simple and direct advice. He liked it. "I have a strong drive to find Jeanie, really it's an obsession. And I know it's hard on my relationship with Lauren and Charlie."

Grace gave him a smile. "What man of you, having an hundred sheep, if he lose one of them, doth not leave the ninety and nine in the wilderness, and go after that which is lost, until he find it?" She paused a moment and added, "Luke, chapter fifteen."

"What you're saying is I'm not unique in my issue."

"I'm saying any man would do it, but I'm cautioning you to not forget you've got kids who need you."

Stallings mumbled, "And a wife."

Grace said clearly, "Who better start to appreciate you."

Tony Mazzetti had been talking for a few minutes about all the possibilities related to the deaths of the fraternity members when he realized he didn't know if he was trying to convince Patty or himself that the deaths could be accidents.

Patty gave him a suspicious look and said, "You sure you're not just protecting your clearance rate?"

Mazzetti gave her a look back and said, "We're not

sleeping together anymore. I don't have to take any shit."

Patty smiled and said, "Like you ever did. I was just wondering and asking questions. You don't have to be an ass about it."

Mazzetti decided to let the whole matter slide. It was awkward enough working with his former girl-friend; he didn't need to fan the flames. He changed the subject completely. "So what did Stall do to get you assigned to me?"

Patty shrugged. "Just got reassigned. I can't read the sergeant's mind."

Mazzetti laughed. "Must've something pretty big to have the LT do anything to her buddy."

"You sound jealous."

"Wish I had a rabbi up the chain. No telling where I'd be now."

"You'd want to do something other than homicide?"

The question took Mazzetti by surprise, and his honest answer surprised him even more. "I guess not." He looked off in space and added, "Thanks, you made me appreciate what I have." When he looked up into her pretty face, he also realized what he had lost.

TWENTY-EIGHT

John Stallings tried to slip into the office like a ninja. He did not feel like speaking to anyone about his troubles. He wanted a couple of files to cover him in case someone asked what he was doing. Grace had set his head straight and he figured six o'clock was late enough to be off duty. Stallings knew exactly where he was headed. But of course even though it was late, Sergeant Zuni was still in her office.

As he walked past he knew she'd look up and see him, so he took the offensive. He stopped in her doorway and looked in.

Sergeant Zuni looked up from the report she was reading and simply said, "I didn't know."

"I didn't mean to put you in an awkward position."

"Instead you made me look like a moron."

"Sorry."

Sergeant Zuni stood up and stepped around her desk. "I'm not a machine. I know what it is to have personal issues. You can talk to me off the record now and then."

"I'll keep that in mind."

"Zach Halston is important to you for personal reasons, but he's also important to our investigation."

Stallings waited for her to finish, but she just stood there until he said, "Yes?"

Sergeant Zuni cleared her throat. "Lieutenant Hester won't check too closely when you're out on the street. She knows you're a hard worker and I don't have to justify what you're doing to anyone." She looked down at two older missing persons files in his hand. "I like that you're smart enough to keep up a façade."

This new sergeant was more complicated than anyone he had ever worked for. And Stallings was starting to like it.

Duval County Assistant Medical Examiner Lisa Kurtz was feeling pretty good about herself as she rushed up the stairs to the second floor of the Police Memorial Building. She had a report from the lab and a photograph that showed she could come up with forensic clues with the best of them. Her instincts about the stain on Connor Tate's shirt had proved to be right on the money. A chemical spectrum analysis of the stain showed it to contain a number of chemicals including ecstasy, strong depressants typically found in sleep aids, and painkillers, in this case a generic form of hydrocodone. In addition, she had a magnified photograph clearly showing a chunk of a ground-up blue Ambien pill.

Lisa waved hello to the secretary, then was brought up short as she opened the door marked CRIME/PERSONS and nearly ran into Patty Levine. The two women had a passing acquaintance and each knew they had one big thing in common: Tony Mazzetti.

Lisa wasn't sure what to say or do so she just smiled and nodded hello.

Patty, always so calm and collected, was able to get out a "Hey, Lisa, what's up?"

Lisa wanted to show the detective the report and what she had discovered, but knew that Tony was the one who needed to see it. She signaled Patty to follow her over to Mazzetti's desk.

Lisa could see the surprise on Tony Mazzetti's face when he looked up to see his current girlfriend and his most recent ex-girlfriend standing before him. His eyes cut back and forth between Lisa and Patty for a moment until Lisa pushed through the awkward moment.

She plopped the lab report and the photograph down on his desk, saying, "Connor Tate drank a potentially lethal concoction of drugs. I had the lab do an analysis of the stain on his shirt."

Mazzetti focused on Lisa. "I know. That's what killed him. Your office did the autopsy, remember?"

Lisa ignored this sarcastic jab and said, "Why drink an odd mixture of sleeping pills and painkillers when you pop them in plain sight of everyone? I think someone fed him the mixture secretly so it would react with all the alcohol in his system."

"Even if it wasn't an accident he could've been trying to commit suicide."

"I looked at the crime scene photographs and noticed there were no glasses around the bed where the body was found. Also the photographs of the tiny kitchen showed three glasses that had been washed and stacked by the side of the sink. That's not the kind of activity you do when you've got a blood alcohol level three times the legal limit and have ingested at least four types of prescription drugs."

She could tell Mazzetti was considering her hypothesis. But he wasn't convinced.

Lisa pointed at the photograph and added, "You can even see a chunk of a blue Ambien tablet on his shirt. He was lying down when he drank it. It dribbled into a puddle on his chest."

Patty said, "C'mon, Tony, she's got something here. That kid wasn't the type to try and take his own life. He was too confident and cocky."

Lisa liked Patty's rational thought and realized the pretty detective didn't hold any grudge about her dating Tony. She could see being friends with someone like Patty.

Mazzetti said, "Who would do something like that?"

Lisa said, "Who was with him the night before his body was found?"

Mazzetti shook his head. "No one knows."

Patty said, "Based on everything we know about the fraternity in general and Connor in particular, it had to be a woman."

Stallings took Grace's advice and the sergeant's coded signal as well as following his heart and sixteen years of police experience. Now he was looking at an ancient block building he remembered as a kid. It looked like an abandoned prison, but local history said it was housing for early migrant workers. When he was a boy, the building had been abandoned and run-down only to be renovated in the early 1990s on the cutting edge of the mini-boom that had gone on in the area. Now it was out of style again and just one of many cheap apartment buildings on the south side of the city.

It was four stories tall with about twenty units on each side and looked to be only about a third full. Stallings had to admit it was better maintained and considerably cleaner than most of the older apartment buildings in the area.

The sun had been down less than an hour, but the lack of outdoor lighting made it feel much later as Stallings approached the door marked OFFICE. He knocked once and rang the buzzer twice, then stepped away from the door, saying out loud in a low voice, "Is this the day that changes the rest of my life?"

The door to his right opened a crack and he realized it was the manager's apartment attached to the office. A thin, elderly man in a flannel shirt peered through a crack with the chain still on the door. Once he got a look at Stallings, he unchained the door and said, "What can I do for you, officer?"

"How did you know I was a cop?"

"I've run this place sixteen years and anyone built like you, with no tattoos and who's taken a bath in the last three days, is a cop. The only thing surprising is that at this time of the night it's usually a uniformed patrolman looking for someone."

The older man invited Stallings inside and his wife joined them as Stallings explained he was looking for two young people and laid out the photograph of Jeanie and Zach Halston.

The woman took a very close look and said, "That's Kelly who lived up on the third floor couple of years ago. And the boy used to come around for a while."

Stallings caught her tone and said, "You don't sound like you thought much of him."

"He was a little bit of an ass. Kelly liked him at first, but she had a thing for a guy named Gator. Nice young man but kinda confused. You know how women like to fix men."

Stallings got all the information he could about Jeanie and Zach, then took the time to ask about Gator.

"I don't know what the young man did for a living. He was tall, about six-one and lean."

The man added, "He would've made an excellent baseball pitcher."

The woman, recognizing what Stallings was looking for, added, "I don't know where he lived, but he drove an older Chevy sedan. He had blue eyes and brown hair."

Stallings said, "Did Jean, I mean Kelly, talk to you or tell you where she was headed once she moved out?"

The woman shook her head. "She was a polite girl and gave us two weeks' notice but never said where she was moving. I had asked her about the one boy, Zach, and she just smiled and said he was a spoiled brat."

Stallings had to smile at that. Some of his values had imprinted on her. He looked up at the old couple and said, "Can I look in the apartment?"

TWENTY-NINE

Patty was supposed to meet Ken, but she had called and canceled. After working so closely with Tony, even in the presence of his girlfriend, Lisa, she found herself thinking about her former boyfriend and was too distracted to listen to Ken babble about some reality TV show or how MDs thought they were so great. She wondered why he hadn't become a general practitioner if he was so jealous of anyone with a medical degree. He had to tell everyone he met how podiatrists attended medical school and were "real" doctors. But his patients still called him "Doctor Ken." That ate at him every day.

Instead of dinner with a petty, frustrated podiatrist, Patty found herself approaching the entrance to the Tau Upsilon fraternity clubhouse at the apartment complex that doubled as fraternity row. Earlier, she had called the house at UF and found out a few more details about the big Halloween party thrown every year in the Jacksonville chapter. The description sounded heavenly for college frat boys and was every parent's nightmare.

She saw Bobby Hollis notice her from the lounger

outside the front door. He sprang to his feet and turned toward the door, apparently to warn the brothers inside.

Patty simply called out in a very loud, clear voice, "Don't."

He responded like a dutiful dog and froze in place. Then he straightened and pulled his shirt, flicking potato chip crumbs onto the ground. He turned slowly and said, "Hello, Detective, nice to see you again."

"Cut the shit. I don't have time for it."

The door to the fraternity house burst open and a young man stumbled out. She immediately recognized him as the one she had thumped out at the beach. He staggered to a stop, looked into her face, and let a goofy grin spread.

He ran his hand across his wild hair and said, "Well, well, what do we have here?"

Patty didn't change her expression when she said, "You don't have much of a memory."

The kid said, "I never needed one until I saw some-one as beautiful as you."

Patty rolled her eyes but acknowledged, at least to herself, she liked the compliment and the kid was smooth.

From behind the drunken moron, Bobby Hollis said, "You remember Detective Levine, don't you?"

The kid was shit-faced, but he remembered, and the color left his face. He backed away, then turned to one side and appeared ready to sprint if he had to.

This time Patty said, "Don't. Sit."

The kid froze, then sat on the lounger next to the front door.

Patty shoved Bobby Hollis next to the frightened

fraternity brother. She looked at the drunken brother and said, "Just out of curiosity, what does a clueless dope like you major in?"

"Pre-law."

"Why?"

"Why else? Money. Personal injury is where it's at, along with decent litigation. Look at the tobacco settlement. Any lawyer involved is rich."

Maybe the kid was right. For a drunken asshole, he made pretty good sense. She turned toward Bobby and said, "I need a few answers from you guys."

"Like what?"

Patty leaned in closer to them to get her point across. "I want to hear all about your Halloween parties the last couple of years."

The fraternity brothers looked at each other. Then Bobby said, "What do you want to know? It's a lot of fun and half the damn school comes to the party."

"That's what I'm looking for. A list of attendees the last two years."

Bobby's eyes opened wide as he said, "That's impossible. I wouldn't know where to start."

"I would start by sobering up and getting together with a couple of your trusted friends. I want a preliminary list first thing tomorrow morning. And if I don't get it, next time I come back I'll bring along Detective Stallings. Your lives will never be the same until you help us out with this. Do my good little dogs understand what I'm saying?"

Both young men nodded their heads in unison.

* * *

When Lynn worked this late it was usually for Dr. Ferrero, but tonight she was behind her desk at the Thomas Brothers supply company catching up on accounts receivable that had been held two weeks, then dumped on her desk in a big pile. She really didn't care because it was peaceful and kept her mind off other, more troubling things.

She finished near seven o'clock and cut through the loading dock to the parking lot, where there were still a number of people scurrying around and closing out their jobs for the day. As she turned into the fleet parking lot she saw Leon wiping down one of Mr. Thomas's Cadillacs.

She stopped and they exchanged helloes as she took a moment to look at the details of the beautiful car. She turned to the familiar sound of the golf cart Dale used to scoot around the giant complex.

He slowed until he was directly across from her and said, "Looking forward to Saturday night. We'll have a great time." He scowled at Leon and said, "You're outside all day tomorrow. Wear plenty of sunscreen." He mashed the pedal of the golf cart and hummed away at a brisk five miles an hour.

Leon looked at Lynn and said, "It's not my business, but why would you go out with that turd?"

Lynn shrugged meekly and said, "I was kind of forced to. I swear to God there's nothing going on between us."

Leon gave her a long, curious look and said, "How'd you like it if Dale was unavailable for your date?"

"I wouldn't be too upset." As soon as she said it, she wondered what Leon might have in mind. Lynn didn't think a simple comment like that meant anything sinister or violent, but she knew the lean, tough-looking man had his own grudge against Dale.

Leon said, "I owe it to your dad and I was going to have to do something anyway. That guy is a total dick." He looked in every direction. "I know everyone in your family can keep a secret. Don't worry about a thing."

Stallings stood in the empty third-floor apartment that Jeanie had once rented. He knew he wouldn't find any evidence or information; he just wanted to be in a space that Jeanie had occupied within the last few years. The whole idea made him shaky and raised an entirely new set of questions in his mind about his daughter's disappearance.

Why had she run away? If she was so close, why hadn't she called? What had gone so terribly wrong? Did she hate him? Had it all sprung from his own relationship with his father?

Stallings's sister, Helen, had been very clear that she'd left because of their father. She was less clear about was what had happened to her after she'd left. That made Stallings wonder what other issues Jeanie might have if, by God's grace, he did find her and bring her home. He had no illusions. This was not the tidy world of the TV hour-long drama. He had to consider the effect on Charlie and Lauren as well as Jeanie's well-being.

So the question came up again, why had she left? It was almost easier to believe she had been taken against her will. At least then there was an explanation. Although the rate of kidnappings in the United States was incredibly small, it still happened. Most detectives went their whole careers without seeing a kidnapping. At least one that wasn't related to the drug trade.

Stallings had developed a certain confidence as a police officer that had served him well the past sixteen years. It could be considered the sixth sense cops are expected to have. A confidence to look at someone and know they are feeding you a line of bullshit. The confidence to know you'll achieve a goal or solve a case. It was the basic personality trait that defined a good cop.

But as a father, he had constantly compared himself to others. One of the reasons was that he never had a decent role model himself. He adopted other fathers as role models. He appreciated dads who not only spent time with their kids but *did* stuff with them too. Played sports instead of watching the kids run around the park. Explained things instead of just showing kids what things looked like. It often made him wonder what he'd be like today if his father had done those kinds of things.

He had a lot of questions about his life and *what if* scenarios. But there was one question that was more immediate and could lead to other answers: Where was Zach Halston?

THIRTY

John Stallings had spent the morning at his desk looking through every database he could think of for a reference to someone named Gator. He also wondered what exactly Zach Halston had done to piss Jeanie off.

He had found so many references to so many different Gators that Stallings knew there was only one place he could go to get any real answers. It was one of the few places in the PMB that most cops avoided. But he had made up his mind and started the trek up the stairs to the third floor where the rubber-gun squad was located. Some of the patrolman didn't even realize there was a unit called Intelligence in the sheriff's office. Years ago the unit had been a dumping ground for cops who had been unable to make a case or work in the streets. But now, with the rising public concern of terrorism and the mushrooming groups of extremists, the detectives assigned to the intelligence unit, or rubber-gun squad, tended to be among the smartest in the department.

Stallings saw Lonnie Freed sitting at the rear of the

squad bay working on a computer. He cut through the empty office and plopped into the chair next to Lonnie's desk, saying, "What's going on?"

The thirty-five-year-old detective leaned back and pulled off his heavy glasses pinching his nose with his fingers, and said, "Stall, you have no idea how close to the apocalypse we really are."

Stallings wanted to rush past this and simply said, "If I gave you a name, could you come up with everything you might have in your files about him?"

"Sure, what's his name?"

"I only have his street name, Gator."

Lonnie laughed out loud and said, "Do you have any idea how many Gators we have listed in reports and intelligence files? Between the goddamn Florida Gators, the swamp people who still love alligators, the rednecks who think it's a funny name, and the felons who don't ever want to use their real names, there must be a hundred and fifty Gators listed in different reports."

Stallings leaned in close and slipped him a sheet of paper that had the description the older couple had given him and said, "I don't care how many you find, I need to talk to one who looks like this."

Sparky Taylor had left his house at six in the morning and managed to miss the seemingly unending rush hour of Atlanta when he rolled in just before eleven. Most of the detectives would've spent the night in Atlanta, but they didn't have two boys like him. He missed every night he had spent away from them and didn't care if he had to work twenty hours just so he could play a quick game in the evening, then tuck them into bed. He'd never realized how rewarding fatherhood could be. It was his solemn duty to produce two intelligent, inquisitive boys who would contribute to society, just like his father had done.

Even though Sparky had gone to college in Atlanta, the sprawling city held no particular place in his heart. It was too impersonal and had the well-earned reputation of being a dangerous city. But it wasn't until this moment that he had ever thought Atlanta had anything but a good, professional police department. He didn't try to hide his deep disappointment in the detective who had written off the death of the Gainesville fraternity brother as an accident without doing the follow-up that Sparky felt was essential to all police work.

He looked at the table and said, "This was everything you have in evidence?"

The lanky detective who had been reluctantly helping him looked at the random clothing, singed pillowcase, and evidence receipt for two separate one-kilo bricks of marijuana and said, "The theory is he was just a stoner who dozed off in bed smoking a doobie."

"It looks like there was more than one point of ignition. How could a guy who just dozed off start a fire in two different places in this apartment?"

"That gave us some problems too. But in the end he was just a kid from Florida who probably shouldn't have been dealing pot in Atlanta."

Sparky browsed through the photographs of the damaged apartment.

The obviously embarrassed Atlanta detective said,

"They've tried to fix up the apartment, but there may be a few of the kid's things left over there."

"Can we go over and take a look?"

"*We* are slammed with two fresh homicides but *you* can go over and look all you want."

Lynn noticed Leon walking toward her near the main office of Thomas Brothers Supply. He gave her a smile and a wink and said, "Something tells me you're gonna be free Saturday night." He kept walking.

She was intrigued by the older man's contention that something might happen to Dale. Frankly, she didn't care what happened to him. She didn't know if her conscience had broken down since she had started on her mission or if the big loading dock manager had just pushed her to the breaking point. As long as Leon handled the issue for her, she could concentrate on other things.

She paused near her office and watched Leon continue to walk out into the lot. Dale whizzed past him in his golf cart. Leon turned and shot the big man a bird behind his back.

Lynn had a feeling Leon wasn't acting solely on her behalf.

The apartment manager hadn't even checked Sparky's badge, just assumed he was an Atlanta cop. He tossed him the keys to apartment 315 and told him to knock himself out because they had not been able to clean it up properly in the nineteen months since the fire had occurred.

Sparky wondered what he meant by that. Until he walked into the apartment with new drywall and was still struck by the horrible, burnt stench. The apartment itself had been cleaned out except for some boxes and trash in the bedroom where the fire had occurred. There were no black smoke marks on the wall or ceiling, but it was clear to him this was the room where it had happened.

One of the boxes contained old clothing and textbooks on physics. There was absolutely nothing of value. Two other boxes had evidence of burn marks on them and contained old shoes and a singed leather coat.

Behind all of these boxes was a much smaller box, which had burned at the top and on one side. It looked like it could have been one of the origins of the flames. He remembered from the crime scene photographs very similar boxes like this on the floor near the bed. The fire had not been a raging inferno, more of a smoldering smoke event with a few open flames.

Sparky was about to leave the apartment when he kneeled down to inspect the small box more closely. The inside was filled with twisted-up newspaper. Exactly the way he would twist newspaper to start a fire more efficiently. He shook his head at the Atlanta cops' attitude toward the deadly fire and reached into the box to pick up one of the twisted newspaper pages.

He opened up the newspaper and realized this was a link Tony Mazzetti might not want to hear about. The newspaper filling the box was the *Jacksonville Times-Union*.

THIRTY-ONE

John Stallings walked into the office at eight o'clock sharp. He didn't feel fresh and ready to attack the day like he often did because he'd spent so much time running down leads on Jeanie, Zach Halston, and now some guy named "Gator." For all his effort he could not say he was closer to finding any of them.

The squad bay was empty, but the lights were on and he could see someone in the conference room. When he poked his head in, Patty Levine and Sparky Taylor had three different easels with large charts and the long table was completely filled with reports and bits of information.

Stallings just stared at the two detectives speaking in short, cryptic sentences that caused one or the other to jump up and write something on one of the charts. Finally Patty looked up.

"Hey, John. What's going on?"

"It really looks like I should be asking you the same question. What time did you get started on this?"

"Sparky came into the office around six-thirty last night and we shared the information we'd found. It made me call the Gainesville fraternity house we visited and get some more information. I also swung by the local Tau Upsilon house night before last and talked to Bobby Hollis again. This is everything we have so far." She waved her hand across the three large handwritten charts.

Stallings shook his head and said, "I'm out of the loop for a day and a half and you guys look like you solved the case."

Now Sparky turned and looked at Stallings. "Hardly solved. But now we have enough information to at least ask the right questions and look in the right direction."

"Are you allowed to fill me in on what you found out?"

Patty said, "We've made a link to a fraternity brother who died in Atlanta, Paul Smiley. The one from Gainesville. Now we're looking at everyone the fraternity brothers told us about and making a time line."

"What does a time line do for us?"

Patty turned one of the easels toward Stallings and said, "The only event that all of the dead brothers had in common was a Halloween party held at the local fraternity house two years ago. Whatever other information we have, Sparky and I believe that this particular party plays a major role in the investigation."

"You think that someone got pissed off at the party, is that what you're saying?"

"Big-time."

Sparky was quick to add, "We still have a lot of work to do."

* * *

Lynn had been working diligently, itemizing the expenses related to the Thomas Brothers supply company's fleet, which included twenty-six tractor-trailers, forty large step vans, forty-four cargo vans, and eleven vehicles listed as general use. Lynn always smiled at the way the oldest Thomas brother listed his Mercedes 450 SL as part of the fleet. As much money as the family had, they still wanted to beat the federal government out of a few bucks in taxes whenever they could.

She looked up from her computer out the window that faced the parking lot. In the far corner of her view she could just see a marked police car pull up to the loading dock. Curiosity got the best of her and she wandered from her office toward the main loading dock.

Before Lynn had even left the hallway she could hear shouting, then saw two men arguing with Dale on the very edge of the wide dock. The two men, dressed in jeans and casual shirts, were by no means small, but compared to Dale they looked like little kids. A tall, thin uniformed police officer stood behind the other two men.

The crowd of loading dock workers and drivers had backed away to the rear wall so Lynn eased up next to the first driver she knew by name and said, "What's going on?"

The older man shrugged and said, "Two fellas there are from the DEA and tried to handle things quietly with Dale. You know how stubborn he can be."

"Handle what things?" Then Lynn heard Dale yell,

"I told you dipshits that if you don't gotta warrant, I ain't sayin' shit. I know my goddamn rights." That's when things took an ugly turn. Dale emphasized his point by shoving one of the smaller men in the chest. The man moved back a step, but that step was a long one because he slipped off the edge of the dock.

That's when the uniformed cop and the other man took action.

It was always easier for John Stallings to find Peep Moran earlier in the morning before he really got moving around the city. For all of his faults, no one could say Peep was lazy. If he wasn't sidetracked by his odd fetish or slowed by use of narcotics, the quirky young man from Detroit would've probably have been a tremendous success in the business world.

He was sitting out in the open on a park bench just north of the main downtown area. He showed no interest in fleeing for a change so Stallings took the bench next to him to find out what his informant had learned.

Peep didn't even waste time with small talk. "No one knows the girl. I been all over Arlington and a couple of the areas I know up north and not one person had ever seen the girl before."

"What about the boy, Zach Halston?"

"That little prick has been all over the city. A couple of the tougher dealers scared him until he focused on the college crowd. Someone told me he got into a beef there too. Another dealer was undercutting him to the college students, which caused a confrontation."

"Can you be more specific?"

Peep shook his head. "I'm not even sure where I heard it. Just gossip on the street. You know how it goes."

Stallings did know how word got out on the street. The shocking thing was how accurate it was most time. No one could ever cite one source, but everyone knew what was going on.

Stallings patted Peep's shoulder. "That's good, Peep. Got anything else for me?"

"The last anyone saw of Zach was he collected a little money someone owed him about four days ago."

Now Stallings gripped the smaller man's shoulder. "Four days ago? So he's still alive?" Then Stallings asked, "Where was he?"

"South of the river, closer to the university."

"Did you hear if anyone was after him or if he was in danger?"

"I haven't heard about anyone being pissed off at him. You know how paranoid pot dealers can be." Peep gave him a half smile showing Stall that his years on the street hadn't robbed him of his sense of humor.

But Stallings hardly noticed him because right now all he could focus on was Zach Halston.

Lynn was amazed how quickly the two cops subdued a man so much larger than them. While one stepped away and pulled a can of pepper spray, the other one threw two quick punches into Dale's massive gut and stepped to the side and kicked him in his upper leg. Dale listed to one side like he was going to fall over just as the tall, uniformed police officer let a stream of orange liquid loose in Dale's face. At first there was no reaction as Dale went down on his injured leg. He gripped his thigh where he'd been kicked and started to yell at the man who had kicked him. Then it seemed like the pepper spray completely occupied his mind as he grabbed his face and started to babble incoherently.

The man Dale had shoved off the edge of the dock was climbing up the stairs, apparently uninjured but eager to get a shot in on the big man who had pushed him down. They rolled Dale on his side like a beached whale until they were able to handcuff his massive hands behind his back.

Lynn heard a voice in her left ear say, "Now you don't have to worry about your date." She snapped her head to see Leon standing right next to her.

Lynn said, "I don't understand."

"One call, a few grams of crack, and a bad attitude will manage to keep him occupied for the next couple of years. Best of all, old man Thomas will can his ass before lunch."

"But how?"

"There's nothing a narcotics agent likes more than a reformed smuggler. Half the numbers in my cell phone are for DEA agents and local narcs looking to make a case. This was so easy I'm embarrassed."

Lynn tried not to smile as the three police officers led Dale away while he was still complaining about his face burning. No one on the dock looked too upset to see the big man leave.

Now Lynn could focus on her real issues.

It'd only taken Patty Levine a few hours to track down three different coeds who had attended a Halloween party two years earlier at the Tau Upsilon fraternity house. She worked alone because she wanted the girls to open up to her and having Sparky Taylor with her would've been just as bad as bringing along John Stallings even if he hadn't been taken off the case.

Sitting in a small sandwich shop on University Boulevard near the University of North Florida, Patty looked across the table at the young lady whose name she had gotten from one of the fraternity brothers in town. The young man had provided a list of as many of the attendees to the Halloween party as he could remember. Not counting the fraternity members, the list had more than seventy names.

Patty had already established that this girl had had a very similar experience to the first two girls she had spoken to.

The girl said, "That fraternity is nothing but a bunch of assholes."

"What makes you say that?"

"I woke up in the bushes after that party. There are girls that found themselves in other *cities* after that party. We have to have a designated sober girl if we ever go to a Tau Upsilon party. That's why they're assholes."

"You think someone slipped you a roofie that night?"

"Who knows? I take responsibility for drinking too much, but the frat boys have so much alcohol on hand. The whole fraternity is known for its wild parties and disappearing the next day."

Patty looked at the pretty blond-haired girl and said, "Are they known for anything else?"

"Just one thing."

"What's that?"

"Pot."

THIRTY-TWO

As much as he hated to admit it, Tony Mazzetti knew he was looking at a string of killings. After talking with Patty Levine and Sparky Taylor and seeing the mounting evidence, he and Sergeant Zuni had concluded that the chances were remote that all of the deaths of the fraternity members were accidents. He wasn't absolutely convinced they were all connected. Someone who used drugs on one victim wouldn't be likely to use a gun at close range on another. Just as it seemed unlikely the same person would burn someone alive. There was no pattern. Mazzetti knew that killers loved patterns and hated change.

Now he was over at the medical examiner's office searching previous deaths ruled accidental or otherwise to see if there were others that could be thrown into the mix. They were starting at October from two years earlier to be on the safe side. Mazzetti and Lisa Kurtz sat at a table in the administration building of the medical examiner's office and carefully looked at each file of any male under the age of thirty who had died in the last two years in Duval County.

The whole squad came up with a number of variables like male victims, within the last two years, between the ages of eighteen and thirty, with any association to the college. These included the numerous deaths that were attributed to drug overdoses, and even suspicious car accidents.

Lisa sat next to him and had been nothing but professional the past two hours. He had wondered if it would be awkward working so closely with the young woman he knew was a freak in the bedroom. So far it was not. He was careful not to call her his girlfriend, especially out loud, because he still wasn't sure how he felt.

Lisa slid an open file across the table to Mazzetti and said, "Here's another one."

Mazzetti looked at the photos of the young man laid out on the procedure table of the medical examiner's office and saw the listed cause of death as "a hunting accident." He placed the file with the other three files they had already pulled for closer examination.

On the very next file, Lisa said, "Here's another one. An alcohol poisoning case two days after the party."

She slid the file to Mazzetti, who looked down and noticed the victim's name was Josh Hickam. The file went on the stack with the others.

Lynn sat at the end of the long table in the lunchroom of the Thomas Brothers supply company. She had takeout from Wendy's, but had just picked at her spicy chicken sandwich and allowed all of her French fries to go cold.

Materializing from the side door, Leon slid onto the seat across from her. He had not spoken directly to her about Dale's arrest since the big man had been carted off, but now he gave her a sly smile and a wink. It made her realize he was younger than she'd originally thought. That weathered skin, the outdoorsy look so many boaters in North Florida developed, made him appear to be fifty when she now thought he was probably not forty.

After a few moments of silence, without any preface or reason, Leon said, "I did all my time in federal prison."

Lynn wondered where this was going and simply said, "Uh-huh."

"State time is tough. No rehab, nothing but lock-up and bullshit. But the federal holding center in Atlanta and my last two years at Eglin gave me a chance to take classes and learn from some of the big-time fraud guys. So now I can read people really well."

"So what?"

"So I can tell you have a secret. A big one."

"That's ridiculous."

Leon looked both ways to ensure no one was nearby. "Coming from someone else I might believe you, but knowing your family I'm pretty sure I'm right."

Lynn was silent.

Leon said, "And I can help."

"Help with what?"

"Whatever you're doing."

Lynn just held eye contact but didn't say anything.

"Look, I need to do something or I'm gonna go crazy. This lack of excitement is killing me."

Without meaning to, Lynn said, "I don't know."

Leon smiled and said, "Trust me. Besides, I never let things go. Now you're stuck with me."

Sergeant Yvonne Zuni felt a hint of claustrophobia with all the blinds drawn and the door closed to her office in the Land That Time Forgot.

Sergeant Zuni had briefed Lieutenant Hester on all the information they had concerning the death of the fraternity brothers. But as she looked across her desk at Lieutenant Hester, crammed into a simple wooden chair, Sergeant Zuni had a sickening feeling in the base of her stomach that the lieutenant was looking at political issues as much as investigative issues.

The lieutenant said, "You understand that the city has worked very hard to attract young people to the universities and events like our growing spring break."

"I'm not sure I see why that's relevant to this investigation."

"Let's just assume that all the information you have is accurate. Let's assume that these deaths were intentional. And that's a big assumption. One death occurred in Atlanta and another in Daytona."

"The victim in Daytona isn't dead. He is in a coma."

"Regardless, the killer, if there really is one, could just as easily live in Atlanta or Daytona or anywhere in between. I'm not sure there's a reason to bring media scrutiny just on Jacksonville. I'd like to see your detectives work on this as quietly as possible."

Before Sergeant Zuni could express her true feelings, which was what she was about to do, there was a rap on her office door.

The sergeant called out, "Come in."

The door swung open and John Stallings stood in the doorway, surprised to see the lieutenant sitting inside the small office.

The lieutenant glared at him and said, "C'mon, Stall, spit it out."

"I, um, I just needed to speak to the sergeant for a moment."

The lieutenant said, "Go ahead, speak to her."

The sergeant looked between the two former partners and saw neither was going to give ground in this standoff.

Stallings nodded and said, "I have some news."

It was the lieutenant said, "On what?"

The way Stallings glanced at the sergeant told her the news was about Zach Halston. He was weighing the dangers of revealing his continued investigation after the lieutenant had taken him off the case.

Sergeant Zuni said, "I let John work on the missing fraternity brother because he's the best there is at finding people. I take full responsibility for putting him on the assignment." She held the lieutenant's stare, not wanting to back down. This was one of the most important jobs a sergeant had.

Lieutenant Hester was silent for a moment as her eyes shifted back to Stallings.

He said, "One of my snitches says Zach was alive just a few days ago."

Sergeant Zuni said, "What else did he say?"

"Zach had been in a business hassle with a couple of other pot dealers. One of them was someone dealing to the college crowd."

"You think that's why he's laying low?"

"It's a reasonable assumption."

The lieutenant's poker face made Sergeant Zuni uneasy. The lieutenant didn't mind sitting in silence either. That made everyone uncomfortable.

Finally Stallings said, "C'mon, Rita, put me back on this thing. I'll find Zach Halston and maybe he can shed some light on all this other bullshit."

Now Sergeant Zuni understood just how close Stallings and Lieutenant Hester were. She had never heard anyone talk to the lieutenant like that before. Sergeant Zuni also recognized the lieutenant hadn't gotten to where she was by sitting back. She got results and knew who could get results for her.

After almost thirty seconds, the lieutenant said in a very even voice, "Will you give me your word you won't look for Jeanie while you're on this case?"

Now it was Stallings's turn to hesitate. He said, "No, I can't do that."

Sergeant Zuni said, "John."

He just shrugged and mumbled, "Sorry, I'm not a liar."

Then the lieutenant said, "Fuck." She shook her head, then stood to face Stallings. "I'll have to take my chances with you. There's too much potential for all of this to blow up in our faces if we don't get a handle on it now."

A slight smile broke across Stallings's face.

The lieutenant said, "Don't count on me changing

my mind too many times. I know what the girl means to you. It broke my heart too when she disappeared. But I've already given the photograph to other detectives and I expect you to pass on anything you find out about her to them."

Stallings just nodded.

Patty Levine sat on a bench in a large common area of the University of North Florida. The campus was one of the nicest in the South and the school had a reputation for looking after its students. On the bench next to her was a junior majoring in business administration and a former girlfriend of Zach Halston's. Patty had found the girl through other students who had been at the Halloween party two years before. That's how most police investigations evolved; one interview led to more and more.

The pretty young woman had a wistful smile when she recalled meeting Zach at the party. "He was down because some girl had just dumped him. You know how it is, a guy who needs fixing is hard to resist."

Patty didn't quite share those sentiments, but she nodded anyway to keep the girl talking.

"Anyway, he was busy during the party keeping everyone happy and the beer flowing. I mean it got wild. Then we started talking and he seemed really sweet."

"Did you see anything unusual? Was anyone getting out of hand or girls upset?"

"Not anything more than usual at a Tau Upsilon party. Zach was also pissed off at one of his brothers, but I don't know why. A couple of them kept telling him to let it go and relax."

Patty kept scribbling notes and asked about potential female partygoers who felt violated after the party. But the girl didn't know anything. Then Patty asked, "Did you know which brother he was mad at?"

"No, but Zach said he was going to have to 'go gangsta' on him. You know how men act tough, but it never works out. I figured it was all talk."

Patty said, "Is there any chance you can recall the name of the girl who had just dumped Zach?"

She thought about it for a few seconds, then said, "I think it was Kelly."

THIRTY-THREE

John Stallings was surprised he felt so nervous, fidgeting by the front door of his former residence, but that was the nature of his relationship with his estranged wife. He hadn't called to give her notice he was coming over and he knew both of the kids were out. Lauren had gone to the movies with two friends, and Charlie was at a birthday party for one of his soccer teammates. Stallings figured he had at least two hours of quiet with Maria. Something told him now was a good time to sit down and work out the problems in the relationship. He still wasn't going to tell her about the photograph of Jeanie, even if it would make her look at him in a different light. It just wasn't right to play with her emotions like that.

He knocked on the door instead of ringing the bell and for some reason felt hopeful. He thought she might view this as a romantic gesture as he looked down at the bouquet of assorted flowers he had bought at Publix for $13.99. For a moment he thought he heard voices; then he clearly heard footsteps on the hard wooden floor of the downstairs.

The knob turned and the door opened inward. He plastered on the best smile he could muster and held up the flowers, but before he could say, "Surprise," he felt shock ripple through his system. He stood there silently, staring at the man who cheerfully said, "Hello there, come on in."

Stallings dropped the flowers to the porch but kept his eyes on Brother Frank Ellis.

Patty Levine liked the upscale restaurant where Ken had taken her to sample Spanish delicacies in the form of tapas. The outdoor balcony looking down on a walkway bordering the St. Johns River only added to the romantic atmosphere. But there was something bothering Patty about her new boyfriend. She couldn't put her finger on it, but looking across at him now didn't fill her with the same sort of excitement she felt when she looked across at Tony Mazzetti when they had been dating. Ken was handsome and refined and everything else a girl would want in a boyfriend. That only added to her feelings of frustration.

She'd already learned to tune him out when he started to blab about upgrading from his BMW to a Mercedes or the expensive speakers he had added to his home entertainment system. Somewhere in the back of her head she heard her name called three times and snapped back to reality.

Ken said, "I lost you there for a minute."

"I'm sorry. Guess I'm just a little distracted."

Ken was about to continue when he looked toward the river and said, "You know that cop down there?"

Patty glanced over the railing to see a young uniformed officer talking to two drunken men. Both were dressed like construction workers and both were larger than the cop. Patty waited until the patrolman turned and she could see him in profile. He had a round face with a wide flat nose, and she had never seen him before.

She looked at Ken and shook her head, saying, "He doesn't look familiar. We have so many patrolman and detectives that I don't always recognize them, especially down here in the southern part of the county."

Ken made an odd face and said, "I just assumed every cop working for the same department would know each other."

"It's a big agency."

Patty glanced back over the railing and saw that the cop was now only speaking to one of the men. The other had walked away. But the body language told Patty that the encounter was escalating from a simple discussion to something more serious. The cop wrapped his hand around the larger man's upper arm in an attempt to guide him away from the water. The man jerked his arm away from the cop and took a step back. Without hesitation the cop did a classic fake with one hand, then drove his knee into the man's opposite leg. Patty had used the move a dozen times herself. The man dropped to his knees and the cop had him cuffed with no more scuffle.

Ken scooted back his chair and said, "Did you see that? That cop just kicked that guy for no reason."

Patty was surprised by her boyfriend's outrage. Had he not seen the same thing? Patty said, "I thought he handled it very well. The guy jerked his arm away from him when the cop tried to direct him where to go. The poor patrolman can't wait for this guy to punch him in the face and run away. He was obviously trying to make an arrest."

"It looked to me like he wanted to kick that guy."

"What would you have the cop do, Ken? You can't just let people decide when they're going to be arrested."

"You don't have to act like a Nazi either."

"Nazi! Now you're just talking from ignorance."

"How can you say I'm ignorant? I'm a doctor, for Christ's sake."

"No, you're not. You're a podiatrist."

Lynn sat at the bar of the Wildside. For most of the year it was a large but tired sports bar, but during spring break you couldn't get into the giant bar that had big-screen TVs tacked all across the walls. The owner had gotten smart in the last few years and closed off half of the bar when things got slow. It saved on electricity and the place didn't look empty all the time. She'd been carefully watching a table where five members of the Tau Upsilon fraternity were sharing two pitchers of beer and watching a Miami Heat and Orlando Magic basketball game. She was having a hard time putting a name to a face and wanted to make sure she made no mistake.

That made her think about her uncomfortable and painful conversation with one of the fraternity members about two years ago. She had run into the young man by accident and he'd already been drinking, but once she'd sat down and really listened to what he had to say, it had changed her profoundly. He'd explained in great detail the horrific event and who had been involved and how it had gotten out of control.

The entire conversation had left her considering the options still available. Should she go to the police? The young man had said no one would talk, including him. Should she tell her parents? They would be devastated and there was nothing they could do about it. The problem ate at her for days until she saw a news story about a University of North Florida student who had committed suicide on campus by hanging himself in a communal bathroom. The young man who had committed suicide was the same young man who had explained to her the details and secrets that were tearing the fraternity apart.

As she watched fellow students come on camera and claim surprise while reciting an almost scripted version of what a great kid he was, Lynn realized something odd. She felt a hint of happiness. Maybe relief was a better word. Whatever the case, the young man's death had eased her misery. And ultimately set her on the path she now followed.

Tonight she found herself sitting in a bar she didn't like, watching young men she didn't want to watch and trying to figure out which one was Bobby Hollis. She also looked around the room, noticing some surveillance cameras in the corners of the ceiling. This would not be a good place to meet her next victim. Too easy to identify her. She'd seen a news story earlier in the year about a bartender here at the Wildside who had killed a couple of spring breakers after meeting them here in the bar. It was creepy to think she could buy a drink from a bartender who had much more in mind. Then she considered her own situation and mission and wondered how different she was from the sinister bartender.

She felt a tap on her shoulder and heard a man's voice say, "Fancy meeting you here."

Lynn turned quickly at the bar and was shocked to see Leon smiling as he sat on the stool next to her.

Stallings had Brother Ellis by the collar of his nice, button-down shirt. He purposely held the shirt tightly in both hands to keep himself occupied. Stallings was afraid if he released the man's collar, one of his fists would make contact with the pastor's face. He had no control. More than one suspect had been knocked unconscious without Stallings's knowledge of his own actions. A dark and ugly rage boiled up inside him. Something he hadn't felt since the days following Jeanie's disappearance. The basis of many of his anger issues. Right now he couldn't think of any coping mechanisms the counseling psychologist had given him after he and the family had visited to help them understand what had happened to Jeanie. He remembered one of the things he was supposed to do was count, but he couldn't remember if it was to count forward or backwards. All he saw was red and the terrified face of the most popular pastor in Jacksonville.

Brother Ellis stammered, "John, I think there's been a misunderstanding." He was breathing so hard it was difficult to understand him.

Stallings said, "You're right. You misunderstood how much bullshit I would put up with. I should've done this after your cheap shot at the fellowship hall putting my partner between Maria and me."

"What?"

Stallings wasn't interested in a debate. It was time to feel bone and teeth disintegrate behind the force of his knuckles. He gave the pastor a slight shove as he released his grip, but it was only to put him at the optimal range for a devastating right cross.

Brother Ellis took two hard steps back and didn't even raise his hands. He looked relieved that he had been released and had no idea what was about to follow.

Lynn didn't mean to sound quite so annoyed when she barked at Leon, "What're you doing here? Are you following me?"

The lean, older man nodded his head and said, "A little bit."

"Why?"

"I already told you that I could help you with whatever you're doing."

"You don't even know what I'm doing."

"I don't care. I just miss the excitement. I miss having something important to do. I don't mind washing a few cars at Thomas Brothers and I don't want to go back to prison, but if I don't do something a little different once in a while I'll go crazy." He placed his hand on Lynn's arm and said, "Please let me help you if for no other reason than to show respect for your father."

Lynn thought about his offer for a moment. "There is something I could use some help on."

"Anything. Anything at all."

"Could you find someone for me?"

"Easy. Especially if he was in the business. What's his name?"

"Zach Halston."

THIRTY-FOUR

Stallings lined up his punch like a professional billiards player lined up a championship shot. But a split second before he balled his fist and threw the punch a woman with curly blond hair wandered in from the living room and said, "Who's at the door, dear?"

Stallings used the distraction to take in the scene. He gave no indication of what his next action might be.

Brother Ellis composed himself quickly, turning to the woman and saying, "This is Maria's husband, John." He gave Stallings a look that said, *Be cool.* "John, this is my wife, Denise. We were just visiting with Maria. She ran upstairs to grab a photo album and will be down in a minute. I'm sure she'd love to have you join us."

Stallings managed a weak smile as he nodded to the pretty blond lady and stepped into the house on unsteady legs. The whole situation freaked him out a little bit.

* * *

Tony Mazzetti lingered in his car as Sparky stepped out of the Crown Vic, waiting for his partner to join him. Mazzetti hated talking to families of dead people. Whether it was an auto accident or a homicide, talking to a family after a case was closed either raised hopes or suspicions. Every parent saw conspiracy in the dead child. No one wanted to admit to the fact that random chance played a vital role in everyone's lives. No one ever wanted to admit the death could be the victim's fault. They wanted answers and scapegoats. They wanted a reason to not feel so desolate. Mazzetti didn't want to do that to someone who'd already grieved over the loss of a loved one and now he had nine files waiting for him to do just that. Nine families whose old wounds would be reopened just by talking to the police.

Add to that the fact that his old partner, Christina Hogrebe, was still teaching at the police academy and he felt real despair. Christina or "Hoagie," as she liked to be called, could talk to anyone about anything and make them feel good. It wasn't just the fact that she was an intelligent, beautiful girl; it was some unquantifiable quality she had that allowed her to deal with people in an easy manner. Patty Levine had a similar quality. The only person in the detective bureau with less ability to speak to someone easily than himself was his new partner, Sparky Taylor. For all his brains and sharp insight, Sparky talked to people like a robot and appeared to have no ability to feel any empathy. That didn't mean he wasn't compassionate. He cared about how people felt; he just had no ability to understand emotions. Now Mazzetti had to interview a family who lost a son two years ago. What a way to start the holiday season.

Mazzetti knocked on the front door of the nice suburban house. He noticed the Star of David over the door. Mazzetti identified himself with his open credentials as soon as the nice-looking, middle-aged woman opened the door. Without hearing anything but his name, just seeing the JSO credentials, the woman started to cry uncontrollably.

Once inside the house and sitting on a couch, the woman composed herself. When she'd stopped crying and only sniffled, she managed to say, "Have you found something new about Robert's death?"

"No, ma'am. We just had a few questions about him. It's sort of a follow-up study were doing on deaths in the county over the past two years. Do you feel up to answering a few questions?"

"If you're asking me why he would hang himself at the dorm shower room, I still have no idea."

Having an entire sleepless night to reconsider how he felt about Brother Frank Ellis had led John Stallings to the conclusion that he needed to listen to people more. He had spent more than an hour looking at old photographs of the family with Ellis and his wife, Denise, and the pastor had never once hinted that Stallings had roughed him up or treated him badly in any way. The fact that the man was visiting Maria with his wife also indicated that perhaps Stallings was wrong about him being interested in Maria. If he was wrong about Brother Ellis, what the hell else could he be wrong about?

Counter to stereotype, many cops liked to focus on the best in people. Stallings had to look for the best or risk drowning in despair at how people could act. The vast majority of people did what was right because it was right, not because of the law or the work cops did to enforce the law. If people started doing whatever they wanted, there weren't enough cops in the world to set society back on the right track. It now annoyed Stallings that the one guy he thought was an asshole turned out to be a decent guy. Shit.

Stallings's cell phone pulled him out of his deep thought. As soon as he flipped it up and noticed a number from Volusia County he immediately recognized the voice.

The woman said, "This is J. L. Winter. Remember me?"

"How could I forget?"

"It would be hard, wouldn't it?"

Stallings could feel her confidence even over the cheap Nextel phone.

J.L. said, "Can we meet? I have information on Zach Halston."

Patty listened carefully as Tony Mazzetti systematically explained everything he and Sparky had learned about the suicide at the University of North Florida two years earlier. The victim had been a member of the fraternity and attended many of their parties. The boy's mother noticed a change in him before Thanksgiving two years ago. He had seen a doctor for depression several years before that. He was probably a true suicide.

Patty asked why he had not had a tattoo.

Mazzetti had thought of that too and had asked the grieving mother. Tau Epsilon never forced anyone to get the goofy logo on their ankle, and the boy was a practicing Jew. He'd skipped the tattoo for religious reasons.

Mazzetti said he then raced over to the medical examiner's office to go through the file with Lisa Kurtz. There was nothing at all to indicate this was anything other than a suicide. Mazzetti had even gone as far as contacting the retired detective who had worked the case. The detective had found three of the victim's friends who had said he was deeply troubled by something. They said it was something that had happened shortly before his death. That put the time frame right around the Halloween party.

The story sounded like classic Tony Mazzetti, emphasizing how hard he worked and how quickly he jumped on leads, but mainly how the death could not possibly be a homicide. However, in this case, Lisa Kurtz agreed with him. Patty was surprised how much she liked Tony's new squeeze. But the less interested she became in her own boyfriend, the more jealous she was of the pretty young assistant medical examiner. Despite her personal feelings, she couldn't deny that Lisa was sharp and dedicated. She represented women well in law enforcement. That meant a lot to Patty.

But now in the conference room, seeing Sergeant Zuni and Sparky staring at Mazzetti, it was clear they had a problem. Mazzetti wanted the problem to be a rash of accidents and suicides, but Patty knew it to be something else. She said, "There is no way these are all coincidence. I don't care if they happened over the course of two years or ten years, the common thread of the fraternity links these deaths together. These have got to be homicides."

Mazzetti shook his head. "Too many variables. A gunshot, all kinds of different drugs, even ketamine. I mean, Jesus, where do you even find that shit?"

Sparky said, "Usually at a veterinarian. But the rampant spread of the drug used recreationally has provided a number of sources."

Mazzetti looked at his partner and said, "What're you, a commentator on a documentary?"

Patty had to smile at the give-and-take between the two partners but noticed that Lisa Kurtz, sitting at the end of the table quietly, was the one who came up with the comment that shut Tony Mazzetti down.

Lisa said, "What if the killer did it specifically so they wouldn't be caught? Change up the mode of death so radically and use so many different jurisdictions that the cops would never catch on? Made it seem like a woman, when it was really a man, or something like that."

The comment earned a frown from Mazzetti, but Patty wanted to cheer the young medical examiner who'd put it all together.

This was the start of something big.

THIRTY-FIVE

John Stallings sat in a booth at a Denny's in the south end of Duval County. He wanted to stay in his official jurisdiction just in case there was a problem. He couldn't fully trust a pot grower, even one as attractive as J. L. Winter. From the window he could see the traffic coming down J. Turner Butler Boulevard. He wasn't sure what kind of vehicle to look for but wasn't surprised when he saw the beautiful woman pulled into the lot driving a Cadillac CTX. Nice, but not too flashy.

He stood when she entered the restaurant and approached him. He held out his hand to forestall any chance of a hug.

J.L. said, "What a gentleman."

When they settled into the thick padded benches, J.L gazed out the window and said, "I try not to come into civilization too often. But it gets so boring on the farm and I have so few visitors, I have to keep occupied."

"My guess is you could have all of the visitors you wanted."

"Given the nature of my occupation, I try to limit

the number of people who actually come onto the premises." She gave him a sly smile. "But you have an open invitation."

"Why do you live in such isolation? There is so much you could be doing."

"If business stays like it is, I can retire in a couple of years and never worry about money again."

Stallings had heard that same line from every prostitute, drug dealer, and thief in Jacksonville. "What do you do when you have enough money?"

J.L. shook her head, causing her black hair to fan out behind her. "I don't know. Maybe public service so God won't judge me too harshly. I thought about teaching. I have my bachelor's in elementary education from USF."

Stallings said, "I was at the University of South Florida on a baseball scholarship."

"When did you graduate?"

"Never did."

"How do you go from baseball to a police officer?"

"Maybe I want God to take it easy on me too."

Lynn couldn't believe how quickly Leon had found information on Zach Halston. She'd already written down where he had been seen down in St. Augustine. Now she looked back up at Leon sitting across from her at her desk.

"How'd you get this?"

"One phone call. You just have to know the right people to call."

"I appreciate this, Leon. But I think you've done everything you could do for me."

The hard-looking man shook his head. "No, there's a lot more I could do. This was too easy. Now that I've done this, we're joined together."

"But I don't need any help."

"Everyone needs help and this makes me feel good. You don't want me to feel bad about myself, do you?" His tone changed.

Lynn could see how effective this man could be in almost any cutthroat industry. But now he was her problem and she had to figure out a way to deal with him.

Stallings sipped his coffee and let J.L. talk about herself for a few minutes before he focused her on what he really wanted to know.

"You said you had some information on Zach Halston."

"You're not going to arrest him, are you?"

"I don't arrest minor pot dealers. Almost no one does. He's a missing person, his parents are worried, and I have a few questions for him. That's it."

"That's what I thought. And I believe you; otherwise I wouldn't be saying anything. The last thing you want to happen in this business is be labeled a snitch."

Stallings just gave her a scowl, hoping to prod her into divulging the information.

J.L. said, "I heard some talk. A few people are not happy with Zach. He's unreliable and owes some money, but it's nothing too serious. The pot-dealing community is not known for its violence. He's just laying low down in St. Augustine."

"Can you be more specific? The tourists alone could keep me from searching all of St. Augustine for one missing college kid."

J.L. let loose with a dazzling smile. "He hangs out at a bar off King Street named the Ponce de Leon Pub. It's supposed to be a small, dingy place with good food and a couple of decent TVs. My source thinks he's staying at a motel close by. He eats lunch at the pub every day."

Stallings wrote the name of the pub in his notepad as he gazed out the window and considered his next move. He knew he'd have to go down to St. Augustine alone. He couldn't have anyone around when he found Zach because his first question was going to be about the photograph of Jeanie.

J.L. cleared her throat to get his attention and when he looked back she said, "I'm not used to men forgetting I'm close by."

"I bet you're not." He laid a twenty on the table and said, "You're probably not used to men leaving you in a restaurant either, but I'm afraid I have to go. I really appreciate the information you gave me."

J. L. Winter lifted her left eyebrow and said, "Oh yeah? How much do you appreciate it?"

Stallings looked at her and said, "Enough to hope you become a teacher really soon."

THIRTY-SIX

Patty Levine had to admit she enjoyed being alone with Tony Mazzetti even if it was in the conference room of the D-bureau. Everyone had left the informal meeting and gone about their day, but she enjoyed the few moments with her ex-boyfriend, purposely scooting her chair closer to his so he'd get a hint of her perfume. She was feeling good about herself because she had gone a day and a night without any prescription drugs. It seemed like that was becoming a more common occurrence. The problem was she felt loopy from the lack of sleep.

Patty said, "The key to this thing is in the victims."

"Still officially accidents."

"Whatever. You know as well as I do how much work we have to prove it either way. I don't care about the political considerations command staff has about labeling Jacksonville the home of another serial killer. We've got to figure this out."

Mazzetti reluctantly nodded his head. "I hate talking to the families. Sparky and I will work on the leads we've developed and talk to the frat boys if you and Stallings talk to some of the families of the deceased."

"John is down in the south end of the county for something today, but I'll start on it by myself. I should have all of it done by tomorrow afternoon and we can see where we are then."

Mazzetti smiled and said, "Thanks, Patty. You're the best."

For no reason Patty went with her urge and leaned across the short gap between them, placed her hand behind Tony's neck, and laid a deep, meaningful kiss on him.

John Stallings took advantage of meeting J. L. Winter in the south end of the county and wasted no time making the short drive down to St. Johns County, then east into St. Augustine.

He liked the historic little town that gave the relatively newly settled state of Florida a link to the past that rivaled New England's. St. Augustine was the oldest European settlement in the continental United States. Every public school student learned that it was settled in 1565 by a Spanish admiral named Menéndez. Most people liked the fairy tale of Ponce de Leon searching for the fountain of youth. The story and man were referenced all over the city.

Almost in the center of the city was Flagler College, which filled up an old Henry Flagler hotel and the area immediately around it. Stallings used to like the good, tiny Florida school until he learned Tony Mazzetti was a graduate.

Stallings had always enjoyed the historical Florida town. He'd brought the kids here on a number of occasions and still brought Lauren and Charlie whenever they had a chance. Charlie was fascinated by the Castillo de San Marcos. All of Stallings's memories now were categorized by whether they'd occurred before or after Jeanie disappeared. He could remember every event so clearly based on if she was there or if not. The last time they were in St. Augustine together she was about thirteen. She'd pretended to be too cool for the tourist attractions but enjoyed walking the walls of San Marcos just as much as the rest of them. Stallings had a photograph of Maria looking off a rampart with the wind blowing her dark hair behind her. He needed to frame that photo and put it on his desk.

Driving down King Street he saw the Ponce de Leon Pub on the right next to Ponce de Leon Pawn and Gun and across the street from the Ponce de Leon Quick Stop. It was not the heart of downtown and there was almost no traffic. His instincts told him to take a few minutes and drive through the area. That would get him familiar with the streets and also give luck a chance to play a part if Zach Halston was walking down a sidewalk.

There was nothing unusual on the quiet weekday. He noticed a blue Suburban with dark-tinted windows roll past him and turn a block west of the pub. He patted the photograph on the seat next to him and looked down at Jeanie's smiling face next to Zach. He felt like he was close to getting some answers.

*   *   *

Zach Halston considered himself mature for a twenty-one-year-old. He had managed a sophisticated business with the number of associates for more than two years. He'd managed two households for a year and a half. Zach had even stayed hidden in plain sight for almost three weeks. That's why it was hard to admit he missed his family. It was fun to talk tough and act like a gangsta on the street. It was even satisfying to tell his dad he didn't need any extra money and to skip the occasional holiday break to go on a cruise with his girlfriend of the moment, but it was no fun to sit in a small hotel room in a crappy town like St. Augustine with no one to talk to. He even missed his annoying little brother.

When he was his little brother's age, Zach thought he would be playing baseball professionally by this time in his life, not hiding like a mole in a cave. He wanted to shudder at some of the decisions he'd made over the past few years. Having the money was nice but not worth what he'd gone through. God, what he would do if he could go back in time.

He realized he was forgetting all the bullshit his father had made him go through at home. Right now he missed that nice, middle-class house in Ormond Beach and his mom making him French toast or pancakes every morning. When he was fourteen, he'd started to skip church on Sundays and told his dad he needed to make money instead of wasting his time. As he got older he learned to make more and more money and thought that it would buy happiness. Looking around the dingy hotel room, he knew how wrong he'd been.

He had to get out and get something to eat.

*   *   *

Lynn was careful not to tell Leon exactly what she was doing. Even though he wanted to come with her, she'd been resolute. Besides, the loss of Dale on the loading dock had thrown the Thomas Brothers supply company into unexpected chaos. The redneck bully had apparently been the linchpin that made the operation run smoothly. No one had heard anything from him since the day the cops pepper sprayed him and dragged him away in cuffs. Mr. Thomas announced that Dale would not be returning to work and Lynn had read a short news story that said he was charged with dealing in cocaine and had faced a federal magistrate who set his bond at a hundred thousand dollars. She almost felt sorry for the big lug.

Leon imagined she was involved in some crazy drug dealer or robbery scheme. Some scam that only a guy who had spent a few years in prison could think up. He had no idea how much weirder the truth was.

The truth had bothered Lynn over the past week, but she was too close to stop now. Something had to ease the pain she felt. Drugs hadn't done it. Neither had spending time with her family. She was sure this was the only way. She didn't need to involve Leon in any part of it.

Leon had been a godsend in other ways. He signed out the Suburban from the fleet manager for her and gassed it up. He didn't even ask where she was taking it. When she said she'd have the car back by midafternoon, Leon just nodded. Now she was getting used to driving the big SUV that felt like a semi tractor-trailer compared to her Nissan. She couldn't help but notice the tiny damage still in the grille where she'd hit Alan Cole. The hospital had been very careful not to release much information when she called. All they would say was that he was still in serious condition. One afternoon about a week ago she was able to speak to a nurse who let it slip that he was still in a coma. She'd always asked for the same nurse and spent a few minutes just chatting with her.

Lynn liked quiet St. Augustine, which always seemed so peaceful to her. She had even considered Flagler College for her undergraduate work, but it was just a little too close to home. Leon had found out that Zach was staying near King Street and frequented several stores and bars in the area. Right now she planned to just drive around and see if she could discover where he might hang out. There was a sports bar called the Ponce de Leon Pub that looked like a nice place to have lunch and maybe run into Zach. She had carried the Buck knife with her since she hadn't used it yet. The circumstances would have to be just right for her to risk that kind of attack.

Driving west on King Street, the only other car she noticed was a black Impala. Looking down through the tall Suburban, she clearly saw the driver. It took her a second, but she realized why he seemed familiar. She had seen him at Kyle Lee's house in Winter Park. She was on the right track. But it looked like the police were too.

She might need a new plan.

THIRTY-SEVEN

Zach Halston walked down the two flights of rickety stairs, pausing to glance out the cracked window of the double doors. It was overcast and puddles from an earlier shower dotted the road. This place wasn't much better than Jacksonville as far as a cheerful climate. An elderly man popped his head out of the apartment closest to the front door and stared silently at Zach. It was a little ritual the old man went through every time Zach left the building. He'd tried to be friendly and engage the old man in conversation, but he was always met with a disapproving glance and the door closing firmly after a quick inspection of who was coming or going from the building. Zach paid two hundred dollars a week to the super who lived in a detached building behind the apartment. The two hundred was in cash and Zach never had to give his name. He figured it was safer that way. He had no idea who might be looking for him, or if someone was watching the frat house, or tapping his parents' phone line and as a result he'd been lying low for almost three weeks. He intended to stay that way.

Zach had run low on cash a couple of times and gone out to make some quick collections from people he trusted. He had enough to last another month or so; then he might have to either get back into business or hope any trouble had been smoothed over. When he'd first decided to flee Jacksonville, he had considered taking an extended cruise, but the travel agency said they would all require him to use his real name. This was one of the few places he'd found where no one cared if he had a name or not.

Zach had no idea if the cops were involved yet or if any of the Tau Upsilon brothers had been arrested or squealed.

His usual routine involved grabbing a meal at one of three places he liked: Sonic because it was cheap; Mario's Italiano, when he was in the mood for pizza; and the Ponce de Leon Pub. After eating, he always walked over to the Castillo and soaked up a little more history. He loved walking the ramparts of the old fort.

Zach stepped out the front door and looked up at the gray sky trying to decide where he would go today.

John Stallings sat at a high-top table near the bar in the Ponce de Leon Pub, assessing the cute young bartender who acted as a waitress too. He was wondering if he should show her the photo of Zach and Jeanie. A cop's entire day was filled with decisions like these. Would she help, or tell Zach someone was looking for him? He glanced around the quiet pub until his eyes fell on a single, older man at a booth, sipping French onion soup directly from the bowl.

Stallings had to admit his patience for finding Zach was running short and he decided it was time to be more overt and aggressive. He pulled the photograph from his rear pocket and came up with a story that he was looking for a friend. Just as Stallings was about to say Zach's name and hold the photograph up to the pretty young bartender, the door to the pub opened.

Stallings casually glanced up and did an actual double take when he noticed Zach Halston walk in and plop down on a stool by the bar.

The bartender said to Stallings, "Know what you want yet?"

"Give me a few minutes and you can wait on your new customer."

The young woman peeked over her left shoulder, then shook her head. "I don't have to take his order. I know he's going to have a hamburger and two Budweisers, just like he does every day."

"Nice to have a regular customer."

"It would be if he ever tried to tip me with anything other than a joint."

Stallings gave her a smile and waited until she walked back behind the bar and into the kitchen before he calmly stood up from the table and took a few steps to the bar next to Zach.

Zach's head snapped to his left quickly as he looked at Stallings and relaxed when he realized it wasn't anyone he knew. Stallings pushed back his light jacket so Zach could see the badge and gun on his right hip.

Zach rolled his eyes in an effort to be cool, then managed to slide off the stool and start to run before Stallings could react.

* * *

Patty Levine had already talked to three distraught families and she could see why Tony had weaseled his way out of the duty. It was daunting and demoralizing and also educational. These poor families were looking for any shred of information or evidence that random chance hadn't taken a loved one from them. They wanted someone to blame. They wanted someone on which to take revenge. There wasn't a single parent who didn't look tired and didn't choke up when they discussed whatever accident had caused the death of their son.

She would've preferred to have her partner with her, but he'd called to say he was on a lead. Patty suggested she would come join him in St. Augustine, but he told her he had it covered and that he'd be back later in the day. Stallings had been acting oddly the last few weeks and she wondered exactly what was going on in his personal life.

The thought made her laugh out loud. She was worrying about someone else's personal life. That made no sense whatsoever. She'd just laid a serious kiss on her ex-boyfriend who was already involved in another relationship. And Patty didn't regret it one bit. Tony Mazzetti was a decent guy, and if it hadn't been for her own issues and her fear about what police work would eventually do to the two of them, she never would've let him go. But she now realized she was not completely over him. She just hoped it wouldn't be funky with him around the office.

Her cell phone rang and she saw it was Ken. She almost didn't answer, but then, on the fourth ring, Patty popped it open and said, "Hey, Ken."

"Hey, beautiful. Are we still on for dinner tonight?"

She thought about their last dinner, then about the kiss with Tony Mazzetti. Patty bit her lower lip and finally said, "I'm sorry. I've got to work late tonight."

John Stallings was used to people running from him and didn't let Zach get more than two steps away before he reached out and grabbed him firmly by the collar of his flannel shirt and jerked him back toward the bar stool. The quick action caught the attention of the old man sipping French onion soup, but he quickly went back to his task. By the time the bartender walked out, Stallings was sitting calmly next to Zach at the bar.

Stallings looked at the bartender and said, "We'll both have his usual."

The bartender gave him an odd look but nodded and turned back into the kitchen.

Zach said, "You're not going to hurt me, are you?"

"Why the hell would I do that?"

"I don't know who you work for."

"I just showed you my badge. I'm a detective with JSO."

Zach relaxed slightly, the white going out of his knuckles grasping the bar. "So you really are a cop?"

"Yeah, that's why I have a badge, a gun, and no time for bullshit."

Zach still looked worried and said, "How long have you been looking for me?"

"A couple of weeks."

"What are the charges?"

"What the hell you talking about? I'm here because your parents are worried about you, idiot."

"Really?" His voice cracked.

"Really."

Then Zach Halston showed he had the ability to surprise Stallings. He started to sob uncontrollably and blew his nose into a wad of napkins sitting next to him on the bar.

Lynn had caught just a glimpse of Zach Halston as he turned and walked into a seedy-looking pub. She reached into her purse and found the Buck knife she'd been waiting to use. She'd found a better way to deal with Kyle Lee and this was still an option. Now the only question was if she wanted to walk into the bar and give Zach a chance to remember her.

The other option was to cruise the area a while longer and see if she had the opportunity to use the big Suburban again. There was no way the cops would link a traffic accident in Daytona and a traffic accident in St. Augustine. She could be back in Jacksonville and at her desk in less than an hour.

And one step closer to finishing her mission.

THIRTY-EIGHT

Zach Halston was nervous because he didn't know if the cop was telling the truth. He'd seen too many TV shows where cops said all kinds of crazy things to get people to admit stuff.

The cop looked tough, with a hard body and stare to match. He pulled the photograph out of his rear pocket and slapped it down on the bar, letting Zach examine it for a moment, then said, "What do you know about the girl?"

"I thought you were looking for me because my parents were worried?"

"I was, but this girl's parents are worried too."

"Kelly? Is she okay?"

"What was her full name?"

"She said her name was Kelly Smith. We only went out for a few weeks and that was the only time she ever came by the fraternity house. She was secretive and didn't share anything about her personal life."

"When's the last time you saw her?"

Something about this guy's tone put Zach on edge

and he knew there was a lot more to the visit than his parents being scared. "I guess about two years ago."

"Tell me about her?"

What kind of a question was that from a cop? The whole situation was making Zach panicked. Who was this guy really? He sure acted like a cop, but not like a missing persons cop. Zach wondered if he was in narcotics or homicide.

Zach finally said, "She was a nice girl. She worked at an antique clothing store. I really don't know much more about her."

"Why'd you two break up?"

"We were never really going together. She met some guy she liked. She just kind of wandered away from me."

"Who's the guy she met?"

This was freaky. Why was this guy asking about a girl? "His name was Gator. That's all I know. I never met him. I'm proud of the fact that I don't know anyone named Gator."

The cop looked him up and down. "Why have you been hiding?"

Zach considered the question and the expression on the JSO detective's face. "I made some stupid choices and didn't want to face them."

The cop nodded. "So why else?"

He hesitated and said, "I made a mistake."

"Is it one that could be linked to the most recent deaths?"

Zach looked up at the cop. "What deaths?"

"You really haven't talked to anyone in Jacksonville?"

Zach shook his head, feeling his stomach turn. "Who died?"

"Connor Tate and Kyle Lee."

He could barely squeak out, "How?"

"Connor overdosed and Kyle, well, he had a boating accident."

The news was like a hammer into Zach's heart. His two most trusted friends. There was no doubt now. Maybe he needed this cop. Zach wondered if he should tell the truth. Admit everything and let the legal system handle his problems. He'd do some time. But then it'd be over. Or would it? What if things didn't change and he just had to spend time in jail? He started to sweat and slid away from the bar, saying to the big cop, "I gotta use the restroom real quick and wash my hands. Can we pick this up again when I get back?" He noticed the cop's eyes dart to the rear of the pub, where the restrooms were located, then toward the front door. Zach knew he was calculating how hard it would be for Zach to escape. Now he knew this was serious.

The cop nodded his head silently.

Zach tried to smile, then forced himself to slowly walk to the restroom. He knew he couldn't bolt for the open front door, but he had also been in the pub's restroom enough to know he had one other chance. There was no way he wanted to leave the Ponce de Leon Pub with this cop. If he got away and called his parents—if that was really why the cop was after him—his parents could call off the search. Then he'd deal with his problems one at a time. But if the cop had other things on his mind, Zach knew he didn't want to be anywhere near him.

Once inside the tiny bathroom, he really did use it, then washed his hands, before cranking open the small, frosted glass window and shoving out the screen with one hand. It was a tight fit, but he could make it. He needed to hit the ground running to put some distance between him and the JSO detective.

Lynn had pulled around the corner and parked, then got anxious and started to drive around the block, passing the Ponce de Leon Pub about once every ninety seconds. The rain had stopped, but the road was still slick. Almost no one was on the uneven sidewalks. As she came up the street on the east side of the pub, Lynn saw someone on foot come out of the narrow alleyway between the buildings. He glanced toward her but turned and kept up his fast pace on the sidewalk. It took her a moment to realize it was Zach. Why had he come out the back? The street was empty beyond her and there were no cars parked next to the sidewalk. She slowed the Suburban and saw Zach glance over his right shoulder before he took a step into the road. She punched the gas and felt the big vehicle lurch forward.

Almost like it had happened with Alan Cole, Zach froze midstride and looked up at the fast-moving SUV. She couldn't keep the smile from spreading across her face. She just wanted to hear the scream.

Stallings sat at the bar looking down at the photograph he had carried and shown to so many people. He wondered what Rita Hester would think of his first questions to Zach Halston being about Jeanie and not about the Tau Upsilon fraternity brothers. He'd have time to go over everything that had happened as soon as the young man returned from the bathroom.

After two minutes the bartender walked back and sat down four Budweisers. Two in front of Stallings and two where Zach had been sitting. She had taken a decidedly cooler stance toward Stallings once she realized he was associated with Zach Halston.

Now he was worried. Zach had been gone longer than he should. Even taking his nervousness into consideration, the young man should've finished up in the bathroom by now.

Stallings stood and walked toward the restroom. The door was locked, so he tapped lightly and called on Zach's name. When he got no response, he jerked on the handle harder, then used a shoulder to force the door open.

The small bathroom was empty. The only thing he noticed was the open window with no screen.

Zach had scraped his hip when he tumbled out of the window. He'd also bruised his forehead landing on the hard asphalt of the alleyway. But he was out and that was all that mattered. He stood up and took a second to brush off the gravel stuck to his side and hip. He wanted to sprint but realized his leg was sore, so he jogged toward the street.

He took a left on the sidewalk. There was no one around. There was only one blue SUV coming up the street slowly. Before he reached the corner, he glanced over his shoulder and decided to cross. The sound of the SUV's engine didn't register with him until he looked up and saw the vehicle barreling toward him. With everything that had happened, his mind locked up and he couldn't decide if he wanted to stop or shoot forward. By the time his mind said, *Start running*, it felt like the SUV was on top of him. He opened his mouth and was surprised to hear the scream come out. It sounded like a little girl frightened by a spider.

He thought he'd made it past the big vehicle, but it turned into his run and caught him squarely in the leg and hips. He felt himself kicked up in the air and briefly wondered how badly his leg would be injured. Before he had any other thoughts everything went black.

Running someone down in the Thomas Brothers SUV was easier the second time she did it. Practice makes perfect. She knew to turn the wheel in the direction he was running but was surprised how quickly he crossed the street. The bumper of the SUV caught his rear leg and hip. But she heard the scream. It was a good solid, if a little feminine, squeal. A satisfying result to her long endeavor.

He flew almost straight up into the air and made one rotation until his head struck the pole of the stop sign and he crumpled onto the ground like a rag doll. She took only a moment to look out the windshield and see the blood starting to pool around his head. She looked each way, then hit the gas, making the tires squeal and slide on the slick pavement.

Lynn looked in her rearview mirror once as she pulled away. She saw someone running down the street toward Zach's body. But there was no way they would ever catch her.

She'd done it again. The thrill raced through her and seemed to satisfy her need for justice.

At least for now.

THIRTY-NINE

Stallings leaned against the St. Augustine police cruiser, telling the traffic homicide investigator any detail he could think of. All he'd seen was a blue Suburban and the first letter on the plate was an A. Not much to go on.

He had waited while they took Zach's body from the scene. There was nothing he could do when he found the boy half on the sidewalk and half on the street. The stop sign he had knocked into was bent at a sickening angle. Blood stained the sidewalk a dark brown and a paramedic was pouring a bucket of bleach and water over it to wash it into the gutter.

Stallings had already called Sergeant Zuni and told her he'd found Zach Halston, but that he had been hit by a car. Her first question was whether it was an accident. Stallings could categorically say it was not. The SUV had driven away too quickly and the blow had been too direct. He was surprised the St. Augustine cops had not sent someone out on the main road to look for the Suburban trying to get on the interstate, but he understood it took time to control the scene and get people moving. Now he was stuck with just one more dead fraternity brother. There was no question they were looking for a serial killer.

Stallings had no idea what his status on the case would be after this, so he wasted no time calling an analyst in the Land That Time Forgot and having her run a report through the Department of Highway Safety to get a list of all the Suburbans with the tag starting with the letter A. He narrowed it down to St. Johns, Duval, Volusia, and Baker counties. With any luck the list in Duval would not be too long. It was the only lead he had right now.

Nothing like this had ever happened to him on the job before. He leaned against the patrol car, unable to focus on what he needed to do next. He realized the thing that had hit him the hardest was that his one known link to Jeanie was now broken.

Lynn calmly drove into the winding rear lot of the Thomas Brothers supply company. It may have been in her head, but it felt like the Suburban was pulling to the right. Could a human body do so much damage to a giant vehicle like this that it made it drift? She doubted it. The grille was intact this time and there was only the slight damage near the headlight.

She drove past a little Hispanic man washing one of the step vans and rolled forward until she could see Leon coming out from the shed that held all the cleaning material and car maintenance equipment. She eased to a stop next to the shed and slipped down from the high seat of the Suburban.

Leon started to walk toward her and then immediately turned toward the damaged front of the car and leaned down to inspect it closely. His weather-beaten face screwed into a puzzle as he turned toward her, not saying a word.

Lynn put on her best innocent act and shrugged, saying, "Just a minor accident."

Leon ran a finger down the front of the car and then under the bumper by the headlight. He lifted his hand, stared at it for a moment, and showed his finger to Lynn.

She immediately noticed the blood, but kept her cool. "Would it be a problem to give it a quick wash and keep the little damage quiet?"

Leon didn't look as eager to help as he had earlier. It took a moment as his brown eyes scanned the parking lot, then fell on Lynn. Finally he nodded slowly and mumbled, "For a price."

"What price?"

"I want in."

"On what?"

"Whatever you're doing."

Lynn felt her face flush as anxiety flooded through her. She tried to come up with a cover story, but Leon was too shrewd. He'd see through any lie she created on the spot. She simply said, "I'm not doing anything."

Leon said, "Then I guess I'll have to report this damage. I signed for the truck. I'm responsible." He turned and started to walk toward the main office building.

Lynn tried to let him play out his bluff, but after he walked about ten feet she called out, "Wait." She watched as he stopped walking but didn't turn around. She said, "There's no money involved in what I'm doing."

Now Leon turned slowly and said, "I don't need any money. I didn't go to prison for free. I only got this job to satisfy my parole officer."

"Then what are you looking for?"

"Some excitement."

"Give me a few days. I'll see what we can work out."

A smile spread across Leon's face. "I'll sign the car back in and see if I can't knock some of this dent out. No one will know a thing."

Lynn wasn't sure she had just made a smart deal.

Yvonne Zuni sat in her office even though the rest of the Land That Time Forgot was empty. She was just waiting for John Stallings to get back. He took things so personally and had been through so much, the sergeant wanted to make sure he was okay. Maybe she'd even get some insight to his marital problems. Any information about the detectives that worked for her was usually helpful. A lot of times detectives did things that didn't make sense on the job. And that was all supervisors focused on. It was almost like nothing existed outside the job and that was where problems occurred. Yvonne Zuni prided herself on recognizing that most of her life took place outside the confines of the Jacksonville Sheriff's Office and she also tried to look at each detective's actions in light of their personal lives.

Not all sergeants and lieutenants felt the same way.

Most patrol sergeants only wanted to know what the patrolmen directly under their command were doing during the eight-hour shift they had on the road. One of her friends who ran the squad in the north end of the county always said, "What happens at home stays at home." She understood that mentality, but it didn't make any sense when you were dealing with human beings.

The sergeant could see Lieutenant Rita Hester walking through the squad bay long before she reached the sergeant's office. That gave Sergeant Zuni a few moments to gather herself and wonder what the lieutenant was upset about now. The lieutenant rarely came into the detective bureau unless there was a problem. And it seemed like usually those problems revolved around something John Stallings had done.

The lieutenant paused at the door to the small office and said, "You hear anything more from Stall?"

"Everything is wrapped up in St. Augustine and he's on his way here."

"How'd he sound?"

"Truthfully, he sounded a little shaken."

The lieutenant nodded. "It's the guys as tough as Stallings who take things the hardest. When I heard what happened and knew how much he had invested in finding this kid and what information the kid potentially had for him, I figured he'd be pretty upset."

"I don't think he got anything from Zach. He said they only talked for a few minutes before he slipped out the back of the restaurant and was struck by the SUV."

"Any word on the search for the vehicle?"

"No luck yet."

The lieutenant let out a long, heavy sigh. "He's not the kind of guy you can send home to clear his head. And I don't want him to feel like he's being punished by being taken off the case again. I already punished him when I found out about the photo of Zach Halston and his daughter. We need something that makes him feel needed but doesn't have much of a risk involved with it."

Sergeant Zuni thought about it for a few moments, then said, "I'll send him out with Patty to talk to families of accident and suicide victims. So far we haven't gotten any leads from it, but the interviews need to be done."

The lieutenant nodded and mumbled, "Good idea." Then she said, "I want you to reassign four detectives to this case quietly. We need to take it seriously without causing a panic. I'll send over two analysts from auto theft." She turned to leave, then stopped and looked back over her shoulder. "It's a good idea to put Stallings on the interviews. Any sergeant who can manage a resource as valuable and as volatile as John Stallings is doing something right."

Sergeant Zuni couldn't help but smile as the lieutenant walked away.

FORTY

Patty Levine tried to relax with her head in Ken's lap. She was stretched out on his leather couch watching the Orlando Magic beat up on the Atlanta Hawks and trying to act interested as he yapped about the dangers of plantar fasciitis.

When he stopped to take a breath, Patty said, "I know what you mean about work being a bitch. We're back to square one on our possible serial homicide case."

"The one that involves the fraternity brothers?"

Patty rolled onto her back so she could look up at Ken's face now that they were involved in an actual conversation and not just one of his monologues about how podiatrists are not given enough respect in the medical community. She said, "Yeah. A witness who ran away from my partner was killed by a hit-and-run before John could talk to him."

"You said there was a possibility that the deaths were all a coincidence."

"John saw the car as it drove away from hitting the witness in St. Augustine."

"Did he see the driver intentionally run down the witness?"

Patty shook her head.

"Then this could be just one more coincidence, couldn't it?"

"I think we've moved beyond the coincidence theory."

"Why would a witness run from him anyway?"

"That's what we're trying to figure out."

Ken thought for a moment, then said, "What was he doing in St. Augustine? That's another county. That's not even in your jurisdiction."

"That's not the point. The problem is a dead witness."

"Who might not be dead if your partner hadn't scared him into running away."

"It's not John's fault."

"It sounds like he played a role in it."

Patty felt a knot of frustration work its way through her stomach. This guy just didn't get it. She felt like she needed a cop to talk to, someone who would understand her and could relate to the job. Uh-oh. She felt the knot of frustration turn to anxiety. She had broken up with Tony Mazzetti because she didn't feel like the job would ever give them a chance at a normal life. Now she was thinking she couldn't talk to her boyfriend because he wasn't a cop.

Oh shit.

John Stallings felt like a homeless person. He could not face the lonely house he rented in Lakewood and he couldn't visit his main residence because he wasn't ready to talk to Maria after the way he had acted with Brother Frank Ellis. The combination of his confrontation with the minister, who had acted like a creep but apparently was an okay guy, and his failure to protect Zach Halston had sent him into a serious funk.

He'd gone by the office, and Sergeant Zuni's calm and sensitive manner had unnerved him. Stallings was used to sergeants shouting at him or threatening him, not giving him a cushy assignment with his partner to interview witnesses the next day. He realized it was their way of taking him out of harm's way without making him feel like a failure. On some level he appreciated it. But he wanted to be in the thick of things. That's why he had become a cop in the first place.

Now he found himself at the community center where his father worked in the evenings. But he couldn't lie to himself. Stallings had not come over here to see his father and be reminded how his failing memory might block him out altogether. He knew Grace Jackson would be over here tonight as well. There was a connection he had with the pretty black schoolteacher, who had seemed to be able to cut through all the bullshit of his job and life.

Stallings had been vague about what happened in St. Augustine and only said that a witness had been killed by a hit-and-run. He went into greater detail about bumping into Brother Frank Ellis and his wife visiting Maria and realizing that Ellis had been trying to help him when he mentioned Maria had a problem with Patty. Looking back on it, Stallings recognized that there was no way Ellis could have gotten that info unless it had come through Maria. It was an issue with Maria even if it wasn't a real-life issue. At some point he'd have to deal with it and talk to his estranged wife about his strong, but nonsexual, feelings for his partner. He would have to talk to Patty as well. He had no idea what he'd say to either of them and right now, setting the table with Grace and looking into her pretty, dark eyes was enough of a distraction to keep him from falling over from a huge anxiety attack.

Grace gave him a warm smile after he finished the story about Frank Ellis and said, "I know this is not the right time to say anything like I told you so."

Stallings broke out into a smile and said, "But."

Grace continued, undaunted. "But I did say that Brother Ellis had a good reputation and you might be jumping to conclusions." She reached across the table and grasped his hand in both of hers. "You are a very fine man, John Stallings. You're intense but calm, you're smart but clueless, and most of all you're a very sweet, loyal husband." Grace sighed and said, "And you know what I think."

"No, but I'd like to know what you think."

"I think you should forget the problems with your wife, Brother Frank Ellis, your dad's Alzheimer's, and even put me out of your mind for a little while and focus on nothing but this case. It will clear your mind, settle your spirit, and maybe keep someone else from getting killed."

Stallings nodded slowly, seeing the perfect sense of the idea.

Grace said, "And once you finish that, you need to figure out what you want to do with the rest of your life and if Maria has a role in it. She *is* your wife in the eyes of God and the mother of your children. I'd be wrong if I advised you to do anything but try and stay with her."

Stallings gave her a smile and said, "I feel another 'but' coming on."

Without saying another word, Grace leaned across the table and kissed him. She let it linger so he could feel her full lips and the emotion behind the kiss. When she was done, she leaned back into her chair and said, "That was so you'd have no doubt on how I feel. And when all of this is cleared up, and I mean everything, I'll still be around."

Grace had made Stallings feel better about everything.

Lynn lingered at her desk, worried about Leon. How was she ever going to satisfy him? He had proved to be persistent and resilient and now he had turned his attention on her. She didn't want to hurt him, but at some point she might have to make the choice between her mission and the former marijuana smuggler. Under those conditions Leon lost every time.

Her other concern was the lingering Alan Cole. She had checked with the hospital on and off and been able to pick up that he was still in a coma and unresponsive. For a while she considered just leaving the injured man to his shattered life, but she kept imagining him rousing from his coma, saying that he'd seen her behind the wheel of the blue Suburban. It was a dream that would wake her up at night. And he definitely had to pay the same price as the others. Now the only question was when to make the trip south to Daytona.

She had another target who lived locally. As she considered him, she realized he could be the last one. It made her think about her life after this horrible quest she'd been on. One of the first things she hoped to do was meet someone. Not just a guy in a bar or one of the doofuses from the loading dock at work but a nice, professional man. Someone like Doctor Ferrero, who didn't care about supply delivery companies or how to effectively murder a college boy.

Lynn could envision raising kids. Sometimes her daydreams were quite specific: two boys with the girl in the middle. If the middle child was of a different gender it might shake up the old idea that the middle child would be a slacker. The oldest was always special because they are first. The youngest is always special because they're the baby. It's the middle kid who needs extra care. She loved the idea of taking them all to the beach or the mall or one of the amusement parks in the state.

Her parents seemed to enjoy raising kids. At least until recently. No matter how old the kids got, her parents still tried to take care of them. She knew her father had created a retirement account for her and said she had nothing to worry about after age fifty-nine. He also had a house fund for her, just like he did for her siblings. But it was understood that the fund was for a house in the Jacksonville area so they would be close to her parents. She wouldn't leave them now anyhow. They were too fragile. It broke her heart. That made her more determined to finish her mission.

She pulled her Buck knife from her purse and stared at it. This last one would be perfect. She'd do it right and finally hear the perfect scream.

FORTY-ONE

Patty thought John Stallings was unusually quiet. That was saying something. He wasn't brooding. John never brooded. He was just more withdrawn than normal and was focusing on the case notes from their first interview of the day.

The mother of a nineteen-year-old son killed in a car accident said he had no connection to the fraternity. These were touchy interviews that could easily open old wounds for the families of the victims. It wasn't until the end of the interview that the woman started to sob uncontrollably. It was moments like this that gave Patty an insight into John Stallings's home life and the sorrow they had all gone through when Jeanie disappeared.

Now Stallings drove his county-issued Impala south on I-95 toward their next interview in Hyde Park.

Finally, Patty had to say, "I know something's bothering you. You wanna talk about it?"

"Do I ever want to talk about anything?"

"You might be surprised to find it makes you feel better."

"For your information, I talked my head off last night. I reached my quota and now I'm going to focus on police work for a little while."

She took his answer as more informative than usual and noted the nice neighborhood as they got off I-95. Hyde Park was an upscale suburb of Jacksonville proper that housed attorneys and doctors. They found the house they were looking for and Patty whistled in amazement. Even by Hyde Park standards this was an opulent home. The two-story house sat far off the street with a winding, semicircular driveway covering much of the front yard. A sturdy, decorative fence ran the length of the property line and an electronic gate blocked the driveway.

Stallings didn't hesitate to pull the Impala into the driveway and press a button on a stone pillar.

Patty noticed a camera on the opposite pillar move as someone inside the house examined the car. After a few seconds the voice came over a speaker in the stone pillar.

"May I help you?"

Stallings looked down at the sheet of paper and said, "Is Mr. or Mrs. Hickam available?"

"Please identify yourself."

Stallings and Patty exchanged glances at the formal and direct command.

He leaned out the window closer to the pillar and said, "Jacksonville Sheriff's Office."

There was a long pause and the camera on the opposite pillar continued to scan the car. After almost twenty seconds another male voice came over the speaker, saying, "May I ask what this is in reference to?"

"We're doing some follow-up on a two-year-old death investigation. We would like to speak to the Hickams. Are they at home?"

Patty always admired how Stallings could put a slight inflection in his voice that seemed to force people to do whatever he wanted without being overtly threatening. She may not have had the same level of experience as Stallings, but her instincts told her something was definitely not right about this house.

Just as the gate started to slide open, the voice came over the small speaker and said, "Drive up to the front door."

Patty heard Stallings mumble, "Is today the day that changes the rest of my life?"

That set her on edge.

Emmanuel White was not as thrilled with his new job as he thought he'd be. He'd worked his ass off to get through Ohio State and worked just as hard for two years to get this job. He was so happy to be out of the Midwest and assigned to Florida that he didn't even care that he had been sent to Jacksonville. He knew in the rest of the state, the northwest city was a little bit of a joke and so far the weather had not proved to be as sunny as he'd hoped. But he was pretty sure he'd make it through the winter without snow and none of the rivers here could catch on fire like the Cuyahoga.

He'd watched the two monitors during the twelve-hour day shift for five days in a row. He was scheduled to be off for the next two days, but on this job he never knew when he'd have free time. In fairness, his job wasn't only to monitor the two cameras; he was expected to review recorded telephone conversations from a number of different phone lines. There still wasn't enough to keep him occupied for twelve hours at a time.

He noticed an Impala drive up and stop at the gate. It was one of the few times there was any activity at the house. The camera he monitored was across the street from the house. Emmanuel could see the security cameras at the house scanning the car before they opened the gate and allowed it to drive in.

Emmanuel was able to copy down the tag and decided to run it instantly, rather than wait until later. He liked watching the national news at 6:30 and always tried to have his work done before Brian Williams came on TV. He turned to a small Toshiba computer, typed in his password, and ran the tag. It came back to a corporation in Jacksonville. He ran the corporation through a separate computer databank and recognized it as a company used to register cars for the Jacksonville Sheriff's Office. The practice was designed to foil drug dealers who tried to figure out who was following them. It didn't slow him down one bit.

He hesitated, then pulled out his cell phone and dialed a supervisor to advise him about the unusual visitors. It was sad that this was the highlight of his last five days. He may have been new to the job, but he expected something different after being an Ohio State trooper for two years and then surviving the DEA training Academy in Quantico, Virginia. Somehow he thought the life of a federal narcotics agent would be more interesting than this.

Emmanuel White advised his supervisor what was going on. All the supervisor wanted to know was if he had finished reviewing the recorded telephone calls from the day before.

Emmanuel wondered if life was any different with the other federal agencies.

John Stallings kept alert and remained very aware of his surroundings as he and Patty followed Mrs. Hickam through the house to a den that overlooked a sprawling backyard and small lake. Several things had caught Stallings's attention during the stroll through the house. It had a surprisingly homey atmosphere with a number of photos of the family. He recognized one of the kids as the victim of the alcohol poisoning case that Stallings had come to investigate. His name was Josh Hickam and he'd been a sophomore at the University of North Florida when he had died in early November, two years ago.

Mrs. Hickam was an ordinary-looking woman of about fifty-five, who had a muted personality that reminded Stallings of Maria when she was using heavy doses of prescription drugs. Aside from introducing herself and asking them to follow her, she had not said a word during the walk through the house.

Mr. Hickam met them in the den and Stallings could tell by the man's darting eyes that he was nervous and making a detailed assessment of him and Patty. The walls of the den were lined with books and framed photographs of the family. One section of the south wall contained a locked, glass display case with more than thirty handguns on various racks and pedestals. This house was secure if Mr. Hickam felt comfortable displaying so many guns so prominently.

Patty and Stallings sat across from the Hickams on two small couches. The older couple held each other's hands tightly, and Mr. Hickam assumed the role of communicator.

Stallings had been careful to advise them right from the start that they had no new information and were simply doing follow-up on a number of deaths in the county over the past two years.

Mr. Hickam said, "We never really thought Josh had died of anything other than alcohol poisoning. We knew the college life could get wild, but we assumed that since he was so close, he was safe."

Patty said, "Did he live here with you?"

"No, we wanted him to have the full college experience even if he was only a few miles away. He lived in the apartment complex that houses the fraternity."

Stallings tried to hide his surprise and calmly asked, "What fraternity was he in?"

"Tau Upsilon."

Tony Mazzetti sat in the corner of the detective bureau with Sparky Taylor, going through reports and other documents relating to their case. The new information, that Stallings had seen a blue SUV driving away from the scene of a hit-and-run in St. Augustine, provided dozens of more leads to follow up.

The cheapskate lieutenant avoided overtime by reassigning four detectives and an analyst to help him cope with the growing investigation, but he knew the break in the case would lie with him or Sparky or one of the full-time detectives on the squad. Experience counted for more than anything else in homicide. He felt like he'd seen just about everything that could be thrown at him, and if you saw something once it was easier to spot a second time.

Sparky was reading reports from other cities, including Atlanta, Daytona, Gainesville, and Orlando. Scanning through hundreds of documents hoping to find a link to this case that could be used to find the killer. As much as he hated to admit it, Mazzetti now realized the deaths of the Tau Upsilon fraternity members had not been accidents. The lieutenant was even now conferring with officials from other cities to decide how they should notify the members of the fraternity that they could be in danger. The way Mazzetti saw it, if the fraternity brothers couldn't figure out something was wrong by the fact that they each knew several dead men, it wouldn't change much when the cops told them they had linked all the deaths. No one ever thinks it will happen to them.

Sparky looked up from a faxed police report and said, "I just found a report from a witness in Daytona regarding the hit-and-run of a fraternity member. The traffic investigator had asked several local witnesses if they had seen any vehicles in the area. Five witnesses listed five completely different vehicles."

Mazzetti said, "So?"

"So one of the vehicles listed was a blue SUV."

That caught Mazzetti's attention. On its own, with no license tag information, the report was useless, but coupled with what a reliable witness like John Stallings had seen, it could be the link they'd been looking for.

"Do we have the list of license plates that start with A?"

"It's two hundred and three vehicles long just for Duval County." Sparky moved some papers around the long table and pick up another print. "Three hundred and sixteen if we include adjacent counties. The number climbs to five hundred and two if we include Volusia County. That's a lot of vehicles to look at. Stallings had the same report run after the hit-and-run."

Mazzetti leaned back in his chair in a sign of frustration. At what point was it useless? These were the kinds of things that the press could use to crucify him later. The reporters had the luxury of time and perspective to look at information. After the dust had settled, they loved to point the finger at detectives who tried to be efficient and prioritize investigative tasks.

As soon as Stallings heard the fraternity mentioned, he couldn't keep from turning and looking at Patty, who gave him a quiet, professional nod and wrote a few more notes on her pad.

Mrs. Hickam said, "They were nice boys. You should've seen the crowd that came to Josh's funeral. Each of them dressed up in a nice suit and they greeted all of the family members, making us feel like one of their own."

Stallings asked a few more questions and discovered that Josh studied business, but the most important thing was they had another body to tie into this conspiracy. It wasn't the right time to explain what was going on to the Hickams, but it could be that their son was the first known victim.

Stallings said, "I have one more question."

Mr. Hickam said, "Sure, anything you want to know."

"Did your son have a job?"

Now the Hickams exchanged glances and after a short pause Mr. Hickam said, "He made a little money doing different things, but he wasn't employed by anyone specific."

Stallings nodded, slowly stood, taking a closer look at photographs on the wall. He said, "You have an attractive family."

"Thank you. We tried to stay very close."

Stallings noticed the Hickams' daughter in some kind of clinical setting. "Is your daughter a nurse?"

Mr. Hickam shook his head and said, "She works part-time at a veterinarian's office, keeping the books."

Stallings moved to the gun collection, noting the man's love of Smith & Wesson revolvers. One entire row of eight handguns were Smith & Wessons from the ancient model 10 to the much newer 686.

Stallings turned to Mr. Hickam and said, "If we have any more questions, can we come by and talk to you?"

Mr. Hickam nodded his head and said, "You just have to call ahead of time. You can see that we cherish our privacy."

Stallings was beginning to wonder about that privacy and if the reasons for it had led to their son's death. Something wasn't right about this house.

FORTY-TWO

It'd been two hours since their interview at the Hickam house and still it was all Stallings could think about. They'd talked to the father of a young man who'd drowned while partying with some former high school friends. The man seemed very matter-of-fact and calm about the whole incident and had never suspected any type of conspiracy. He had accepted his son's death and moved on with his life. Although they hadn't been extraordinarily close, the father knew his son had never been involved with the fraternity and all details of the accident had made sense when the friends talked to the police.

Now Stallings and Patty were just finishing a sandwich at a Firehouse Subs off I-95. Patty looked up and said, "Are you still thinking about the Hickam interview too?"

Stallings nodded.

Patty continued. "It was just weird from start to finish. All that security. And the guns. It looked like the armory of midsized police department. Who has that many guns? Who puts them on display like that?"

Stallings nodded as he said, "I'm going over the same details in my head. This kid is definitely part of whatever is going on at the fraternity. He may have been the start of it."

"What's our next move?"

"Something tells me the first one of these fraternity brats we talked to, who was also the last one we talked to at the house, is holding out on us."

"Bobby Hollis?"

Stallings snapped his fingers. "That's his name. Bobby fucking Hollis. This time we talk to him my way."

"And if he was telling us the truth?"

"I'll apologize."

"That's quite a promise coming from you." Patty nodded her head as if she was resolving herself. "I agree, this is too important to let some snot nose from the fraternity throw us further off track. But this time we're in it together. And don't you try to protect me from command staff if something goes wrong."

Stallings's phone rang and he dug it out of his pocket and flipped it open without looking to see who it was. He heard Sergeant Zuni's voice say, "You guys need to come back to the D-bureau."

"Why?"

"Something to do with IA."

"Did they say what it was?"

Sergeant Zuni said, "No. Is there something you want to tell me about now?"

"Not that I can think of, but you never know how people take different comments." He closed his phone and turned to Patty, saying, "We've got to get back to the office."

"Why?"

Stallings just shrugged and said, "The usual."

Lynn sat at an outdoor break area behind the main building of the Thomas Brothers supply company. She'd been on her cell phone for almost twenty minutes as she chatted with the nurse she'd befriended from the hospital in Daytona where Alan Cole was being treated. She didn't rush the conversation and listened as the nurse told Lynn about her own family problems involving a teenage daughter who was smoking pot and skipping school. Lynn wasn't so cold as to not care about the nurse's problems. But the reason she'd spent so much time talking to her was she was the only one who ever gave her any information about Alan's condition.

Lynn had explained that she was Alan's pregnant girlfriend and that his parents didn't approve of her. She didn't want to cause drama and avoided coming to the hospital. She had just enough detail to make it sound right and had caught just the right nurse with a story.

After the nurse had finished telling her about her daughter's most recent incident, Lynn said, "I had a few issues in high school too. It's probably just a phase she'll grow out of. My biggest problem now is the fact that Alan's parents think I'm some kind of slut."

The nurse said, "Don't worry, sweetheart. They'll

warm up to you. Once they have a grandchild on the scene there's no way they'll be able to stay away. I'm just sorry you and I haven't been able to talk in person."

"You weren't on duty the couple times I've been down there."

"I'm sorry. I would love to sit and talk with you."

Lynn said, "How was Alan today?"

"The doctor sees more activity. He's conscious but not completely responsive yet."

"I'll come down closer to the weekend."

The nurse said, "I'm off on Saturday so try to come either Friday or Sunday."

Lynn thanked her and they said the usual good-byes. As she closed her cell phone, Lynn realized she had to avoid the nurse at all costs, which meant she'd be driving down to Daytona on Saturday. She had plenty to do to keep her busy until then.

Before Stallings had reached the main doors to Professional Standards, or, as most cops called it, Internal Affairs, he and Patty had been met by Senior IA Investigator Ronald Bell. As usual, he was dressed in some expensive suit and looked more like a maître d' than a working detective. That wasn't the only thing that bothered Stallings about the fifty-year-old investigator. They had a long history. Stallings recognized that Bell had a job to do, but he didn't like the way he went about it. When Jeanie disappeared three years ago, Bell had thought the circumstances of her disappearance were suspicious. In a way he was correct. But it was actually only the reporting of her disappearance that was suspicious. Stallings had been late reporting the missing teenager because Maria's drug habit had gotten seriously out of control. By the time he was able to cope with his near-catatonic wife, almost a full day had passed before he realized Jeanie wasn't around the house.

Bell had also been a little too zealous in his efforts to find some missing prescription drugs from the office. He had put Patty under the spotlight, and that had not sat well with Stallings. To his credit, Bell had apologized when the drugs showed up in an undocumented evidence locker, but Stallings still thought he was a prick.

Bell smiled and held out his hand like a slimy used-car salesman. "It's nice to see both of you appear when you're not under the gun for something."

Both Stallings and Patty ignored his offered hand. Stallings said, "Cut the bullshit, Ron. We got things to do, and once again you're wasting our time."

"It's Ronald."

"Whatever. Why are you bothering us now?"

Bell let a sly smile slip over his face and said, "It's not me this time. I have a visitor in my office who'd like to talk to you both. This time I don't think you did anything wrong except being oblivious." He turned and the two detectives followed him back through the offices of Internal Affairs into a rear conference room.

When Bill opened the door, Stallings saw a casually dressed man with a lean, hard look sitting on the far side of the table.

Bell said, "John Stallings and Patty Levine, this is Ed Wiley with the DEA."

Lynn listened intently as her mother sniffled on the other end of the phone line. The first few minutes of the call had been very disconcerting as Lynn tried to understand exactly what had happened. Finally Lynn's mother had calmed down enough to say that two detectives from the Jacksonville Sheriff's Office had visited the house. That made her even more nervous until her mother explained that it had to do with her brother Josh's death.

Lynn said, "Did they give you any other reason for the visit?"

"No. Just follow-up on Josh. Why, are you worried they had a hidden reason?"

Lynn knew her mother's concerns about the police and her own were two entirely separate things. Then Lynn said, "So they have no new leads on the incident? I mean, no new information."

"No. Why? Do you think it was something besides alcohol poisoning?"

Lynn sure as hell *did* think it was something besides an accidental alcohol poisoning, but she couldn't say anything to her mother. She couldn't risk throwing her back into the emotional abyss that had almost destroyed both her and Lynn's dad.

Lynn's mother said, "They did ask a few questions about the Tau Upsilon fraternity."

This time Lynn felt like the phone had literally shocked her. She tried to regain her composure but realized whatever she was going to do she had to do it fast. She still had time to finish her mission and return to a normal life.

Ed Wiley looked like the typical DEA supervisor, dressed in jeans and an untucked, button-down, long-sleeved shirt. He was about Stallings's age but had more of a weathered appearance to him. Stallings guessed the guy had spent some time down on the Mexican border and the sun had taken its toll. He had a lot more gray in his short cropped hair than Stallings.

The DEA always worried more about being effective and less about being formal and official than many of the other federal agencies. The agents tended to work long hours and bonded closely with the local cops in every area. Every cop agreed that they enjoyed working with both the DEA and the ATF. They never really had anything particularly positive to say about the FBI. Stallings chalked it up to the fact that most of the DEA and ATF agents had been street cops at one time in their career. They understood how dangerous and difficult the job could be. They hadn't lost touch with what was important about law enforcement. And certainly one of the things that wasn't important to this DEA agent was how nicely he dressed when talking to the local cops. Stallings appreciated that kind of attitude.

Stallings sat directly across from the silent DEA agent. No one at the table spoke. Stallings had a slight smile because he knew he could win at this game.

Finally the DEA agent said, "Can I ask why you visited the residence in Hyde Park today?"

Stallings gave Patty a quick glance that told her not to answer. He intended to have a little fun in the IA offices for a change. He tapped his forehead and said, "We did a lot of interviews in the last week. Maybe if you told me what the house looked like I'd have an idea of where you were talking about."

The DEA agent was not amused. But he didn't have to cut his eyes over to Ronald Bell for assistance. This was a tough guy who dealt with tough people. He said, "Okay, then I guess I won't be able to help you on your investigation with everything I know about the Hickams." He scooted his chair back and stood.

Stallings raised his hands in surrender and smiled. "Okay, okay. You win." He waited for the stern agent to take a seat again.

"We're in the middle of a possible serial killer investigation and part of it involves looking at deaths previously ruled accidental. The Hickams' son, Josh, died a couple of years ago from alcohol poisoning. We were doing follow-up on that."

The DEA agent nodded slowly and said, "I remember when the son died. Tragic."

Stallings could tell by the way the man said it, he didn't mean it. One of the problems with working narcotics was you developed a battle-like attitude toward the dealers. There was no middle ground where some people were right and some people were wrong. It was just good guys and bad guys. Stallings could tell the DEA agent thought Mr. Hickam was a bad guy.

The DEA agent said, "The whole Hickam family are big-time marijuana smugglers. Bill Hickam and his brother are responsible for almost thirty percent of the marijuana that enters the United States along the southeast seaboard. We've had cameras up on the house for months as we put together a major RICO case. You can imagine our surprise when an unmarked JSO car rolled into the family's driveway."

Stallings said, "Was the son, Josh, ever involved in the family business?"

"It looks like the father wanted to keep that entire generation out of the family business. I know the boy was suspected of selling some pot on the side while he was at the University of North Florida. I don't think he ever progressed further than that."

Just that piece of information, the fact that Josh Hickam could've been a minor pot dealer, made Stallings look at the case from an entirely different perspective.

The DEA agent said, "Is there anything that we can help you with?"

Stallings shook his head while he still looked off in space and said, "I'm not sure, but it's given me some ideas to look into."

The young doctor looked down at his watch and realized he should've eaten dinner by now. That explained his headache. At least today he had a reason to feel lousy. When he'd accepted this job right out of the University of Southern California, he'd had no idea what a shit hole Daytona was. He'd pictured it like Southern California. Now he thought of it as more a waterside Western Appalachian community. Nothing but bikers and rednecks and no chance to study the diseases of the brain he had hoped to. Plenty of trauma from motorcycle accidents and fistfights and the occasional boating accident, but nothing any ordinary doctor couldn't handle. And the fucking University of Florida. The graduates from UF medical school were like the stormtroopers from *Star Wars*. They were everywhere and they never shut up about the fucking Gators.

He paused in one room and sat down to write a few notes. Then he looked up at the patient who had been brought in almost a month earlier. When the doctor stood, he noticed the patient's eyes move toward him. He stepped closer and said, "Can you hear me, Mr. Cole?"

The doctor noticed him nod his head ever so slightly. He'd been able to do some math the last few days. Yesterday, Mr. Cole had cleared his throat and tried to speak for a moment. This was both encouraging and scary. A series of infections had inhibited the accident victim's recovery. He was still in terrible danger. But his brain function seemed to be improving. That's what the young doctor felt positive about. At least he was making progress. All the doctor could hope for was to help the few patients he could while he was stuck in this backwater hellhole. In the past months he'd lamented several times that he had never been on spring break here. If he had, he never would've accepted this job. He should have known when they were so thrilled to get a USC grad that there wouldn't be much here for him to do.

He looked down at the patient and said, "Mr. Cole, tomorrow you and I are going to actually speak." He thought he noticed a slight smile on the man's face. He hoped the conversation wouldn't be the man's last words.

FORTY-THREE

It was still early in the evening and Lynn had a good idea where this young man would be. These fraternity members had proved to be extremely predictable. She was too close to stop now, even if the cops looked like they had an idea of what was happening. She sat alone at a high-top table next to the bar, sipping on a glass of red wine and enjoying the relaxed feeling of knowing she'd be done soon. Lynn had her unused Buck knife in her purse. With all the work she'd put into learning how to use it, she couldn't leave it unbloody. Even if it looked like the police were starting to put things together and maybe her efforts to conceal herself weren't as good as she'd thought.

The young man walked out of the restroom and across the nearly empty bar floor and plopped back down in a seat at the table between his two friends. He was shorter than most of the fraternity brothers, with dark hair and the circles under his eyes like a student who worked too hard and slept too little. From her surveillance work, she got the idea that he didn't party nearly as much as the other brothers. But she'd been told he had been there that night and hadn't helped her brother when he'd needed it most. Having grown up in a household that was told to be secretive so no one would ever figure out exactly what her father did for a living, Lynn was impressed all these boys could keep their mouths shut for so long. And she had used that to her advantage.

She'd already decided that when she was done here she'd deal with Alan Cole. One short trip to Daytona and everything would be done. She could get on with her life and maybe her parents could too.

But first she intended to plunge the three-inch blade of the Buck knife into Bobby Hollis's neck.

Stallings still felt uncomfortable taking Patty with him when he intended to step so far outside the JSO investigative guidelines. But she had persisted and pointed out the fact that they were partners and he did trust her completely. Looking back on his sixteen years with the sheriff's office and all the partners he'd had from road patrol through homicide, Patty was the best. She was head and shoulders above most other partners. He had learned early in his career, when Rita Hester patrolled the streets of Arlington with him, that gender had no bearing on being a good partner. The lieutenant of the D-bureau had backed him up in any situation and never talked about anything they did. That's why he had a hard time getting anything past her now. Not only did she know all the tricks, she knew how far he was willing to go to solve the case.

His other issue taking Patty on some of these authorized assignments was that he did not want to hurt her chances of promotion. He didn't want her tainted with the accusation of undue force or lying to a superior officer. Stallings was willing to take on those stigmas if it helped him catch a killer or find a missing child, but he didn't want Patty's ruined career on his conscience as well.

Stallings drove through the huge parking lot of the apartment complex that housed the fraternities serving all the universities of the area. Loud music came from a dozen different doors in every building and kids were everywhere on the property, drinking beers or tossing footballs. And this was a weeknight.

Patty said, "He has a Dodge Neon registered to him. I haven't seen it in the lot."

"Do we want to just barge into the house and ask where he is or keep things a little more covert?"

"Do we have time to stay covert?"

Stallings smiled because he realized Patty was thinking more and more like him. "Not only do we not have time, I intend to scare this fraternity geek so bad that he won't hold back anything. He'll have nightmares about this conversation years from now." He caught Patty's smile at his comments.

Stallings pulled his Impala across a sidewalk, blocking the entrance to the building where the Tau Upsilon fraternity clubhouse was located. They walked through the front door and saw three young men playing pool in the corner of the empty room.

The boys didn't even ask who they were. Stallings was sure Patty was a legend among the fraternity for the way she'd handled the smart-aleck boy out on the beach the first day of the investigation. Stallings said, "Is Bobby Hollis around?"

The three boys looked at each other, trying to decide if they should speak with the detectives.

Stallings didn't raise his voice, keeping it even but putting an edge on it when he said, "I need to talk to Bobby Hollis right . . . now." Just putting a pause between *right* and *now* made all three boys scramble to speak first.

The tallest of the three boys said, "I saw him leave about an hour ago."

Stallings snapped, "What's his cell number?"

Lynn felt an edge of excitement sweep through her body as she saw Bobby Hollis stand and wave goodbye to his friends. She had sensed he was getting ready to leave for some time and had paid for her drinks. As soon as he stepped away from the table she slipped off the stool and headed out the door in front of him.

She was surprised by how much the temperature had dropped outside. It sent shivers through her as she dug in her purse for the Buck knife. The parking lot was half full of cars, but there was no one outside right now. She saw Bobby's green Dodge Neon at the far end of the parking lot. Her Nissan was about three cars away. That would be the perfect place to wait and call him over like she was having car trouble of some kind. She could picture what it'd be like to send the knife straight up into his neck and pull it out in a slashing motion as he flopped onto the ground like a fish out of water and blood turned the white sand and gravel of the parking lot a tacky red.

She hustled over to her car and unlocked the door. Moisture clung to her blouse as she waited longer than she'd expected. She should've learned that all fraternity brothers take a long time to say good-bye to each other.

Finally, she saw the front door to the bar open and Bobby Hollis walk out. He pulled his sweatshirt over his head. He didn't even look around the parking lot as he stepped out from the overhang that covered the front door to the bar.

Lynn leaned against her car like she'd had too much to drink and grasped the open knife in her right hand, shielding it from Bobby's view with her body.

Bobby Hollis conducted his own personal sobriety test that the fraternity had developed. He stood erect and lifted his left foot so he had to balance on his right foot. Then he said the alphabet slowly and clearly. He'd only had four beers, but he couldn't afford a DUI on his record. He would graduate this year and the job market was already too competitive. He didn't need some manager at Smith Barney or even Charles Schwab—if all else went wrong—to have to worry about hiring someone who drank too much and got stopped by the cops.

He looked at parking lot to remember exactly where he had parked his car. The first thing he intended to do once he was in the working world was to get rid of that piece of shit and buy something with a little style—maybe not a BMW, but at least not the absolute bottom-of-the-line, basic-transportation American car. He had looked at the Mini Cooper, but was now leaning toward a Nissan Z car.

He felt his phone vibrate and pulled it out of his pocket. He didn't recognize the number, so he didn't answer.

He took a deep breath of Jacksonville's night air and noticed a woman who looked like she might be drunk leaning against a car near his. He wondered if he should offer his help.

Stallings didn't leave a message on Bobby Hollis's phone. Instead, he looked at the three boys staring at him from the pool table and said, "One of you give me your phone."

The boy who had been speaking with them said, "What?"

"I said give me a phone. Bobby didn't answer and it might be because he didn't recognize my phone number." He snapped his fingers to speed them to action.

The boy said, "I'll call him." He dug a BlackBerry out of his pocket.

Stallings said, "You can dial, then hand the phone to me."

The boy did exactly as he was directed.

Lynn's heart rate increased as Bobby Hollis walked closer and closer. His gaze switched from the Dodge

Neon to her. She could tell he was debating whether to walk over and see if he could help her get into the car. She yanked on the door handle with her left hand making it seemed like there was a problem. She still had the knife hidden in her right hand. Once he turned and stepped between her car and the pickup truck parked next to her, she didn't intend to hesitate. She would turn and face him and before he realized what was happening she'd have the knife rising in a deadly arc.

He stopped in the parking lot not far from her car and turned slightly toward her. Lynn heard a familiar song but couldn't place it. It wasn't until he reached in his pocket and pulled out his phone she realized it was a ringtone. He stopped where he was and started talking on the phone.

FORTY-FOUR

Stallings heard a voice on the phone say, "Hey, Chucky."

Stallings said, "Bobby, is that you?"

There was a hesitation; then he said, "Yeah, it's Bobby. Who's this?"

"Bobby, this is Detective John Stallings from the Jacksonville Sheriff's Office. We spoke a couple of times."

"I, I remember you, sir."

Stallings was satisfied the boy's stammer indicated how terrified he already was. "I need to speak with you."

"Okay." It was hesitant at best.

"I need to speak with you tonight. I'm over at your fraternity house now."

There was a long pause, and then Bobby said, "I, um, didn't plan to be home until late."

"How late?"

"Sometime after midnight."

Stallings didn't like the way this conversation was headed. He could tell the boy was scared of something and may be hard to pin down if Stallings went looking for him. He needed a few minutes to think.

Stallings was silent longer than he meant to be and Bobby said, "Do I need to speak to an attorney?"

"Why would you need to speak to an attorney? I was looking for one of your missing fraternity brothers and asking a few questions about some unusual deaths. Why are you so hesitant to talk to me?"

"I'm not hesitant. I'm just busy. I'll give you a call tomorrow."

The phone line went dead.

Lynn considered stepping away from her car and surprising him while he spoke on his phone. She was anxious to get this done. He turned and faced the building while he spoke on the phone. Bobby sounded scared. She set her purse on the ground and took three steps to the very front of her car. She was now about ten feet away from Bobby Hollis, who was facing the other direction.

She tightened her grip on the knife, ready to spring forward. Now she knew what a great white shark felt like when he saw a seal right in front of him. It would be so easy to plunge the knife into his exposed neck.

Stallings was frustrated and whipped the Black-Berry back to the kid with more force than he'd intended. He looked at Patty, then over to the boys, and said, "Where was he going tonight?"

No one answered.

This time Stallings slammed his hand down on the pool table, grabbed a nine ball, and slammed it into some loose balls at the other end of the table. "This isn't a game, fellas. I need to speak to Bobby Hollis tonight. Now where the fuck is he?"

One of the boys blurted out, "He's over at the J Tavern, off University."

Stallings looked at Patty.

She said, "Call me when you see him over there. I'll wait here with this nice young man to make sure no one calls him and warns him. Then I'm quite certain one of them would be nice enough to give me a ride over there." She turned her laser-like eyes on the boys and said, "Isn't that right?"

All three boys nodded their heads vigorously.

Bobby Hollis tucked his phone back into his pocket and hesitated in the open parking lot of the J Tavern. He could feel just a mist of rain start. He had intended to head back to his apartment, but the call from the cop had spooked him. He forgot all about the woman at the car and started to walk back toward the Tavern for another beer with his friends.

He knew the cops would catch up to him eventually. He had no idea how much he should disclose. Kyle Lee had told them all to hang tough and keep quiet. He didn't want to be the one who broke and got everyone in trouble. On the other hand he didn't want to be one of the ones who ended up dead. No one said anything about the curse, but everyone knew it was somehow related to that night two years ago. He couldn't believe no one had ever put it together before. It was no secret their party was the biggest in the city on Halloween.

He had a lump in his stomach that made him feel like he might vomit. He took a quick look around the parking lot and noticed the woman was closer to him. He didn't want to turn around and spew right in front of her.

He knew he had to stay here at least for another hour or two. He could figure out what to do tomorrow after a good night's sleep.

Stallings knew the bar the boys were talking about. It was only five minutes from the apartment complex. There was almost no traffic on the roads and the falling temperature and rising moisture created a wintry effect on his windshield. It had only snowed in Jacksonville a couple of times since he was a kid. But it always seemed to be cool and clammy during December and January. This was the kind of night he used to love to light the fireplace and sit with the kids playing a board game. He wondered what was going on at his house tonight. He could picture Maria in one of her pretty nightgowns, watching a movie with Charlie. Then he thought of what Grace told him to do. He had to focus on this case before he could focus on anything else. She was right. He pressed the gas on his Impala a little harder and switched on the blue light after the turn on University.

Bobby Hollis was going to talk no matter what Stallings had to do to make it happen.

* * *

Lynn looked at the young man standing in the middle of the parking lot and wondered if he was so drunk he was disoriented. He just stood there, motionless, facing the bar.

Her eyes scanned the parking lot. Amazingly it was still empty. There didn't seem to be any cars on either of the streets next to the bar. It had to be a sign that it was time to move and move decisively.

As she was about to spring on him, Bobby turned slightly and looked at her, then looked across the entire parking lot. He wobbled on his feet. She thought he might be about to vomit.

It was time to move.

Then Bobby took one hesitant step away from her. And another. And another until he was walking in a relatively straight line back to the building. She hesitated just long enough for him to get out of her range.

Damn it.

Now she would have to wait until he came out again.

FORTY-FIVE

Patty turned, leaned down, and spoke through the open passenger-side window to the fraternity brother who had driven her to the J Tavern. The other two brothers who had been playing pool with him were crammed into the back seat of the beat-up, eight-year-old Camaro.

Patty said, "I think you fellas understand how important it is to keep all this quiet. That is, unless you want Detective Stallings and I to come back out and visit you."

All three young men nodded and the driver mumbled, "I swear we will all try to forget this evening as quickly as possible."

Patty couldn't help but smile as she patted the car and sent the boys on their way. She had made them drive her over here as soon as Stallings called to say he had secured Bobby Hollis at a corner table inside the local tavern. She was surprised the place didn't have TVs or music blaring. It had a nice, homey atmosphere. Stallings sat at a round table in the far corner of the low-ceilinged room. The only other patrons sat at a high top near the bar, three college-age boys who kept looking over their shoulder at Stallings. They were probably the friends Bobby had been visiting before Stallings showed up.

Patty slid into the chair next to Bobby as Stallings said, "You remember Detective Levine." Stallings looked at Patty and said, "We were getting to know each other and setting up the ground rules for our conversation. So far it hasn't sunk into Mr. Hollis's head how important this is."

Patty saw Stallings nod and knew that he wanted her to take over the interview. She took a moment to let Bobby calm down and ordered a pitcher of Miller Light from the plump waitress who came from behind the bar to take their order. The place stank of cigarette smoke and that meant they didn't serve food.

After a couple of minutes of silence, and having served a mug of beer to each of them, Patty got Bobby Hollis's attention with a warm smile. She knew Stallings would sit there silently like a big dog on a chain ready to be released. She liked toying with hostile witnesses. She let Bobby's imagination consider all the things Stallings might do while he sat there silent and still. It was an act the two partners had used a hundred times before.

When it was time, Patty said, "You lied to us, Bobby."

Now the boy looked her in the face and said, "What did I lie to you about?"

"You know there's a lot more to the accidents that have been going on with your fraternity brothers."

Bobby hesitated, then said, "You mean the curse?"

Now Stallings barked, "Cut that curse bullshit out. It's embarrassing to the Florida public school system."

Bobby swallowed hard, his Adam's apple bobbing up and down. He looked from Stallings to Patty, but didn't say a word.

Patty said, "What are you worried about?"

Still the was no response.

"Why this code of silence? I know there's a certain brotherhood in fraternities, but you guys are taking it to the extreme. Don't you understand that we don't think your friends died from accidents?"

Bobby grabbed the mug of beer and took two big gulps. It was hard for him to set it back on the wooden table without showing how badly his hand was shaking. But he still didn't say a word.

Stallings changed his tone and leaned forward, saying, "I can see you're scared about something. I would be too. And I think you're worried that you and your friends are going to get in trouble for something. I swear to you, Bobby, we're just interested in getting to the bottom of these deaths. I don't care what else you guys did. I don't care if you sell pot, if you launder money, or if you cheat on your fucking final exams. I'm going to give you immunity for anything you say."

Patty gave him a look to make sure he didn't go too far with his promises.

Stallings acknowledged her look with a subtle nod, then faced Bobby again, focusing on the boy. "I will not let anything happen to you. Just tell us the truth. You know more than you're letting on."

Patty watched as Bobby's eyes came up to meet Stallings. He started to say something, then stopped. Patty hadn't seen someone in this much turmoil since they had caught a pedophile who had to face what he had done and admit it to the detectives.

Stallings said, "Come on, Bobby. It's not like you killed somebody."

With that Bobby lost all color in his face, looked panicked, turned his head, and vomited onto the linoleum floor in the back of the J Tavern.

Lynn sat in her car, huddling against the cold, waiting for her engine to run long enough to warm up and work the heater. As she sat there, an Impala rolled into the lot and into the first spot that was open near the front door of the J Tavern.

A tall man with a blue Windbreaker stepped out of the car and she immediately recognized him. He had been at Kyle Lee's house in Orlando. She'd seen him in St. Augustine too. He had to be a police detective and that meant her time was up. She knew they couldn't point to her as a killer because the police would've come to visit. But they had figured out the deaths of the fraternity brothers were connected.

The only link that could hurt her was Alan Cole in Daytona. He had seen her behind the wheel of the big blue Suburban. If he was improving like the nurse said, Lynn would have to deal with him. She might also have to put off finishing her mission until Bobby Hollis was no longer on guard and the police less interested in the case.

She put the car into gear, knowing she couldn't be seen waiting here.

* * *

Stallings had quickly taken some paper towels off the roll on their table and thrown them over the vomit on the floor. Bobby Hollis's quick motion and fluid puking action—no doubt developed over many nights drinking hard—had not attracted any attention in the bar.

Bobby wiped his face with another paper towel, then his eyes, and looked back up at Stallings and Patty.

Stallings said, "I hope you realize you're not the best at keeping secrets. If we were playing poker I'd say you just gave away your hand."

Bobby nodded slowly.

Patty placed a hand on his arm and said, "Tell us what's going on, Bobby. You're not under arrest and you're free to go if you really need to."

Stallings appreciated how subtly his partner laid down a statement that could be used in court later. From watching TV, people thought the police have to read Miranda warnings to everyone they spoke to. In fact, the circumstances under which the Miranda rights were given were very narrow. A suspect had to be in custody or imminent custody. Once Patty told him he was not under arrest and was free to go, anything he said from here on out would be legally admissible in court. Stallings wasn't always good with the subtleties of building a case, but he admired a detective who could stick to the rules without inhibiting a witness.

Bobby cleared his throat and said, "It was really between Zach Halston and Josh Hickam."

"What was?"

"It was sort of a feud. They both had their own sources for pot. But Zach considered himself some kind of a kingpin. He used to joke that he was the Tony Montana of Jacksonville. He and Josh went back and forth about who had the right to sell pot to different groups. Josh was quiet and really didn't argue the fact with Zach."

Stallings wanted to hurry the story along. This is what he had been waiting for. But he kept silent, knowing Patty was better at coaxing reluctant witnesses.

Patty said, "So what happened between Josh and Zach?"

Bobby swallowed again, took another sip of beer, and said, "It just went back and forth. A bunch of the guys worked for Zach. It was like a pyramid scheme. No one sold much, but it ended up being a lot of money for Zach." He paused and took another gulp of beer. "We didn't mean for it to go so far."

"For what to go so far?

"It started at the Halloween party. Josh drank way too much. He mixed beer with rum punch and shots of tequila."

The long silences between each fragment of information were driving Stallings crazy. He waited for Patty to nudge the boy along.

Bobby said, "So once it got rolling, Zach had us all keep feeding drinks to Josh. He had some stupid idea about putting him behind the wheel of the car and letting him get arrested for DUI on campus and thrown out of school. Some kind of crazy plan like that. Zach thought it would keep them from poaching the same customers." Bobby just stared straight ahead for a few moments, then started to cry. He pulled off another paper towel and blew his nose.

"It just got out of hand and, in the early morning hours, when a couple of us went to put Josh into a car, he felt like a sack of potatoes. It took us a few minutes to realize how cold his body felt. Then we realized he was dead."

FORTY-SIX

Patty Levine could hardly believe the incredible story Bobby Hollis had laid out before them. Although the fraternity brothers had intentionally pumped Josh Hickam full of alcohol, he could see it was an accidental death. But that meant that Josh Hickam was not a victim of the conspiracy to kill members of the Tau Upsilon fraternity.

Bobby Hollis had regained his composure and said, "Zach stayed real calm and told each of us what to do. We put Josh in his car and parked it in one of the rear lots of the university so no one would find him until the next day. Then he told us how we could all be charged with murder. Basically it scared us all into silence."

Patty said, "Who was involved from the fraternity?"

"There were a whole bunch of us. Some of the guys were from other chapters but had all worked with Zach distributing the pot. The guys from Gainesville depended on him as part of their income."

"Do you know if anyone ever talked about this?"

Bobby shook his head. "I know no one ever talked

to the police. I doubt they ever said anything to anyone else either."

"But you can see that someone has been killing your fraternity brothers."

"I can now."

At least Patty didn't think they were chasing shadows anymore.

It wasn't even eight in the morning and John Stallings felt like he was accomplishing something. He should have been exhausted but spent the night ensuring Bobby Hollis packed a few things and went to visit his aunt in Kentucky. Stallings hadn't allowed the boy to speak to any friends or fraternity brothers. After Patty and he had shown the terrified fraternity member what had really been happening, he was able to say that there were no obvious victims left in the fraternity house. Some had graduated and moved away, and, of course, several were dead. They had briefed Sergeant Zuni and Lieutenant Hester so they could make the best decision about how to inform the fraternity. In the meantime, a JSO patrolman had been assigned to sit at the fraternity house. If that didn't send a message, nothing would.

Stallings walked into the seedy International House of Pancakes off J. Turner Butler Boulevard and smiled. The lean, weary-looking man in the booth did not seem to be in such a good humor.

Stallings said, "I appreciate you meeting me."

"We do things on a slightly different schedule at the

DEA." Ed Wiley took another sip of coffee, then wiped his face with his hand. "I don't mind getting up early, but gathering all of this information in one evening kinda wore me out." He slid a manila envelope with Stallings's name written in Magic Marker across the front. "You swear you'll only use this information on your homicide case?"

Stallings raised his right hand, suppressing a smile. "On my honor as a certified law enforcement officer in the state of Florida, I will use any information you provide me for the sole purpose of a homicide investigation. I will eat the paper the information is printed on before I allow anyone in narcotics to see it."

Wiley chuckled. "You have no idea how competitive the world of narcotics investigations can be."

"My experience is that all law enforcement is competitive. Narcotics is one of the few areas that's easy to measure. Arrests or seized narcotics. Both play well in the news."

"And thank God for it. If we didn't get decent airplay now and then the FBI would steal every penny of funding we have coming our way."

Stallings started to get up, saying, "I appreciate this. I have a meeting in less than an hour and this information will be vital."

Wiley smiled. "If Ronald Bell says you're a hard ass, you're okay with me. If you were a little younger we could use you."

"I'm happy where I am." He stood and paused by the table, looking down at the DEA agent. "You don't think Josh Hickam's father is responsible for these deaths? I know we talked about it and you said he didn't have it in him. I just don't want to miss something."

Wiley shook his head. "No way. You gave me the dates and places of the deaths and I checked all of them against our surveillance. He was at home. He's hardly left that house for two years. We've got cameras, trackers, and the occasional live surveillance. Plus our intelligence from informants says the old man's all done. His son's death just took it out of him."

"But you're still going after him on a case?"

"Have to. He was a boss. He brought in a lot of product. You'll see in the packet I gave you a list of associates. It's long. A dozen of them have already been to jail. We can't pick on the little guys without going after the kingpin once in a while."

Stallings held out his hand and said, "You're okay."

Wiley took his hand and shook it, saying, "The DEA doesn't hear that much. Thanks."

Tony Mazzetti bristled every time someone else brought up a piece of information that supported the serial killer theory in the Tau Upsilon case. It wasn't that he didn't believe the goddamn theory. It just felt like they were rubbing it in his face. Sitting around a big conference room table with everyone remotely involved in the case staring at him, he felt like a jackass. Somehow the only thing that mattered to him right now was that Patty Levine didn't think he was a jackass.

That asshole John Stallings had provided a list of associates related to the pot smuggler whose son appeared to be the first victim in these lines of deaths. The victim, Josh Hickam, died of alcohol poisoning. Even Mazzetti's current girlfriend, Lisa Kurtz, had confirmed that assessment. But now they were all pushing the angle that the deaths were somehow related to the pot business being run out of the fraternity.

Mazzetti picked up the list of more than forty names and said to Stallings, "What the fuck do you want me to do with this?"

Stallings stayed very calm and said, "First, check it against the list of Suburban owners whose license plates start with the letter A. We might get lucky and find the driver of the truck that ran down Zach Halston on the list. It's just another group of suspects."

Mazzetti was frustrated, but what Stallings was saying made sense. He still had to say, "Why not look at old man Hickam?"

"The DEA is all over him. I gave them a list of dates corresponding with the deaths of different Tau Upsilon members and he was at the house every single time. In fact, they say he very rarely leaves the house."

Mazzetti shook his head and took a quick second to look at the face of each person at the table. Then he turned and handed the list to his partner, Sparky Taylor. Sparky had been quietly taking in the different conversations but had yet to say a word.

Mazzetti said, "Can you look through this bullshit, then use your computer brain to make sense of it?"

Sparky looked absolutely delighted.

Mazzetti realized this was a good assignment for his odd partner. He didn't have to interact with anyone or anything other than a computer. It was perfect for him.

* * *

In an effort to kick-start the investigation, each pair of detectives took a list of names developed from owners of Suburbans that had license plates starting with the letter A. The entire effort made Stallings a little nervous; he hoped his eyesight was sharp enough that he had picked up the right letter on the license tag.

Sparky was still sorting out many of the names and intended to run them against the list of Hickam associates the DEA had provided. For now, Patty and Stallings had drawn eight names in the central part of the county. They were going to do simple knock and talks. They'd find the owner of the vehicle, knock on the door, and hope the person confessed or, more realistically, refuse to speak to with the police. That would earn them a spot on the suspect list. Another set of detectives was visiting local body shops hoping to find someone who had repaired front-end damage to a blue Suburban. The Department of Highway Safety and Motor Vehicles didn't accurately list the color of vehicles. Detectives had found that often vehicles were repainted in different colors or simply listed with the wrong color at the date of registration. In a case as important as this, they couldn't rely on the simple designation on a vehicle registration.

Just as Stallings was about to exit the D-bureau he saw Lonnie Freed, the detective from the intelligence division whom he had asked to find out anything he could on someone named Gator. It seemed like an eternity since he had approached the detective and asked for help. He'd never told Lonnie the help had to do with finding his missing daughter, Jeanie.

The thin detective with wire-rimmed glasses smiled at Patty as she walked by and said, "How are you this fine morning, Detective Levine?"

Patty gave him her standard smile and nod. She was so used to men hitting on her she didn't even acknowledge it most days.

Stallings saw some papers in Lonnie's hand and told Patty catch up to her a few minutes. He looked at the intel detective and said, "Whatcha got, Lonnie?"

"I've been working on the description and street name 'Gator' that you gave me."

"You mean you found him?"

"Not exactly. Based on the information you gave me and the description I've come up with twenty-eight possibilities in North Florida. These are just men who've been mentioned in police reports or indexed news reports through any of the indexing services we subscribe to." He handed the thick bundle of papers to Stallings.

Stallings looked down and saw that there was a photograph associated with every report. Some of the photographs were from booking at the jail, some driver's license photos, a few surveillance photos, and a few from sources he couldn't identify. He looked up at the scrawny detective and said, "This is great, thanks." He turned to place the papers on his desk.

Lonnie said, "Is this on the fraternity case? I heard it might be big."

Stallings shrugged and said, "Sort of."

"Do you think you might be able to get me involved in the case?"

"It's not up to me, Lonnie."

"I busted my ass to find all the stuff. Come on, speak up for me. Maybe I can tell the lieutenant how helpful I've been already?"

Stallings quickly turned to keep the intel detective from doing anything stupid. "No, no, I'll see what I can do." He knew the sergeant wouldn't turn down help, but he was hoping to keep it quiet. Then Sparky Taylor walked by and an idea popped into Stallings's head, making him reach out and grab the portly detective by the arm. "Sparky, you know Lonnie from Intelligence, don't you?"

Sparky nodded and said, "I am familiar with the detective."

"I think he could be a big help working with you on the lists of names."

Sparky gave a slight scowl and said, "I can handle it."

Lonnie cut in, "But I'm good with databases."

"I am utilizing Microsoft Access for most of this."

"I know Access inside and out. We could use the databases we're hooked into in intelligence if we need to." Lonnie looked like a puppy waiting to be patted on the head. "I'd love the chance to work with you. I applied to go into tech, but never got in."

Sparky's face softened and he finally said, "Okay. You can help."

Stallings felt like a matchmaker as he watched the two eccentric detectives walk off together. Their body types reminded him of Laurel and Hardy. Before he could race off to meet Patty, Stallings couldn't resist taking a moment to thumb through the photographs of the young man Lonnie had given him. Had Jeanie really ran off with one of them?

He moved from leaning on his desk to sitting in his chair as he thumbed through report after report. His cell phone rang. When he picked it up, Patty said, "I thought you were meeting me in the parking lot?"

"I am. I'll be there in a minute."

"That's what you said over an hour ago."

Stallings looked at the time on a cell phone and saw that he had been sitting at his desk for more than an hour. He'd have to be more careful to keep leads on Gator from distracting him on big cases like this.

FORTY-SEVEN

Lynn sat at the desk in her small, cluttered office at the Thomas Brothers supply company gazing over a stack of forms explaining why products had gone bad before delivery. She'd noticed an increase in spoilage since Dale had been arrested and fired from the loading dock. That went hand in hand with the current disorganization. She couldn't believe the big, slow-witted redneck had been so competent and so essential to the company. The first report showed that a load of dairy products had not been refrigerated properly. The next report was just a case of holding eggs past the expiration date. These were simple errors that didn't often occur when Dale was in charge.

She heard a light rap on her doorframe and looked up to see the lean figure of Leon smiling at her. "What's going on?"

Lynn sighed and said, "Since you managed to get Dale arrested, the company has gone to hell."

Leon quickly stepped inside the office and held up his hands. "Hey, girl, don't say shit like that. Even joking."

She saw how serious he was, and in a way that made her feel more confident. This was a man who had spent his adult life in a business that demanded secrecy. Lynn mumbled, "Sorry, you're right."

Leon smiled as he sat down and rubbed his hands together. "Now, what's our next move?"

"You've already helped me enough."

"Nonsense, I was just getting into it. My life is so boring now compared to what it used to be, I want to rob a bank just to see what it's like. At least with you I'm helping an old friend's daughter. Even if I don't know exactly what you're doing."

"And going by your secrecy rule, it's best that you don't."

"I understand. But that doesn't change the fact that that I'm going to help you whether you want it or not. The alternative for either of us is not pleasant."

Lynn could also see how this man would have been subtly threatening in his former career. Finally she nodded slowly and said, "I was going to drive down to Daytona Saturday."

Leon smiled and said, "I'll check out the Suburban from the fleet."

"I was just gonna drive my personal car down there."

"Why? I work till two on Saturday and have to go down to one of the warehouses in New Smyrna to pick up some paint and fencing material stored down there. It'll all fit in the back of the Suburban." He gave her a sly smile and said, "I'll even drive you like I was a chauffeur."

Lynn shook her head and said, "I still don't get it. Why do you care what I'm doing?"

"I'm no idiot. The time will come one day when Bill Hickam repays favors. I know the man. I want to stay on his good side. The only question now is, what should I bring on Saturday?"

"What do you mean?"

"Knife, gun. Your call."

Lynn rolled her eyes. "It's not like that. I'm just going to the hospital."

Leon snorted like he didn't believe her. "You're going to have to learn, girl, you always need something as backup. Something more than the person you're going to talk to. Maybe we could get by with just a baseball bat or a Taser."

"You own a Taser?"

"Technically, by law, I don't own any weapons. But there's nothing I can't get ahold of on a moment's notice."

"Fine. Bring a pistol. Just don't let me or anyone else see it." Lynn didn't mind having Leon come with her as a security blanket. Alan Cole was a loose end she couldn't ignore. Looking up at Leon's smiling face in her own office, she wondered if he wasn't a worse loose end.

The doctor barked at the nurse when she bumped Alan Cole's bed as she replaced an IV bag.

The doctor worked hard to suppress his slight Indian accent because he'd heard some of the rednecks in the hospital imitate him. "He's very unstable. That's why we have him in the ICU. If it was safe, I'd have him transported up to Shands in Gainesville, where he might stand a chance."

The nurse said, "He seems like he's been more responsive in the last few days."

"He wants to say something. I've heard him mumble the same thing two or three times. But aside from his injuries, we're dealing with a serious infection now." He flashed dark eyes at the nurse and said, "From now on only you or the nurse who replaces you on shift are to be in here. Take every precaution to keep from exposing him to anything unusual. I'll check back every three hours. The next three days are critical. We must keep him stable with no excitement. He's conscious enough now that he would react."

The nurse said, "I understand."

The doctor nodded, thinking the nurse wasn't a local. She didn't have the annoying twang many of the nurses raised in Daytona or its suburbs had. He felt confident she was the right nurse to look after the most challenging case he had had since he arrived in purgatory.

Sparky Taylor had to admit he enjoyed working with the intel detective. Lonnie Freed shared his love of computers and even knew his policy pretty well. They started by sorting the names of associates provided by the DEA. The federal agencies had always been quite secretive about how they obtained information. Of course the FBI was the worst. An informant could provide them with hearsay about one person talking about another person and both of the people would end up as criminal associates to some known terrorist or fraud kingpin.

The world of narcotics was even more nebulous. Names were batted about by informants and over wire-taps and entered into DEA reports, making them each become an associate of a known drug dealer. At least the DEA attempted to rate the reliability of informa-tion. They had a proprietary database that no other agency could access. But this report the local DEA su-pervisor had given John Stallings detailed the reason each name was on the list.

Sparky noted how efficient Lonnie was in determin-ing who was a viable suspect based on if they were in jail or living in some distant area. He had managed to narrow the list to eleven names.

Now Sparky was separating the various owners of Suburbans into three separate piles. Each pile repre-sented a geographic area with the largest one being Jacksonville.

Lonnie pointed to a stack of five registrations and said, "What's that fourth pile?"

"Those are vehicles registered to businesses. We may not have to worry about them."

Lonnie said, "Why don't you give them to me and I'll see if anything matches up."

Sparky smiled and nodded at the efficient, intelligent idea. He wished this guy worked in crimes/persons.

Patty Levine and John Stallings had already cleared three Suburban owners off their list simply by driving by the vehicles. One was white and two were red. Stallings had insisted they stop and inspect one of the red Suburbans to ensure it hadn't recently been painted.

Now Stallings wanted to stop when he saw a blue Suburban backed into the driveway of a small house in a newer section of Jacksonville known as Argyle. Developers had put their mark of bland, identical houses across broad swaths of former ranch land. Zero lot lines made the houses look more like apartment buildings.

Even though the chances were miniscule that this was the right Suburban, Patty felt her heart rate increase with anticipation. This was the first car that was even the right color.

She stood at the end of the driveway as Stallings bent over and inspected the grille and headlight on the front. Patty saw damage on the driver-side bumper, but it looked more like he had struck a low wall.

Patty was startled by a shout from the front door of the house.

A beefy bald man in his mid-thirties yelled, "What the hell do you think you're doing?"

Stallings straightened, reached into his back pocket, and pulled out his ID, letting the man clearly see the badge.

The man said, "I don't give a damn who you work for. This is my property. Unless you want a shit pot of trouble, you better back out of my yard and get a warrant."

Patty saw the way Stallings stuffed his ID back into his rear pocket and started to march toward the man. She could read Stallings's body language better than anyone else. This was about to turn ugly, and more important, cost them valuable time.

Patty stepped forward, holding her hand up to stop Stallings like she was a traffic cop and he was an approaching truck. She turned to the man and said, "We're sorry, we didn't mean to upset you. This is a countywide effort to identify the driver of a specific blue Suburban."

The man the man cut his eyes from Stallings to Patty. "Why are you looking for a Suburban?"

Stallings said, "Why are you being evasive? Doesn't matter why we're looking for it, we just are."

Patty turned so the man couldn't see her expression, but she was able to convey to Stallings that she needed him to shut the hell up for a minute. As she turned back to the man, Patty put on a calm expression and stepped closer to him. "We're looking for someone involved in a hit-and-run of a young man in St. Augustine. A witness was able to see part of the tag, which is the same as yours. If you can tell us where you were yesterday about two we can cross you off our list."

The man relaxed slightly and said, "I was on my route in Fernandina Beach yesterday."

"What kind of route do you have?"

"I'm an independent business machine repairman. I have the contract for Konica in North Florida."

Stallings said, "Can you prove where you were?"

The man scowled at Stallings but stepped over to the car and opened the passenger-side door. Patty maneuvered to be able to see inside the vehicle and brought her hand to the gun on her hip covered by an open

Windbreaker. She noticed Stallings step to the other side so he could look through the driver's window.

The man came out with two sheets of paper. As he showed them to Patty he said, "This is the receipt from the office where I fixed two copiers. And this is my vehicle log that shows I left the house at eight-fifteen, made three stops, all at Fernandina Beach, and got back home at four-forty-five."

Patty checked the paperwork and saw that it all matched up. But the paperwork gave Patty an idea. What if the Suburban was part of a fleet? It could be very hard to track down. Both Zach Halston and Alan Cole in Daytona had been struck during the middle of the day. There was the strong possibility that whoever was driving was using a vehicle from their employment.

She looked at Stallings and said, "On the next set of names we pick up, let's take vehicles registered to businesses."

FORTY-EIGHT

John Stallings and Patty Levine had identified five businesses they would visit tomorrow. Somehow Stallings wasn't surprised that Sparky Taylor had already separated out vehicles registered to businesses. As usual, the portly detective gave no indication of whether he thought it was a good idea to visit businesses. He had found a likable, capable new assistant in Lonnie Freed. No one from the D-bureau even asked why Freed was up there helping out. Even Sergeant Zuni accepted his presence without a word.

Stallings had chosen the businesses they would visit based on their size. Because tomorrow was Saturday he chose only the big offices that would have someone there on the weekend. He knew command staff viewed this case as vital by the ease with which he and Patty got permission to work on a Saturday. No one even asked about overtime.

Stallings had purposely left all information Lonnie Freed had provided on suspects named Gator on his desk. He didn't trust himself not to abandon the case in his search for Gator and a link to Jeanie. He hoped they could resolve the fraternity case soon; then he'd contemplate taking a leave of absence to focus on finding Gator and healing some of his own personal issues. He wasn't sure how he could explain it to Maria, if he even bothered. As distracted as she'd been recently, he wasn't sure she would realize he was not going to work.

Just thinking of Maria caused him some anxiety. He knew his personal life was a mess. He knew he was still hopelessly in love with his estranged wife. What he didn't know was how she felt about him. He was trying to be patient with her issues. But he didn't know how much longer he should let things drag out without resolution. Stallings didn't want to let another woman like Grace Jackson walk out of his life. That was one of the reasons he was visiting the community center this late on a Friday evening. Although he wanted to visit with his father, he was hoping Grace might be volunteering tonight as well.

His father was in the rear of the kitchen putting away some clean pots and serving dishes. The crowd had thinned to a few older men playing cards and some kids playing basketball at the far end of the giant room.

Stallings's father turned around and smiled, saying, "Hey there, John. What brings you by this hour?"

"Just wanted to see how you were doing, Dad."

"I'm hanging in there, for an old fart." He motioned Stallings over to a couple of stools. As they sat down, James Stallings said, "You might need to spend more time with your wife and kids than you do down here with me. I wouldn't want you to make the same mistakes I did."

"Sometimes it seems like you're the only family that wants to see me."

"At least you're not turning to alcohol for the answer. I swear to Christ, son, I wish I had never had a drink. Maybe it would've made Helen's life a lot different. My problem is I joined the military so young, and had such a strict father, that I never understood how to deal with your mom or you two. I'm just glad it wasn't too late to fix things with you. Maybe Helen will come around someday."

Stallings nodded, too choked up to speak. After almost a minute he said, "It's meant a lot to me to get to know you the last few months. I'm glad you're getting to know your grandchildren too." Stallings didn't want to waste a night of his father being lucid.

"I only wish I could help you more with Jeanie. I know I met her, but I can't for the life of me remember any more details."

"Did she ever mention a name to you? Maybe a boy she was seeing."

"I can barely remember the visit at all now. And some of my memory comes from you asking me questions about what I said before. I know things are fading in my head. I know what my future holds. That's why I'm trying so hard in the present."

Stallings saw the old man was having trouble controlling his emotions too. "I found out Jeanie hooked up with a guy named Gator."

"Gator? What kind of a name is that?"

"We call it the *street name*. You would've called it a nickname."

"So you're convinced she's alive."

"She was more than a year after she disappeared. I won't give up until I find out what happened."

His father reached over and patted him on the shoulder. "I must've done something right. I couldn't be more proud of you."

Stallings didn't want to ruin the moment by saying that his mother had done something right. He just gave his father a weak smile, then asked, "Has Grace Jackson been by here tonight?"

His father gave him an odd look and said, "That name rings a bell. Who is she again?"

Patty sat on her comfortable couch with papers spread out across her long coffee table and her cat, Cornelia, splayed across copies of vehicle registrations. Patty reached over and rubbed the long-haired tabby's stomach, saying, "I know I haven't been paying enough attention to you. I'm sorry." The cat curled up and playfully caught Patty's hand in her front paws.

It was another Friday night and Patty was alone, but at least it was by choice. She had been reenergized by the leads on the fraternity case and was excited that her idea to check businesses had gotten so much support from her partner, John Stallings. Now she was making notes and checking the list of names provided by the DEA. She would know exactly what to look for tomorrow morning when they started visiting businesses in greater Jacksonville, asking about the Suburbans registered to them.

The whole squad was working well together and the sergeant seemed pleased with their progress. Patty knew how much command staff worried about a case like this blowing up in their face. The two factors that had to make them uncomfortable were the fact that no one discovered a connection in the deaths until two years after they started and the victims were generally well off financially. The children of wealthy parents garnered the most media coverage, and, as a result the strongest possible police response. That was the case in almost any crime. A burglary in Hyde Park got more attention than a shooting in Arlington. That was the reality in virtually any police department in any city in the country.

Patty was about to tidy up her papers and slip them into the battered metal case she carried everywhere when her doorbell rang. She was careful to check the peephole before opening the door and greeting Ken.

She appreciated his handsome, smiling face, but the moment was still awkward. Patty had not returned his calls and then had waited until she'd known he was at the gym to leave a message saying she was too busy to see him tonight.

Patty said, "I didn't expect you."

"I thought I'd be romantic and surprise you." He stepped into the town house, glancing in every direction.

"Look, that's sweet, but I have a lot of work to do and an early morning tomorrow."

"Work is more important than me?"

"It is right now."

"Does that mean you're asking me to leave?" He had a cold, arrogant edge to his voice and took a stance like he was about to be in a fight.

"No, I'm *telling* you to leave."

Ken folded his arms and shook his head. "You're blowing something good. I'm quite the catch."

Patty sighed. "In order to be a catch, you can't *know* you're a catch. You need someone who'll love you as much as *you* love you. That's going to be a long search." She crowded Ken and slowly started forcing him back toward the door.

She could tell he was trying to think of something clever to end on, but nothing came out of his mouth. It was probably lucky for him. As she closed the door firmly behind him, she had a pang of doubt. She'd just broken up with her second boyfriend in three months for two opposite reasons.

Patty took a moment to regain her composure and wondered if a Xanax would make her feel better or if she needed an Ambien to sleep. Then she decided she felt too good about herself right now to screw it up.

The doctor was beyond exhaustion. His other three patients in the ICU were all stable and their prognosis was favorable, but this young man, Alan Cole, was giving him fits. He'd already explained the immediate dangers to Alan's mother, who'd been at the hospital almost continuously the last few days. At the first sign of any consciousness from Alan, his mother had appeared like a magic genie. But the doctor had been honest with her and explained that Alan's condition was grave and his chances of survival less than fifty-fifty. The plump blond woman had stifled a sob but accepted the news she seemed to have been expecting for more than a month.

The doctor wasn't good with family. He was the top of his class in every aspect, but there was no class on interpersonal relationships and dealing with grieving parents.

He hated to lose. At basketball, at golf, or with a patient. It wasn't really compassion. He didn't try to fool himself. It wasn't an ego thing. He was the smartest guy in this hospital, not that that was hard to achieve in Daytona. But he was top of the food chain. His dark skin had made him stand out and he knew that some of the other doctors looked down on him because of it. They couldn't even pronounce his name properly. The only way he could prove them wrong and win was to hold the most effective survival rate of any professional in the hospital. So far he had achieved it.

Now he sat in the generic recliner next to Alan Cole's bed, watching the monitor. It didn't look good for the young man who'd been struck by a car only a few miles away. He'd slipped in and out of consciousness all day. The doctor wished he could have a few minutes of clarity to say whatever he wanted. He was probably asking for his mother like so many dying patients did.

The doctor yawned, stretched, and realized he needed to get some sleep so he could be back by eight in the morning. He'd already canceled his regular Saturday golf game. This was more important.

He had to win.

* * *

Leon Kines waited for the office manager to come back to the window with the keys to the Suburban. He didn't know why the half-door was closed to this one office, but he suspected they didn't want the Guatemalan car washers wandering in and out.

The thin, balding man named Larry, who always wore the same drab white shirt and blue polyester pants, came back with a clipboard and the keys to the SUV.

The manager said, "Where you going today, Leon?"

"Down to the warehouse in New Smyrna Beach."

"Good idea to go on a Saturday. Traffic shouldn't be bad at all except down there by International Speedway Boulevard where that giant flea market is."

Leon nodded, anxious to get on his way.

"What time do you think you'll be back?"

Leon shrugged. "I don't know, maybe two o'clock?"

"Why would it take so long to run down to New Smyrna and back?"

Leon didn't want to stick around with this jerk all day. He had things to do. "I was going to visit a sick friend at the hospital in Daytona. It won't take too long and I didn't think anyone would mind."

The manager looked around at the empty office behind him and said, "There's nothing going on around here today. If I'm not here, leave the keys in my mail slot."

Leon waited for Larry to make a few notes on the clipboard, then accepted the keys. He hustled out toward the rear lot where he knew Lynn was waiting for him. She was a nice girl and certainly pretty, but that wasn't why he was going out of his way like this. She was the key to getting back in with Bill Hickam. Old Bill might have taken some time off, but guys like that never quit and they never failed. He'd be back in business soon enough and Leon wanted to be right there with him.

He didn't care what he had to do to help Lynn; he wasn't cut out to work jobs like this the rest of his life.

John Stallings and Patty had already been to three businesses and checked three Suburbans in the greater Jacksonville area. One of the vehicles was old and rusty and the shop manager said he wouldn't trust it more than five miles from the business. The second was green and the last was white with a hideous painted logo of a kangaroo carrying building supplies and wearing a work apron that said, WE JUMP ON EVERY JOB.

It was almost ten in the morning when they pulled through the main gate of Thomas Brothers supply company. Everywhere Stallings drove he saw step vans and semi-tractor trailers with the company's tasteful logo. The complex was massive with administrative offices in the front.

Patty didn't say a word as Stallings turned onto an access road and headed immediately toward the rear lot where work vehicles would be stored. He didn't have time to go through nine layers of bureaucracy just to look at a truck. Besides, on a Saturday morning it didn't look like too many people were in the main building.

The gate was open and Stallings drove into the acres

and acres of paved area. A dozen semi tractor trailers were parked in the far corner with several step vans next to them. As he followed the small road toward the rear loading dock he saw a blue Suburban backed into a spot.

Stallings pulled the Impala directly in front of the car as Patty jumped out and trotted to the rear of the Suburban. A few seconds later she was back in the car and said, "Wrong tag number. But the registration says the company owns six Suburbans. Only one has a tag that starts with the letter A." Patty pointed toward the loading dock and said, "Let's go ask someone."

Lynn liked being driven. There were a few times, when she was a kid, that her parents used a driver. Back then she'd had no idea there was a security consideration. Her father tried to do business with the same people over and over, but occasionally he had to work with people outside the normal, polite, marijuana industry. She could envision Leon being one of their drivers.

She also felt like she could trust Leon. Maybe more than she could trust anyone else in the world. She certainly couldn't tell any of her brothers what she had been up to. But Leon asked few questions and obviously kept his mouth shut. As they were coming up to the exit in Daytona she said, "Leon, do you have any idea what you're helping me with?"

"I'm not an idiot. I know it has something to do with your brother, right?"

Lynn nodded. She was surprised he was so accurate on this first guess. "How'd you know?"

"I saw who you were watching the night I found you in the bar. I heard rumors that someone set your brother up and they listed his cause of death as an accident. I'm sure your father blames himself. He never wanted any of you kids to go into the business or be touched by it in any way."

"You're very insightful."

Leon shrugged and turned his weather-beaten face toward her. "You have to be to survive in this world. If I didn't know it before, four years in the federal pen in Atlanta and a year in a halfway house taught me how to read people." He looked back on the road and said very casually, "It wouldn't hurt if you give me some details. It's not like I'm going to blab to anyone."

"Let's say I'm dealing with it because the cops won't."

"The old street justice. I'm very familiar with it. And it's as good a reason as any to help you."

Lynn didn't answer. She was so impressed with his grasp of the situation, she realized how valuable he could be. She also realized he still had contacts in the law enforcement world. He wouldn't have been able to set up Dale as easily as he did if he wasn't trusted by someone in law enforcement. That made him a liability. Maybe one she could live with.

But probably not.

FORTY-NINE

Now that they were inside talking to a manager, Patty took the initiative. She didn't want to risk Stallings getting annoyed or impatient and threatening an employee of a big company like this. But the fleet manager, Larry, was very accommodating. He immediately invited them behind his counter to sit and have a cup of coffee and ask him any questions they wanted. Larry was the kind of guy who looked older than he really was. His thin face and bald head and unfortunate choice of plain white short-sleeved shirt made him appear closer to forty-five, but Patty realized he was only about thirty.

Larry said, "We only have one other blue Suburban and it's on the road right now."

Patty said, "Where is it?"

Larry looked down at the clipboard and said, "Volusia County."

Patty said, "Was anyone driving it Tuesday afternoon?"

Larry flipped through a couple of pages on his clipboard and said, "Yeah, it was gone from eleven until three-thirty. It may have been on the lot before that if the guy who checked it out might have washed it too."

Stallings said, "Did the same person check it out both days?"

Larry didn't need to look at his clip board for that. "Yes, sir. A guy named Leon Kines. He does general stuff and maintains the grounds and vehicles."

The name rang a bell with Patty. She ignored the manager for a moment while she opened the lid to her metal notebook case and shuffled through some of the pages the DEA had provided Stallings. She froze when she saw one profile under the name Leon Kines. She pulled the sheet of paper with the photograph in the corner and silently showed it to Stallings, who displayed no emotion but gave her a slight nod.

She held up the photograph to the manager and said, "Is this the man who checked out the Suburban both days?"

The manager took a closer look, then appeared stunned. He just nodded and mumbled, "Yeah, that's him."

Now Stallings stepped in and said, "Where exactly in Volusia County was he going?"

"We have a warehouse in New Smyrna Beach. He said he had to pick up some fencing material stored down there." Then the man snapped his fingers and added, "He also said he was going to visit a friend in the hospital in Daytona."

Patty looked at Stallings and knew exactly what he was thinking. Alan Cole, the victim from the hit-and-run, was still in the ICU in Daytona.

They were going to have to move quickly.

* * *

Lynn gave Leon a quick wave as he dropped her off at the front of the hospital, then pulled the Suburban to the rear of the parking lot. Lynn knew there were several issues facing her, mainly slipping into the hospital without having to give any identification or being noticed.

She stepped through the front door and saw a bored-looking woman with a Tammy Wynette hairdo looking down at a copy of the *National Enquirer*. Lynn let her eyes skip past her and see the corridor extending into the hospital. The woman still hadn't looked up to see who had come in the door.

Lynn rushed up to her and said, "I'm sorry, this is embarrassing, but where's your nearest restroom?" She hopped up and down a little bit to emphasize the urgency of the request.

The woman didn't hesitate to point down the hallway and say, "Down there and to the left, sweetheart."

Lynn didn't wait for her to ask if she'd be back. She just walked quickly and slipped into the restroom. That had been much easier than she'd thought it'd be. She knew from her conversations with the nurse over the phone that the ICU was on the second floor and that Alan Cole was in room 201. She waited a full three minutes before quietly slipping out of the restroom and turning toward the elevators instead of the security checkpoint. The female security guard never even looked in her direction.

She stepped out of the elevator on the second floor and followed the sign to the intensive care unit. The security door was propped open. She slipped past and took a moment to survey the nursing station. She could

tell 201 was in the next hallway to her left. This hallway had even numbers on the right side of the wall.
There were three nurses and a dark-skinned doctor at
the station, but no one noticed as she walked past con-
fidently to the end of the hallway, then turned to her left
and her real objective.

She felt the excitement course through her as the
room numbers counted down until she could see 201 a
few doors ahead. She had to make this fast and neat.
Her only real concern was setting off an alarm that
might draw the nurses. She'd work that out when she
was in the room.

John Stallings had already called ahead to the Daytona Beach Police Department as he and Patty raced
south on I-95. He had given a description of the Suburban and Leon Kines to the patrol sergeant on duty and
advised him that there was a chance he was going to
the hospital to deal with a witness in ICU. He made
sure he added that Leon Kines was a convicted doper.

In the seat next to him, Patty was trying to get a
photo sent over to the Daytona Beach Police Department to help identify Kines.

Stallings hated these situations, but the one bright
spot was that it was Saturday morning and traffic was
light. He also felt confident they had identified the
killer of the Tau Upsilon fraternity brothers. With luck
this case could be over soon and he could concentrate
on Gator.

*   *   *

Lynn took another quick look down the hallway toward the nurses' station, then slipped into the room. It seemed bright with the curtains drawn back and it took her a moment to notice the bed was empty. There were flowers in one corner and two plotted plants. The card on the flowers had Alan's name on the outside. Had they taken him for some tests? Then she had a sick feeling in her stomach. Had he recovered enough to be moved to another room? Could he talk? She was certain he'd seen her face just before the car struck him outside his bank. She'd met him more than once, the last time being Josh's funeral. He knew who she was and could identify her.

Lynn had no other choice but to ask where he was and risk someone else being able to identify her.

The young sergeant with the Daytona Police Department had grabbed another patrolman and a motorcycle cop who usually handled traffic out at the flea market. There was no way he was going to let a chance like this slip away on a quiet Saturday morning. It wasn't bike week. It'd been a quiet Thanksgiving and he needed some action. No matter what happened, he could always claim he was just helping the Jacksonville Sheriff's Office. His chief was big on helping other police agencies.

He spotted the big blue Suburban parked in the rear of the front parking lot as he pulled off Beville Road. He casually drove through the lot, past the Suburban, to make sure it had the right license plate. That's when he noticed someone sitting in the driver seat. Holy shit. Not only had he found the car, he'd found the guy too.

The sergeant quickly called up the other two officers and told them over the radio how he wanted them to close in. He told them to buckle up because it looked like they could be heroes today.

Leon Kines noticed the cop cruise past. His past employment had taught him to pick up on any law enforcement officer in the area. This guy could be on normal patrol. He'd gone through every aisle in the lot. But it could be just a ploy to lull Leon into a false sense of security. He had a Taurus nine millimeter in the waistband of his jeans. It was left over from his days in the business. He'd stashed it along with some cash in a safety deposit box. It wasn't registered and there was no way it would ever be traced back to him.

He didn't like the idea of having to shoot it out with the cop. He also didn't like the idea of a cop catching him with a pistol. Both the state and federal government frowned on convicted felons carrying firearms. Even if he was doing it mainly to impress the daughter of his former boss.

He didn't want to turn around and be obvious, but just looking in his rearview mirror he couldn't see the cop anymore. Maybe it was just a random patrol. His backup plan was to toss the pistol into the low hedge bordering the parking lot. The key was he had to see the cop coming again to have time to dump the gun.

Leon noticed a second cruiser. This one was a

Dodge Charger. It was on the street across a small field directly in front of Leon. The cop wasn't looking his way, but it made him nervous all the same. He started to sweat. Dealing with the cops was not generally part of the marijuana business. If he had wanted this kind of stress he would've gone into the more profitable co- caine business. He had very little experience dealing with the cops. Other than being arrested by a Customs Inspection team that stopped his go-fast boat with three thousand pounds of pot, his only interaction with law enforcement had been as a snitch since he got out of prison. There was a guy at the ATF he could trust. That was whom he'd passed on the trumped-up infor- mation about Dale to.

He had no business holding a handgun. He didn't care if the two cops had no interest in him or not, the gun was going in the bushes. Leon pulled it from his waistband and carefully wiped it down with his loose T-shirt. He used two fingers to hold it by the edge of the grip and opened the door to the Suburban. Just as he was stepping onto the asphalt surface of the parking lot he heard someone shout, "Police! Don't move."

Lynn thought the young doctor looked tired. He was Indian and wore stylish metal frame glasses and his name tag said Dr. Hamamllama. She didn't want to risk pronouncing his name. She cleared her throat until he looked up. Then she said, "Excuse me. Could you tell me where the patient in 201 is?"

The doctor's eyes darted to each side; then he said, "Are you related to Mr. Cole?"

"I'm his cousin. I came right here from the airport and haven't talked to anyone." She had been thinking of the ruse for several minutes.

The doctor nodded and said, "I see."

She could tell he had a slight accent. It was elegant and formal.

The doctor said, "I'm sorry to inform you that Mr. Cole passed away during the night from his injuries."

Lynn felt a burst of energy and joy surge through her, but she knew not to express it. She gripped the edge of the nurses' counter and said, "Oh my God, I just missed him." She thought the doctor might say some words of comfort, but he remained silent. Lynn looked up at the doctor and said, "Did he ever regain consciousness?"

"Not fully."

She wasn't sure what that meant. "Was he able to speak at all? Did he have any last words?"

The young doctor shook his head. "No, I'm sorry. He never spoke."

Lynn couldn't believe her good fortune. She managed to fake a sob, wave to the doctor, then march off to the elevators.

It was over. Now all she had to deal with was Leon.

Stallings swerved to miss a car that didn't acknowledge the small interior blue light flashing on the dashboard of his Impala. There were so many things running through his head it was hard to concentrate just on driving. Would they be able to link this guy, Leon Kines, to any of the deaths besides Zach Halston? Would he talk? Had he done it at the request of Josh Hickam's father? It wasn't unlike most of the cases he'd worked, but this one had come together much faster.

Patty, as usual, had kept her head and done all the practical tasks. She called Sergeant Zuni and advised her where they were and the lead they were following. Then she called Tony Mazzetti, who was predictably bent out of shape at the prospect of being left out of another major arrest. Stallings would have to remind him how he protested wasting detectives on interviewing owners of Suburbans. Mazzetti had all but accused Stallings of dreaming up the entire Suburban scenario. Mazzetti couldn't deny that Zach Halston was dead as a result of a hit-and-run in St. Augustine, but he'd argued that Stallings could have seen any car, not necessarily the one that hit Zach. Stallings hated to admit it, but the look on Mazzetti's face would be very satisfying if this all worked out.

The Daytona Police sergeant's plan had worked beautifully. He'd sent the patrolman in a marked unit down the main road to attract the suspect's attention. The sergeant and the motorman traffic cop had walked through the lot, then crept down below car level until they were almost on top of the Suburban. It looked like the suspect's attention was still through the windshield. The sergeant pulled his issued Glock and motioned for the motorcycle cop to stay low behind the Cadillac parked next to the Suburban.

The sergeant was surprised when the door of the

Suburban opened unexpectedly. Holy shit, the guy had a pistol in his hand. Out of instinct he shouted, "Police, don't move." In an instant he let his eyes scan behind the suspect to make sure there were no pedestrians or cars on the access road or in the field. The suspect turned, looking as shocked as the cops, but he still had the pistol.

The sergeant knew he didn't have time to give another command and let his training take over. At this range he only focused on the front sight of the pistol, tried to breathe naturally and squeezed the trigger of his forty-caliber. He fired twice at the man's chest. Center mass. He'd had to explain to too many people, at too many parties, that shooting the gun out of someone's hand was just a Hollywood invention.

On the other side of the Cadillac the motorcycle cop also fired. But he kept pulling the trigger. It sounded like an automatic weapon even though he was firing the same model Glock. It seemed like it went on forever with the sound hammering his eardrums. Finally there was silence.

The sergeant stepped from behind the trunk of the Cadillac. The suspect was flat on his back and made one wheezing sound as he went limp. He'd been hit at least five times in the chest. The sergeant did a quick look to see where all of the motorman's extra rounds had gone. There were at least three holes in the open door of the Suburban.

The other patrolman in the marked Dodge Charger had jumped the curb and was racing across the open field toward them.

The sergeant took a deep breath to calm himself,

pulled the radio microphone off his shoulder, and hesitated, knowing whatever he said would be recorded. This was an opportunity to show how cool he was under stress. He depressed the mic button and said, "Clear traffic, clear traffic. We have a signal zero, shots fired and a suspect down in the parking lot of the hospital." It would have been the perfect thing to say if his voice hadn't cracked up two octaves to make it sound like he'd been breathing helium. Damn it.

FIFTY

It had taken most of the day and three separate buses coming up US 1, but Lynn was now back at her car in the front parking lot of the Thomas Brothers supply company. She was lucky she'd parked in a lot that didn't require an access card. No one would even notice her car. If anyone did, she'd claim a dead battery and giggle like she didn't know what she was supposed to do about it.

No one had seen her leave with Leon. She'd been careful about that earlier in the morning. After her surprise at learning Alan Cole had died, she was startled by the commotion in the parking lot with police cars arriving every minute. She casually waited inside until she heard the security guard telling a nurse the police had killed someone in the parking lot. She knew exactly who the victim was. She wondered if Leon was wanted or if it was related to her mission. She'd find out soon enough. Lynn was surprisingly unconcerned about the whole situation. In fact, she felt lighter and happier than she'd felt in some time.

Lynn had come to the concrete decision that no matter what happened she was done with her mission. Bobby Hollis had suffered and could be forgotten. She hoped. That left her free to pursue whatever she wanted. It could be a domestic life raising kids or going back to school and learning to do something else. She was pretty certain she didn't want to be a bookkeeper the rest of her life.

Once she was out of the Thomas Brothers Supply lot, she turned toward the interstate. She decided to visit her parents unannounced.

Just the idea made her smile.

Stallings sat next to Patty at the conference table in the D-bureau. He felt like he often did when one of these cases was resolved. He was exhausted. The physical and mental drain always caught him on that final day. Now it was up to Mazzetti to do the real work and piece everything together, but knowing the crafty New Yorker, he'd find a way to clear virtually every unsolved homicide in the history of the county. Leon Kines would be responsible for murders that had occurred before he was born if Mazzetti had his way.

Mazzetti was already trying to determine Bill Hickam's role in the killings. Initial assessments indicated that Leon Kines had acted alone. The DEA could find no contact between the two men. That helped a lot.

Everything had come together so quickly, Stallings had not digested all the information.

Sergeant Zuni stood at the end of the table, saying, "They could use this at the police academy to show

how little details lead into big breaks in the case. We've had three analysts running all types of information since Kines was shot in the parking lot of the hospital. We've gotta get everything together in case the Daytona cops let something slip at their news conference. We're all hoping to keep this as quiet as possible."

The sergeant looked down at some notes and Stallings realized she was going to tell them everything she couldn't say in front of the cameras.

The sergeant said, "Kines worked for Josh Hickam's father. He was doing time in Atlanta for smuggling pot and was released to a halfway house just before one of the fraternity brothers died in the fire in Atlanta. He came back to Jacksonville one month before the shooting of the auto parts store manager. Even though he used a different gun, the time line matches up perfectly. We have him in the Suburban for the St. Augustine hit-and-run of Zach Halston." The sergeant looked up at the attentive detectives. "We're hoping to get more records from Thomas Brothers Supply showing that he had the Suburban on the day Alan Cole was struck. The problem is the record-keeping at the company is very shoddy."

Mazzetti clapped his hands together and, with a big smile, said, "Looks like it's another case closed, nice and neat."

Patty gave him a scowl that shut him up.

The sergeant nodded and said, "Command staff hasn't determined how we're going to approach the case or what we intend to tell the media about the activities of Kines. None of you are authorized to talk about it. Is that clearly understood?" She let her green eyes meet everyone at the table. There were nods and mumbles of agreement all around.

Patty sighed and pushed away from the table as the meeting broke up. She turned to Stallings and said, "This is one Saturday night I'm glad I don't have a boyfriend."

Earlier she'd told Stallings about her quick and painless breakup with the podiatrist. He noticed she had said the last comment loud enough for Tony Mazzetti to hear. By the look on his face, the homicide detective wasn't disappointed in the news.

Patty said, "What about you, any plans tonight?"

"I'm going to sleep and sleep hard."

"You earned it clearing up a case like this so quickly and completely."

Stallings nodded, but he wasn't convinced it was so completely cleared up. Something didn't feel right.

FIFTY-ONE

It was midafternoon Sunday and Tony Mazzetti noticed that Lisa Kurtz had hardly spoken to him since they had gone out to lunch at a local sports bar. Maybe she wasn't used to the letdown after a case was broken. He'd have plenty to do in the next few weeks, but at least no one was in danger now. Lisa seemed disappointed she was completely left out of the final aspects of the case.

It felt weird to be around the talkative medical examiner when she was in a quiet and contemplative mood. He wasn't sure he liked it any better or worse. They'd gone out Saturday night, but it had felt more like something they both expected to do rather than something either of them wanted to do. She had worn simple jeans and a blouse to go to the movies and dinner and had shown no inclination to take them off afterwards. That had been fine with Mazzetti, who was also tired after the case had been wrapped up.

She sat on his couch and made no comment while he stroked her bare foot in his lap. Mazzetti said, "You wanna watch some football?"

She looked up, smiled at him, and said, "No thanks." She had her shoes back on and was at his front door before he could even ask her where she was going. She mumbled a quick, "See you later," as the door shut behind her.

Mazzetti shrugged, put the TV on CBS, and hoped the Jaguars had sold out the stadium so he could watch the game from the comfort of his living room.

Stallings pulled up to the house just as the sun was setting on Sunday evening. His long night of uninterrupted sleep and then a day spent with his kids bowling at the new lanes down in Deerwood Park had reenergized him like nothing he could remember. Charlie and Lauren seemed to enjoy their regular Sunday visit. As the kids slid out of his car he decided he needed to see Maria. He had no idea what kind of mood she'd be in or if she even wanted to talk to him.

He'd been surprised how little news there was of the shooting of Leon Kines. The Jacksonville Sheriff's Office had let the Daytona Police make the announcement. The official story was the police officers shot a suspicious person who pulled a gun on them. They had a booking photograph of Kines and made sure to mention that he had spent time in prison. On the face of it there didn't appear to be much to the story that reporters would care about. Leon Kines's secrets would apparently go to the grave with him.

Stallings felt like he was sneaking into a concert as he followed the kids through the front door without announcing himself. It seemed the least awkward of his options. Charlie immediately raced upstairs and Lauren plopped down in front of the TV. Maria stepped in from the back porch with a book in her hand and her hair in disarray like she had dozed off reading. She offered him a smile.

Maria motioned him out to the back porch, where they sat in matching lounge chairs. Maria said, "Did your father go bowling with you?"

Stallings nodded. "The old coot is a good bowler too."

"It looks like the kids had fun."

Stallings nodded, appreciating the few quiet moments with his estranged wife.

Maria stayed quiet for another second, then said, "I'm sorry I've held so many things inside. I'm sorry I didn't talk to you directly about Patty. I know it's stupid and it was my own issue. Brother Ellis seemed like a good person to talk to. I'm sorry that it caused you any concern at all."

Stallings said, "I wish we didn't have any secrets."

"It was secrets that almost ruined us."

Stallings looked off in space and nodded slowly.

Maria said, "I know that look. What's bothering you?"

Stallings hesitated, completely torn on what he should say or do. Finally he sat up in the lounger and turned toward her. He reached into his back pocket where he kept the photo of Zach Halston and Jeanie folded in his wallet. He swallowed hard and said, "I have a secret we need to talk about."

FIFTY-TWO

Lynn sat at the cluttered desk in her office that was less cluttered because she'd spent two days staying occupied by going through file cabinets and stacks of documents to see what could be discarded. Every time there'd been a knock at her door she tensed, wondering if the police had come to arrest her.

The police had questioned her father and his connection to Leon, but they seemed satisfied her dad had no idea what was happening. She was prepared to step forward if the pressure was too much.

She'd heard through the rumor mill at Thomas Brothers Supply that Leon had pulled a pistol and that was why he was shot by the police in Daytona. She'd also heard he was wanted for the hit-and-run that killed Zach Halston in St. Augustine. Even though Larry ran a messy office, she worried about someone finding the vehicle log where she checked out the Suburban the day she hit Alan Cole. It wasn't difficult to slip in and remove the vehicle log. She hadn't even brought it back to this office. She used the main office's shredder to dispose of the paperwork once and for all.

Now, almost a week since Leon had been shot, she realized she'd literally gotten away with murder. Several times. Everyone had paid a price for Josh's death except Bobby Hollis. And he could wait years. But for now she felt like a weight had been lifted off her. Even her parents seemed brighter. Lynn was ready for her life. The one she'd earned.

She signed off on some accounts receivable and started to think about lunch. She intended to leave the office today and eat with a couple of the girls from admin. There was a new Sweet Tomatoes that had opened down the street and Lynn planned to have a long, leisurely, healthy lunch.

A soft rap on her doorframe made her look up at a man, and it took her a moment to recognize him. She had seen him before, but it still took some time to register.

The man gave her a charming smile and said, "I'm John Stallings with the Jacksonville Sheriff's Office." He held up a badge and flipped it open so she could see the identification card with his photograph. He didn't say anything else. He just looked at her with a crooked smile on his face.

Lynn said, "May I help you?" It was calm and professional on the outside, but she felt her heart rate increase and her stomach start to knot up.

Finally the detective said, "Thought you got away with it, didn't you?"

Lynn forced herself to calmly shake your head and say, "I'm not sure what you're talking about."

"You almost did. But you're not quite sneaky enough. You don't think like a real criminal, and I admire that."

Now she was smart enough to keep quiet. She didn't want to give her position away and blurt out something stupid like, *I want to speak to my attorney.*

The detective casually stepped in the office and eased into the chair directly in front of her desk. He kept his eyes on her the whole time. Lynn had the clear feeling that if she made any sudden movements this man would take action.

The detective said, "My partner will be here in a minute. She was just checking a few things up in your administrative offices. I wanted to show you a photo and ask you a question first if you don't mind."

Lynn remained silent but nodded slightly.

The detective held up a creased photo of Zach Halston and a pretty young woman. Then he asked her something she didn't expect.

"Do you know the young woman?"

Lynn shook her head, swallowing hard. She doubted she could speak even if she wanted to because her mouth was so dry.

The detective said, "I didn't know how much time you spent with the fraternity brothers back when your brother was a member. I was hoping you might recognize the girl. It's not related to our case in any way and you'll have plenty of time to worry about that in the coming weeks. So forget I even asked about the girl."

Lynn finally summoned up the courage to say, "Why do you think I did anything wrong?" It was generic enough that he couldn't use it against her, but maybe she'd have an idea of what evidence they did have.

The detective said, "Leon Kines is a good scapegoat. His motives made sense, no one was going to stand up and fight for him, and it clears our case. But there were a couple of things that didn't add up, and I did some checking." He gave her a chance to say something or add a comment. She just kept staring at him.

He said, "The first thing that bothered me was the fact that Leon had a nine-millimeter with him when he was shot by the Daytona police and a thirty-eight was used to shoot the auto parts manager. I realize some people have more guns than they need, but a guy like Leon tends to stick with one. I also noticed your dad had a collection with several thirty-eights in it. We've got someone over at his house right now with the search warrant.

"Then I happened to notice your name on the company employees list. That's a big coincidence. I was able to subpoena your cell phone records. You made several calls down to the hospital in Daytona." He paused and waited for a response.

Lynn felt like she was going to vomit.

The detective shrugged and kept going. "We had always assumed that a woman was with Connor Tate and that was the only reason he'd drink something with so many pills crushed in it. Then there is the case of Kyle Lee."

Lynn looked up and wanted to say something. The cop noted her attention.

"Do you remember being stopped for speeding by a patrolman near the marina?" He paused for effect.

Lynn kept still and quiet.

"He didn't ticket you, but he made a note of the stop. That's the kind of circumstantial evidence that stacks up in court. Then there are the other little details like the paper you used to start the fire in Atlanta. It was the *Jacksonville Times-Union*. Leon wasn't allowed to leave Atlanta without checking with his parole officer. If he started that fire, where did he get a newspaper from Jacksonville? He could do it, it just seems unlikely."

Lynn swallowed again and realized her hand was shaking, giving her away.

"The last thing," the cop stated in that same even voice, "ketamine. It was too obscure. The fact that you work in a vet's office in the evenings, and have access to it, gave us enough for the search warrant for your father's guns as well as giving me a chance to talk to you." He looked at her like he expected her to say something.

The detective said, "I'm sorry things didn't work out the way you expected."

Now Lynn found her voice and said, "No, they worked out about like I thought." She still was oddly unconcerned. Did that make her a sociopath?

She wondered if that might make a good defense.